THE REPLICA

A NOVEL

RENAE LYNK

Name: Lynk, Renae, 1999 - author
Title: The Replica / Renae Lynk
Description: First paperback edition March 2024
Identifiers: ISBN 9798990640139 (paperback) ISBN 9798990640108 (hardcover) ISBN 9798990640122 (paperback) ISBN 9798990640115 (hardcover)

ISBN 979-8-9906401-0-8
979-8-9906401-1-5
979-8-9906401-2-2
979-8-9906401-3-9

"The Replica will pull you in and immerse you in its sinister world... one that looks eerily similar to ours."
-Jason Letts

"The Replica is chilling, and had me sleeping with the lights on. Lynk has crafted a terrifying and emotionally resonant tale that will linger in your mind long after the final page. The vivid, atmospheric writing style immerses you in a world that feels both familiar and deeply unsettling."
-Corrie Romer

"The story sucked me in deeper with every chapter as secrets of the home and characters were revealed, and the ending's plot twist left me in tears."
-Lacey Clampitt

For Lacey.

Thank you for all of the many things that you contributed to this book and to my motivation for writing it.

Thank you for being my best friend, my number one supporter, my editor, and my biggest fan.

The man I loved
Refused to hear my pleadings-
He abandoned me and now
My life fades away.

-Ise Monogatari
English translation of The Tales of Ise

Both the victor
And the vanquished are
But drops of dew,
But bolts of lightning-
Thus should we view the world.

-Ouchi Yoshitaka
1551

Author's Note

...

The Replica contains mature and graphic content that is not suitable for all audiences, including but not limited to: self harm, suicide, violence, and blood. Reader discretion is advised.

THE REPLICA

One.

Before

To be a good parent is to kill each part of yourself that is not for the benefit of the child. To put it away, somewhere deep, where the child will never see it. Never suffer its wrath.

Jewel was born to be a mother, that's what Maren always said. She taught him many parenting lessons just by being there, with no parts of herself that needed to be put away. She was simply perfect. He watched from across the room where she held their sleeping daughter in her arms.

The love that Maren held for his wife poured through her like surging ocean waves. It danced with every part of her being and into Lily, their beautiful baby girl, who stirred softly in Jewel's embrace. Lily was always restless, even in sleep.

Their house was small and cozy, full of trinkets, colorful baby toys, eccentric art pieces, and multi-textured throw pillows that Jewel insisted added dimension to the couch. She was right, of course, but her husband teased her anyway.

Jewel had a habit of collecting seemingly meaningless things from each place that she visited. A strangely shaped rock from each of their many hiking trips, a cracked shell from the beach, a piece of scrap metal that she had plucked from a parking lot of a rest stop and swore resembled some American president.

Her treasures riddled the house, along with the treasures that they had collected for Lily. Even at less than two years old, she was a spitting image of her mother. The only detail of Maren's that had reached their daughter seemed to be the small freckles on the top of her tiny pale nose. Jewel's blonde hair was sprouting from Lily's head and her same blue eyes shined from her face. The same breathtaking smile.

Even the sound of Lily's tiny voice and the echo of her laugh rang in Maren's ears the same as his wife's did. Looking at her, Maren could sometimes only see Jewel staring back. His chest could burst at any moment with the love that he had for them both.

The two of them, Maren and Jewel, rarely stopped to breathe before Lily was born. Jewel had constantly dragged her husband along on her adventures, or whatever crazy idea that she might have had. With Lily, they now spent most of their days at home, watching her grow.

Jewel dedicated herself to her daughter, pouring every ounce of affection into her. Maren watched as motherhood soaked deeply into his wife. His heart swelled.

She was perfect. Fleeting.

"Isn't she the most beautiful thing you've ever seen?" Jewel would ask. Her husband nodded each time, kissing her cheek.

"She's just like you," he would reply.

Two.

Present Day

The house was small and white and boring. A house much like all the others that Lily had lived in over the years. Eleven years and three—no, four houses. All small, mostly white, all boring.

The houses had been more fun when Lily was very young, too young to know that a new house meant an absence of the old one. That a new house meant a new school and a new collection of strange people to live around. That a new house meant another lonely beginning of a lonely life.

Her father, Maren, led her delicately by the hand through the new, small, white, boring house and introduced her to each room. Lily stared straight ahead while they walked, focusing her attention on her father's short dark hair and trying her best to ignore the house around her. His tall frame took up most of the hallway as it towered over Lily's four-foot-five-inch perspective.

Maren Caplin was a tall, strong, intimidating man. His eyes were soft and wise, a smooth brown that hinted flecks of gold in the sunlight. His face was littered with pale freckles, high cheekbones, and a thick, crooked nose. His hands felt even larger than they were as he held Lily's, which looked small and fragile in his grasp. She hardly resembled her father, overtaken by the many pieces of Jewel wedged between her soft features.

Lily was beautiful, as her mother was. Long blonde hair fell in straight locks past her shoulders and down her back. Her eyes were bright and blue, made even more striking by her smooth pale skin, her father's freckles sprinkled over the top of her thin nose.

She was smart and fiercely independent, another trademark of Jewel. She half-smiled at her father, who glanced over his shoulder at her while they walked through the empty house. Their shoes clicked softly against the wooden floors.

The textured brick that dressed the exterior made the home seem smaller than it was. The house was two stories high, with an attached garage and a basement. Lily never had a basement before.

Up the stairs awaited three bedrooms, all blindingly white and connected by a curving hallway. There were two bathrooms, one upstairs and one down, and an open living and kitchen area on the lower level. Bright morning light streamed in from the windows and two large glass doors that led into the backyard.

Every inch of the house that Maren showed her, Lily despised.

She escaped her father halfway through the tour, leading herself aimlessly through the house in silence. It was completely sterile, crisp, and clean, with not a single speck of dirt or surface that had not recently been repainted.

"It's like a hospital," she breathed, tapping the toe of her shoe against the smooth white baseboard.

She stood in the small bedroom at the end of a curving hallway, which would now belong to her. Each of the walls were soullessly white, the same as the rest of the house, with two windows facing different sides of the road. Lily imagined her bed nestled in the corner, and her desk near the door, against the largest wall. She imagined her clothes hanging inside of the closet.

In each house that her father had forced her into, Lily always arranged her bedrooms in the same way. It made it feel better, more like home.

She kept only a handful of decorations, having lost most of her trinkets and keepsakes to garage sales and donation bins over the years. She was used to that, by now.

As she dragged her shoes across the carpet of what would soon be her bedroom, she hoped that maybe if she muddied it up, her father might change his mind. They might hop back into his truck and drive all eighteen hours back to Utah. They might stay there for another few years or so before being ripped away again.

She walked and walked, cleaning her shoes on every sterile surface of the house.

Lily's father had been in the military since before she was born, always insisting on how fun and exciting it was to move to a new house every few years. How she got to explore the country in a way that not many children were able to do. That Lily was "lucky." She didn't feel very lucky; she felt alone.

Her mother, Jewel, had been a stay-at-home mom for most of her childhood, attempting to make up for the lack of attention that Lily would get from her lack of friends and lack of siblings. Her mother was home, sure, but hardly present.

Jewel was a writer, a novelist as she liked to say, though her books never sold. Nonetheless, she had rarely left her home office before 5:00 p.m., when Lily's father returned home and Jewel emerged to join them for dinner. She was always overexplaining some new book idea that rarely made much sense.

When Lily was about seven years old, the time that Jewel spent in her office began to turn into time away from home. Her visits to the doctor slowly took over their lives.

"Don't worry, sweetheart," she would say. "Mommy will feel better soon. Mommy will get better and we can go to the park then."

Lily gave up asking to go to the park when she was seven, but her father started taking her again himself after Jewel had passed away.

She was angry at her mother for leaving, and even angrier at herself for being angry. She missed her every day.

Mommy would have liked Michigan, she thought, staring out the window into the new green yard. *Mommy loved trees.*

"So what do you think, Lily-pop?"

She turned on her heel toward her father's voice, booming through the empty house, too lost in thought to have heard his footsteps ringing on the kitchen tile.

"It's . . . fine," she mumbled. She hated this house, but she hated the defeated look on her father's face slightly more. "It's cool. My new bedroom is a little bigger, I think, with two windows instead of one."

Maren smiled a bit, relaxing his wide shoulders. He took two long steps toward her and tousled her hair with his hand.

"I knew you'd love it. Wait till you see the park around the corner. Good place to hang out with all the new friends you'll make at school."

Lily smiled as convincingly as she could muster. "Can I see the basement?"

...

The basement lived in its own world, different in every way from the home above it. A chain-pull of the lightbulb in the doorway revealed old wooden stairs leading down and to the right. Each step recited its own unique tick or creak.

Instead of freshly painted walls, they were scuffed, muddy, and made of old wood and cement, with pipes running every which way. In exchange for the updated appliances from upstairs, there was a mismatched washer and dryer set that, by the looks of it, had not been used in years. Two tiny windows caked in dirt sat almost to the ceiling, letting in dull light that barely illuminated the tightly packed rectangle of brownish-orange dirt. The whole room smelled like old rain and dust.

Two wooden doors barely hanging on their hinges hid two equally dirty rooms behind them, with their own chains with lightbulbs dangling from the ceiling.

"This is so cool . . ." Lily approached the closed door and pushed it lightly with her fingertips, glancing back at her father for permission to continue on. He picked at a scab of mud from the wall with his fingernail, one foot still planted on the bottom stair. He was paying no attention.

She gave the old wooden door a good push until it *thumped* against the wall behind it.

The room was dark, windowless, and damp with humidity. The glow from the still-swinging lightbulb at the top of the stairs barely peeked through the doorway.

Lily hesitantly directed her foot over the threshold, not yet wanting to slip into the thick shadows of the room. Her arm stretched straight ahead, fingers twitching in the air as they searched for a chain to pull. One, two, three more slow steps into the room, and her heart rate picked up speed.

It's just a basement, she thought to herself. *I'm not a kid.*

She shot a desperate look back toward her father, where his attention still locked into the mud on the wall. He still picked at it with his thumbnail, staring mindlessly, as if he'd forgotten where he was. Lily pushed on.

She took one last brave step forward, holding her breath as her fingers finally stumbled upon the chain and pulled so hard on it that she worried it might break. The small room illuminated slowly, sending the darkness crawling back toward its corners as the lightbulb bloomed to life. She stood proudly in the middle of the dirt floor, soaking in her surroundings. Her fear quickly melted away.

Lily's eyes widened at the sight, gleaming in the soft orange cast of the light. The hint of a smile teased her face.

"A dollhouse." Maren spoke tenderly from over her shoulder, almost as quiet as his footsteps must have been as he approached. Lily startled, snapping out of her trance and snatching her gaze from the dollhouse and back toward her father. She caught her breath.

"It's . . . cute." He stared at it, tapping his finger against his leg while he spoke. "I wonder what it's doing way down here."

"Yeah, it's cool, I guess . . ." She took a slow step forward, breaking through the quiet of the room. The dust settled slowly from the air like snow. "Looks like it's been here for a while."

The room breathed around her, exhaling a breeze through the wooden-slat ceiling.

"Probably not for very long. This house was owned by an older man a few years before it went up for sale." Maren twisted the tip of his finger against the wooden roof of the dollhouse, clearing a circle of dust. "He must have built this for his kids or something and left it behind."

Lily knew that this was adult-talk for "An old man died in this house before he could give this gift away to whomever it was meant for," but she felt comforted by the dollhouse, like she was somehow meant to have it. Like the dead old man had built it for her.

The small wooden house was covered in a thick layer of dust and grime. The colors underneath dulled with gray through the muck, revealed only by a thin line that Lily drew with her index finger across the length of it. A dark-brown roof, a tiny attached garage, and fake white bricks on the whole exterior. The small brown front door stared at her.

"Can I keep it?" she whispered to the room, stretching out her hand toward the smooth wood of the miniature door. It was the kind of dollhouse that folded closed to look like a real house, but opened on hinges to reveal the inside. Slowly, afraid that it might fall apart in her hands, she gripped both ends and guided it open.

The inside was perfectly preserved. On the second story, it held three carpeted bedrooms. The dining room and connected living room on the first story had slick wooden floors and a tiny red faux-brick fireplace against the far wall. Hand-carved miniature wooden furniture peppered each room, with tiny closets and two tiny bathrooms with windows and closed blinds. Lily soaked it all in with twinkling eyes before landing her gaze on the dolls.

"Um, yeah. I'm sure you can keep it. I can clean it up for you first, I suppose. It's filthy." Maren watched cautiously as his daughter grasped both dolls with curious fingers, plucking them from their places in the dollhouse. His eyebrows twitched together at the sight of them.

The girl doll, porcelain-skinned with bright-blue eyes, was sitting up in the miniature wooden bed before Lily took her from it. Her tiny head was wound slightly to the left, as if looking blankly out the window of her bedroom. Her yellow dress cascaded down her torso and over her shiny pale legs, with short blonde hair falling just above her shoulders. A bright and cheery smile was glued tightly to her porcelain face.

The second doll looked half-made, put together in a hurry and seemingly discarded. Its hard porcelain skin was a dull and sickly gray. Its face had no eyes, nose, or mouth, not even hair. It had black shoes and what looked to be a tiny gray sweater and tight gray slacks, almost too neat and taken care of to belong to it. Even with no face, it seemed to be staring—cold and straight ahead.

"What a creepy-looking doll." Maren laughed nervously. "Who would even make something like that?"

Lily held both dolls in her hands, admiring them equally, while her father held tightly to an uneasy feeling.

"I bet we can find you some new dolls at the store to play with," he continued. "These look like something we can donate."

He loved that word, *donate*. Lily scowled.

Maren reached swiftly for the dolls in his daughter's hands and she recoiled them just as fast. Her face twisted with offense, like these were her dearest friends already, while her father's impatient hand wavered in the air.

"What do you mean? This is their house," she said defensively. Her eyebrows twitched above a narrowed stare.

"What about this gray thing?" Maren pleaded. "It doesn't even really look like a doll. Doesn't seem like it would be much fun to play with." The gray doll continued staring.

"I want to keep *both* of them, it's only fair." She glared at Maren as he glared at the dolls. Humidity clung to their skin, slicking Maren's palms as he released his extended arm from the air. It sank down to his side in defeat.

"Fine." He exhaled a deep, exhausted breath. "You're right, don't want them to be lonely." His eyes held something solemn that quickly evaporated as he forced a smile down at Lily, scooping up the dollhouse in his strong arms. He turned quickly and ascended the stairs, leaving his daughter alone with her new dolls.

She held them close to her face, breathing them in. Dust and humidity and the choking basement scent seemed to have ignored them. They smelled like laundry soap. The girl doll reminded Lily of herself, the same blonde hair and blue eyes, like her mother's. The gray doll warmed in her palm, vibrating with energy.

Was it looking at her?

"What happened to your face, Mr. Doll?" she whispered where the gray doll's ear should be. She liked the way his new name rolled from her tongue. It fit him well.

She looked at the blonde doll in her opposite hand and her glossy eyes that stared into nothing. Her porcelain skin felt cold against Lily's palm, even through her tiny yellow dress.

"Lily-Doll," she said assuredly. Her pointer finger stroked the doll's small chilled forehead. "Lily-Doll," she said again as a soft smile formed on her face. Her mind floated far above the basement floor.

"Lily-pop? You coming?" Maren stood at the top of the staircase, drumming his fingers against the side of the wooden dollhouse. Lily cringed at the nickname, the one he seemed to save for days that he felt guilty, or sad.

She reached up and pinched the end of the chain with two fingers, pulling softly. The sudden darkness was not quite as thick as it was before as she turned to follow her father back up the creaking steps. Her two new friends were nestled snugly in her palms, one in each hand.

Three.

Piece by piece, the house gradually began to resemble a home. With each item that had found its way into the house, Lily was forced to come to terms with the fact that, now, it was hers.

Moving men armed with dollies, tape, and plastic wrap darted in and out of the house, obviously paid by the job rather than per hour. Lily watched from her seat on the bottom stair as they wheeled in and unpacked the many boxes, whispering to each other things that Lily couldn't hear. She held Mr. Doll and Lily-Doll tightly in each hand for comfort.

The sleeping bags and blankets that they had slept on the night before had been replaced with their same old beds. Their same old couch and their same old dining table, and the rest of their same old things now littered the house, haphazardly placed in the general areas that they might belong in. The dining table could move a few feet back and to the right, the couch a bit closer to where the TV would soon be hung. A box of miscellaneous kitchen items would soon be retired to the inside of the new junk drawer, already marked by whatever surfaced from Maren's pockets that he no longer wanted to hold.

The front door opened directly into the great room, with a closed stairwell on the left. The living room, dining room, and kitchen all connected together into one large space, with dark wooden floors, tan tile in the kitchen, and white walls throughout. The kitchen had a tall wall of cabinetry that touched the ceiling, with lightly colored wood stain. The kitchen island sat in the middle, with tall bar stools perched at the edge. The dining room to the right had a long wooden table with six chairs, which would likely get no use. The Caplins rarely had company.

The light from the windows was bright and warm. Even with the frigid October air whirling around outside, the yard was still brightly green. Dewy grass, three medium-sized trees, and several round bushes decorated its edges. There were thick round stones stretching from the door, around the corner, down the walkway and out the gate to the front. A small white shed sat in the corner.

Lily stared at her new house, soaking its energy into her skin.

"Lily, can you come here, please?"

She blinked, rising from her seat on the stairs and searching for the source of her father's voice. It echoed, seeming to bounce around the house like it was launched from a slingshot. She could barely tell if he was upstairs or down, but decided that the kitchen was the safest bet.

She rounded the corner to where Maren stood, studying the overflowing kitchen island beneath him. Small boxes were strewn over every inch of it, each with old mugs, utensils, pots, or pans. Photo albums, extension cords, books, and office supplies had all somehow found their way inside of the boxes labeled "kitchen." Lily frowned at the sight.

"You'd think that I would have this moving thing down by now, huh?" He cracked a toothy smile in an attempt to hide his bubbling frustration, but his fingers tapped the edge of the counter anyway.

"Yeah, I guess not." She half-smiled at him, grabbing an empty box from off of the floor. She neatly set Mr. Doll and Lily-Doll on top of the counter, propping them up against the empty paper towel holder and beginning to separate the non-kitchen items from the mess. The hollow cardboard shells were thrown thoughtlessly around the kitchen floor, crumpling under Lily's sneaker with a *crunch* as she stepped backward to open a drawer.

Maren slowed, staring at the dolls, while Lily took over most of the work.

There's something about that gray doll's face, he thought. *Or lack thereof.*

As expressionless as it was, the doll always seemed to be staring at something. There was always a thick line of attention drawn between it and the thing that it tried so hard to see. Or was it trying at all? Was it seeing exactly as it wished while whatever it was focused on was blissfully unaware?

Maren scoffed at the thought. A doll, just a doll. A doll with no thoughts and no intentions and certainly no invisible, staring eyes.

It's just this house, he scolded himself in his head. *I will not succumb to its superstition.*

With a deep breath, he waved the thought away and continued with the boxes, knowing there were still many more to go.

...

Soon enough, the movers were all gone, leaving behind the freshly unwrapped furniture that had been placed in the right positions. The kitchen island was clean, the junk drawer was completely full, and the rest of the boxes patiently waited until tomorrow. Chinese takeout was on the menu for dinner, as it always was after a long day. It had become an unspoken rule with the Caplins.

The family of two sat on the couch while the freshly hung TV sparked to life with some cheesy movie that neither of them liked. Another tradition that never died, even though Lily's mother was the one who created it: Hallmark movies.

Maren watched Lily from the corner of his eye as she danced a fork around a piece of orange chicken, which stopped being her favorite over a year ago, unbeknownst to him. He frowned.

The movie blared through the room loudly while images bounced over the screen.

"How could you not see what he's doing to you?" The man held her by the shoulders, gently shaking her in his passion.

"I love him; you don't understand!" the woman replied. She shoved him away from her and ran, crying.

The man chased after her, reaching desperately for her hand.

"I love you! That is something that YOU don't understand—love." He gripped her fingers gently within his own, drawing them to his chest. She felt his heartbeat.

"My heart . . ." he continued, "it only beats for you. His barely beats at all! He doesn't love you, Abby!"

Abby withdrew her hand from his, turning away from him once more. "You don't know him!" she cried.

"I know that he is only using you. He doesn't even know you!" he scoffed. "He sees what he wants to see. He will only hurt you, Abby. I won't let him."

Abby extended her arms to him, but stopped herself, considering.

"The choice isn't yours to make," she whispered. A single tear rolled down her cheek as she walked away, leaving the man alone. He fell to his knees.

Maren rolled his eyes at the film, desperate for a distraction.

"So." He cleared the sauce from his throat, setting his empty takeout container into his lap. "Are you excited to start school next week?" He tapped his fingers against the plastic sides.

Tap tap tap tap tap.

School was a touchy subject for both of them, as Lily was anything but excited, and Maren knew that it was mostly his own fault. School never seemed to go well for Lily. She never caused any trouble, but mostly stayed in the shadows, keeping to herself. Making friends proved to be difficult, especially when she started in the middle of the year, and felt even more challenging when she would rather be alone in a corner than with the other children. Her notebook had always been her closest friend.

"Yeah." She held her eyes to the same dry spot on the chicken that she had been staring at for a couple of minutes now, suddenly no longer very hungry. "Yeah."

Repeating things never made them more true, but Lily hoped that her father might be more convinced if she said things more than once. Similarly, tapping his fingers didn't actually make things any easier, but Maren thrummed them against his takeout container anyway as he spoke.

"I know it's always hard moving in the middle of the year, but October isn't such a bad time to start." His words were nervous and quick. "There's Halloween coming up, all the candy you'll get in class. Maybe they will let you dress up at Oak Park Elementary, like they did at your last school."

Tap tap tap tap tap.

"I've heard good things about this school, Lily," he continued. "The teachers are really nice and the kids all seem to get along."

Lily said nothing, continuing to nod and stare forward at the television as it flashed. Maren's anxious fingers moved with a mind of their own.

"A smart kid like you, you'll figure everything out really quick. You'll make lots of friends, I bet." Tapping and talking, that's all he could ever do, these days.

Tap tap tap tap—

"Dad?"

"Yeah, sweetheart?" His finger stilled on the porcelain as the tapping noise dissipated. "What is it?"

Lily paused, confused.

"What are you doing?" she asked.

Concern scrawled over her eyes. She swept them between her father's face and his hand as it curled anxious fingers around Lily-Doll. His tapping finger hovered over her face.

The silence rubbed raw between them. Suddenly, the TV was much too quiet, the AC no longer a soft hum. The wind and the rustling leaves outside appeared to have halted completely.

"I—" Maren gawked at his open palm, where the blonde doll rested weightlessly on his salty-slick skin.

When did I pick this up? He couldn't remember. Worry tasted sour on his tongue.

He grew very aware of another set of eyes, or what *should* be eyes, burning through his skull. The gray doll sat patiently on the couch cushion beside him, perfectly between his daughter and himself. Its head was turned slightly to the right, staring.

Lily snatched Lily-Doll from her father's open hand while a thick look of confusion and offense spread like hot oil on her face.

"Why did you do that? You squished her dress." She patted down the doll's blonde hair and frilled yellow dress with a careful hand, wary of upsetting her.

"I didn't mean to hurt her, just holding her, is all. I'm sorry, Lily-pop." The nickname dropped off his tongue in the warm air, splattering on the cushion between them where Mr. Doll seemed to patiently watch the scene unfold. Maren hardened his eyes at it, suddenly angry at nothing. Angry at a small gray doll.

"You could have broken her, Dad." Her face was hard, eyes narrowed.

"I would buy you a new one, sweetheart, of course. I can get you any new doll you want." The suggestion of new dolls melted like sweet butter on his tongue. He dipped his words carefully as he continued.

"These old dolls are a little . . . *creepy,* don't you think? They've probably been trapped in that basement for years." He paused, hoping for each word to stick. "They have these really cool dolls at the store that come with loads of outfits and accessories, much cooler than these old things. How about we go tomorrow, before—"

"They've been lonely down there, Dad!" Anger and hurt welled in her eyes. "I can't just get rid of them now; they're my friends!" She drew the dolls close to her chest in defiance, turning away from him.

"Lily, these dolls aren't real. They're just toys. They don't have feelings and they surely won't be sad. Wouldn't you at least rather have another pretty girl doll instead of this gray thing?" Maren was suddenly concerned with the bubbling passion Lily had for her new dolls. She had always been a strange kid, but this seemed different. More intense. She stayed quiet.

I am not a superstitious man, he thought.

"You're eleven years old. Don't you think you're a bit too old for dolls, anyway?" The words felt more like a prayer than a question as they passed his lips. His fingers were growing desperate for something to tap on in this suffocating quiet.

"No. They're mine. Mr. Doll *isn't* creepy. And they *do* get sad. He told me." She kept her blue eyes on the ground, tears stinging as they refused to fall.

The stories of the house rang in his mind like an old telephone, the whispers of the moving men flicking his skull.

Haunted.

Creepy.

You hear about the old man?

I bet that door leads down to the basement . . . where it happened.

He snatched up the remote and switched off the TV, which had somehow become too quiet to hear, though the volume never changed. His food sat cold in his lap.

"It's been a long day." The weight of the moment settled deep into his shoulders as he spoke. "Maybe we should get some rest. We can talk about it later." He slipped off the couch, grabbing both takeout containers to take to the trash. He wondered how much life their little traditions had left before they, too, died out.

"I'm sorry if I . . ." His words trailed off, floating in the air. "I just worry about you, Lily-pop."

That nickname had gotten more use lately than Lily was accustomed to, and the sound of it began to sting in her ears.

"It's okay." Lily-Doll sank deep into the pocket of her pajamas as she stood. Mr. Doll sat stoically in the crook of her elbow, gazing into nothing. "I'm tired. I think I'll go to bed."

"Yeah, okay. Get some sleep, and maybe we can stop by that park tomorrow that I told you about. Maybe go shopping or something." His smile faltered, and his blood began to vibrate with a wave of guilt, exhaustion, and fear. A fear that he couldn't quite place. "Goodnight."

Lily turned toward the stairs. "Goodnight," she whispered. Mr. Doll was warm against her arm, steadying. She didn't feel like going shopping tomorrow, or to the park, but she knew that her father would forget by the morning anyway. They still had quite a bit left to unpack.

Maren collapsed against the reclining chair in the corner as Lily stalked up the stairs to her bedroom. He stared down at his open, empty palm.

I am not a superstitious man.

Four.

Each house that Maren had lived in, which was a great many, had its own unique sounds in the night. The creaking of the settling floorboards, the shifting of the attic, the grumbling of the ice machine in the refrigerator. Sometimes there were trees that stood a bit too close to the house, with branches that extended into windows and scraped with the wind. Sometimes it was a tricky air conditioning unit that buzzed at all hours of the day. This house, however, seemed to speak.

The walls breathed around him, with long, deep inhales and exhales as they swelled and caved. The basement had a constant breeze running through it that whistled at all hours, a haunting melody. Each room held its own concoction of energy and a thickness to the air. He could feel it each time he breathed, and taste it on his tongue as he spoke.

The first nights in this house were long and restless, at least for Maren. Lily slept peacefully in her bed while her father tossed and turned in his. Even now, with the furniture freshly moved in and a new familiarity with the space, every night was still the same. Long.

He lay with open eyes that pressed into the blackened ceiling above, rocking back and forth in his reclining chair. It had always felt more comfortable than his empty bed, but not here.

Creak. Creak. Creak.

The thick leather chair leaned back and forth, pushing into the floorboards below. Each creak danced with the sounds of the house around him, digging their nails into his ears and whispering through the air. The living room was thick with shadows, and the night imprisoned them. Even submerged in it, allowing his eyes to adjust, he still could barely make out the details of the space around him. Sitting there inside of it, he was slowly forgetting what it looked like.

The corners swayed at each edge, pulling and stretching the room into odd shapes. The kitchen cabinets looked open, then closed, and then open again. The dining table seemed to slide across the hardwood like a boat on the water.

Reflections from outside seemed to cast shadows of faces over the windows, with eyes that glowed in the dark and watched him squirm. Everything moved constantly around him, rippling the blackness. His skin crawled.

At all times, this house was crackling with life. Each surface watched patiently and waited for him to turn away. Maren was sure that if he wasn't watching, each piece of this building might stand and close him in. He feared to shut his eyes and miss something. He could barely blink.

This chair had grown into his favorite place to sleep, and it followed him in and out of each place that he had occupied. But here in this eerie, dark house, its comfort evaporated.

Maren slipped off the curve of the seat and retreated from the web of darkness, barely escaping the bony fingers of the shadows as they reached for him. The staircase drew him onto it and up each stair, spitting him out at the top and hurling him down the hallway to his bedroom. He swung the door closed behind him.

The crackling aura of the house didn't seem to reach this room. The carpet was plush beneath his feet as he walked, quieting his footsteps and sucking away the noise from the rest of the house, wrapping it up tightly.

In here, it seemed just like any old home, with any old air filling the room. The wind swiped at the glass of his window like light fingers, streaking down the face of it, calming his restlessness. The shadows here seemed thinner, and the corners didn't sway or shake. It was just a room, lulling him slowly to sleep.

…

Morning sun peeked from the sky and through the windows. The air was cloudy and gray, but tiny streaks of yellow light protruded through, leaking into the space around him.

Maren's eyes fluttered open, absorbing his surroundings. Each piece of furniture was placed strategically, almost exactly the same as every other bedroom of every other house he had lived in. Each drawer was always filled with the same clothes, and the same sparse decorations and accent pieces were set in the same spots.

Pants and jeans in the top left drawer, socks and underwear in the bottom. Folded t-shirts were stuffed in the top right, and miscellaneous items in the one below. He had a small, shiny orb on a stand at the end of the dresser, easily seen from any corner of the room.

It was a gift that Jewel found for him on one of their many adventures, a polished geode that she got from a street vendor. The man had sworn that it was special, once owned by some princess of the mountain and blessed by the gods or something of the sort. Jewel ate up the description, though they both knew he was lying. She bought it anyway.

It sat proudly at the edge of his dresser, the only other decor in the room besides a framed photo on his nightstand. It was taken on Lily's second birthday. Maren held Jewel as Jewel held Lily, and they all smiled wide for the camera. A bittersweet memory.

There weren't many things of Jewel's that Maren could bear to display. Most of her belongings had been lost slowly to time. She once had piles and piles of books, clothes, boxes of trinkets, artwork, and seemingly meaningless keepsakes that she had collected over the years. Dragging them from house to house after her death was just too painful for him, and for Lily. The geode, a handful of manuscripts, photos, and the book were most of what remained.

Maren slipped out the door and into the hallway, still much too early for Lily to be awake. He toed past her closed door and back down the stairs.

The eerie mess of the great room all unfolded in the morning light. The pulsing energy, deep breaths, and creaking noises of the house from the night before had been replaced with a comforting emptiness. Birds chirped outside and clouds dragged across the sky. It was peaceful.

Maren made himself a bowl of cereal, falling back into his favorite chair and exploring his newly decorated house with sleepy eyes.

Everything was neatly placed and unwrapped, shining like new in their positions around the room. It looked like they had been living here for much more than just a few days, as they were quite used to the routine of unpacking. They settled easily into new places, or at least Maren did. Lily did as she was told.

He rocked in his chair, sending gentle waves of cereal back and forth inside of the bowl between his fingers. The crunching of the food in his mouth filled his ears, drowning out the rest.

Suddenly, a soft hum penetrated through the noise, sharp and long through his ears. Maren's jaw stilled, dissipating the crunching sound from his teeth. He sat still, pressing a foot to the floor to stop the chair from swinging, and waited for the sound again.

It rang once more, slightly longer this time. A thin melody of a breeze slipping through the cracks in the old wood of the basement walls. It echoed in the silent house, squirming through his head.

He stood, setting down the bowl on the side table and following the noise to the basement door. It stood tall in the kitchen, freshly painted white like all other surfaces of the house. A cold chill ran up his spine as he reached for the handle.

It's just a basement, Maren thought, *like any other basement, at any other house.*

The doorknob turned slowly, leaning the frame into the cramped stairwell of the damp, dark room. It beckoned him farther inside like a portal to another world.

The humming sound grew louder as he descended the stairs and dipped into the basement, with wind snaking through the cracks around the windows where the caulking had gradually stripped away. Maren stood at the center of the dirt floor, soaking the creeping feeling through his skin.

The walls had eyes, watching him as he inspected every inch of the basement. The room around him vibrated, prickling his bones.

Creeeeeeak!

The sound shot straight through him like it was right in front of his face. It was loud and piercing, much too stern to be the breeze, reeling his eyes up to the ceiling and dragging them over each piece of wood that held it together. His attention landed on the large supporting beam at its center, ringing with life like it stared back down at him.

The breeze teased him, peeling through the cracks to swirl and extend to each corner of the basement. The sounds taunted him, waiting for him to react. The house laughed at him.

Just a stupid basement, he thought, forcing his nerves down his throat. *Just a—*

Creeeeeeak!

The sound erupted again, and cold sweat dripped down his back. The dirt hugged his feet, holding him in place, but he shook free of it. He stormed back up the stairs, leaving the dust to settle behind him before his cereal softened.

…

The day was long and uneventful, full of tedious tasks and cleaning. Boxes slowly emptied and found their way to the trash, or piled next to it once it ran out of room. Some of the larger boxes were tossed into the side room of the basement, waiting to be used again for the next move. Maren's trips to the basement were always quick, in and out. He never took longer than he needed to.

Once Lily had woken up, she mostly kept to herself, or to the dolls, at least. She made a quick breakfast, same as Maren, and ate in her room as she unpacked. Most of her boxes laid open, leaving her to dig through the contents to find what she needed when she needed it, rather than putting everything away all at once. Her own system.

Her room was a whirlpool of things, clothes, toys, and books. She was never one for organizing. Her bedrooms were always messy and chaotic, but she didn't seem to mind. Mr. Doll and Lily-Doll both sat at the cleared edge of her overflowing desk, watching her sort through her things.

"These are my clothes," she said, shuffling through a large box. She pulled out a soft blue shirt, holding it out into the air for the dolls to see. "This is one of my favorites." She smiled.

Only the favorites made it into the closet, hung proudly from the rack. The rest remained in the box, which was shoved into a corner and ignored for months at a time.

She grabbed another box from the pile in the doorway, popping up the edges of the tape and revealing the items inside. She never labeled her boxes with anything other than her name, so each one would be a surprise when she opened it. It was the one part about moving that she could bring herself to enjoy.

Her hand dove excitedly into the box, sliding around and grabbing the first thing that it landed on: a picture frame. She plucked it from the box, running her fingers over the thin layer of bubble wrap. Her fingernail dug under the tape, peeling it away and unraveling the frame from its wrapping.

"That's my mom," Lily said softly. She held the thick photo in her hands, displaying it to the dolls. "Her name is Jewel. She died a couple years ago . . . She was sick." Her words were slow, solemn. She tilted her head, examining the photo. She didn't have many pictures of her childhood other than the early years, when she was small. Her parents stopped thinking about taking them when things got too bad.

Within the frame, Jewel smiled widely at her as she held baby Lily in her arms. Her father was behind the camera, like he was in so many of the photos she had seen.

Lily looked up at the dolls, turning over the frame and placing it gently back into the box. She didn't want to feel sad right now. She grabbed their small porcelain bodies in her hands and hugged them to her chest.

"I'm so happy I found you here. I bet you were lonely down there, in that little basement." She dropped her eyes. "I've been lonely too."

The dolls sat in her hands, staring up at her. Mr. Doll's porcelain skin warmed into her palm, and she grinned.

"At least we have each other now," she whispered softly, so only they could hear.

...

Once most of the unpacking was completed, Maren slumped against the couch, wet with sweat. Almost all of the boxes had been cleared out and all of the things put away. The only spot left empty was the kitchen, with a few microwave meals and breakfast items that had found their way inside.

It was getting late, nearly dinnertime, when Lily finally appeared downstairs. Her lunch had consisted of a second bowl of cereal, some pretzels, and an entire bag of Cheetos. Lily always had free rein of snack choices on the trip to a new house, and she took full advantage. They were almost all gone.

"Pizza?" Maren asked as Lily melted into the chair that perched at the end of the kitchen island.

She nodded, resting her head against the palms of her hands. "Pepperoni and sausage." Her usual.

Once the pizza was delivered, they fell onto the couch to watch TV. Lily chose the film this time, some animated children's movie that Maren only used as background noise for whatever scrolling he did on his cellphone. His sagging eyes were ripe with exhaustion from the day, and the pizza grew cold in his lap. The aura of the dolls separated him from his daughter like a fence.

Maren wondered, as Lily bore her eyes into the screen, how she had grown so attached to these dolls so quickly. She had had many toys in her life—birthday presents and things she had seen in the store that she just couldn't bear to leave without. Each time she would carry them around for a day or two, and play with them for a week, tops. Soon enough they would be lost to the chaos of her bedroom, surfacing again just to be rounded up in a box and off to the donation bins.

As he watched the dolls perched in her lap, he hoped that the pattern would repeat. He hoped that it was only a passing phase, and soon enough these dolls would be gone. He could throw them in a box and drop them off somewhere, far away, like all the others.

Somewhere deep, the thought nagged at him that these dolls were different, and her attachment was different too. He saw the way she looked at them, like they were more than just toys.

Once the movie was over, the credits rolled over the screen and his daughter fell back into the cushion of her seat. Maren flicked the TV off, leaving the black screen to buzz, fizzling around the silent room—the kind of silence that reminded them they had nothing really to say to one another.

Lily rose hollowly from the couch, dropping her empty paper plate into the trash before returning to the empty seat where the dolls awaited her. She bent down, scooping them both into her arms, and disappeared up the stairs to her bedroom. The house soaked her in.

"Goodnight," she mumbled over her shoulder as Maren followed her with his tired eyes.

"Goodnight," he replied, watching her fade away.

He crawled from the couch and into his reclining chair, melting against the headrest and letting out a long, steady breath. Most nights his bed just seemed too far away. He had fallen into a habit of sleeping in this chair, comforted by the smallness of it. It curved around him, embracing him with warmth. His bed was too large, too empty. The cold sheets scraped his skin.

Something was missing from it. *Someone*.

He ignored the energy of the house this time. He ignored the shadows and the dark waves and the whistling wind of the basement. It all faded into blackness as he submerged into sleep.

Five.

***H**e pushed the heavy yellow door open with his palm. The thin wooden frame dangled away from the wall where it had split at the force of the crowbar, which now lay sideways at the doorstep. His wild and unfocused eyes scoured the lonely room.*

He struggled to adjust his shaky vision, which saw only darkness and blurred walls. Shadows tiptoed across the wooden floor and danced at the corners of his eyes. He obsessively inspected every inch of the room, over and over again, half expecting the shadows to grab at his wrists. It was eerily quiet, the middle of the night, but he knew that turning on the light would cause trouble.

No one was home, he was sure of that, but the neighbors might notice, he thought. He stumbled around in the blackness, fumbling over his feet as they walked.

His heavy hand pressed against the wall at the base of the stairs, steadying himself. Slick fingers slipped against the frame of a painting, sliding the thin string off its nail and sending it tumbling toward the floor. The wooden frame cracked at its corner before he could catch it. His stomach curled at the shock of the sound as he hurriedly snatched it from the floor, hanging it back against the nail haphazardly. His tense body slowly turned, wide eyes stinging as he ascended the stairs.

What he was here to find, or so he was told, should be upstairs in the master bedroom. Cash and jewelry, thousands of dollars' worth. It was down the street, third house on the left, upstairs bedroom with the window facing the road. Down the street, third house on the left, upstairs bedroom facing the road . . . down the street, third house . . .

He swallowed roughly.

Was it on the left or on the right? His mind swam in panic. Climbing to the top of the stairs, he glanced around the dark hallway. A lump formed in his throat.

This doesn't look right at all.

He stood in the mouth of the stairwell slowly spinning in a circle, panicked. Sweat trickled down his back, and anxious fingernails scratched mindlessly at his arms until his skin burned. Tapping the cold thing in his grasp against his temple, he mumbled in terror to himself.

"Down the street, third house on the . . . third house on the . . . right . . . Fuck! Fuck, fuck, fuck!" He smacked a closed fist against his forehead. Burning red eyes darted around the dark and empty hallway as the door handle behind him turned slowly. The shadow of a small figure emerged, and a disembodied, gravelly voice panged through his brain like a siren.

"Get out of my house."

The low voice cracked through him like lightning. Like it was living in his head.

Maren shook violently awake as the nightmare fizzled away, sending the chair swinging back and forth beneath him. A soft creaking sound lifted through the air, and the glowing clock on the side table pierced through the darkness, reading 3:26 a.m.

What was I just dreaming about?

He couldn't remember. He could barely recall falling asleep. The leather chair was moist beneath his shirt, soaking through with sweat, and the moonlight pressed against the closed blinds.

The house always looked different at night. The shadows pooled on the floor around him, casting dark waves that pushed and pulled as the house breathed. The night licked the white from the walls, smudging them with gray. A crescent moon was imprisoned behind the wooden slats at the windows as blackness infiltrated its absence.

Maren sat, swaying softly in the chair and bubbling with impatience as he waited for the *bad thing* to happen.

What bad thing? He wasn't sure. But he knew where it was. He knew what it wanted.

Standing slowly, he took deep breaths in and attempted to gather himself from the nightmare he couldn't shake off. None of this was real, of course. A nightmare, an anxiety-induced delirium. There was no *bad thing;* there were only shadows. Shadows in *his* house that he would not fear.

One flick of the light switch revealed that the dark waves had receded. The shadows sank back into their caves, and the warm glow of the kitchen light birthed a quiet, empty house. Maren ran a shaky hand through his dark-brown hair.

It's this damn house.

The only decent house in the only decent neighborhood that Maren could afford. He refused to drag his only daughter to the military housing that she so despised, if it was the one thing he could do. So what if the house had a reputation? All he cared for was the price tag; everything else was just talk.

Just talk.

He scoffed at his childishness. They were rumors, ghost stories to scare the children. He was just an old man, after all—a troubled old man. Troubled old men have died in most of these houses, he was sure. Why should this house be any different?

But he wasn't that old, was he? he thought. *It wasn't old age that took him.*

Maren refused to tell the story to Lily since she was just a child. Children believed that houses could be haunted, that basements could hold darkness in the walls. Children would have nightmares and paranoia and fingers that *tap tap tap tap tap . . .*

He withdrew his restless hand from the counter, rubbing it roughly with the other. His nervous habits had come back full force with the stress of the move.

"Stop it." His words pushed out through gritted teeth as he flicked off the light and stood in an unfamiliar darkness. The shadows resumed their positions, blanketing the room. He tensed.

Maren retreated upstairs to his new bedroom, where freshly washed sheets stretched over an eight-year-old mattress that bowed beneath his weight. He needed sleep, he was sure of that. Darkness had a way of seeping through him in a manner he was unwilling to admit, but he was strong, unmoving, unbreakable. He needed to be. There was only one of Lily's parents *left* to be.

He closed his eyes and breathed in deeply through his nose, out through his mouth. His fingers pulled a heap of blankets up and over his cold torso as he climbed into bed, all the way to his shoulders. The wind rolled against the windowpane, scribbling a desperate message over the glass. He ignored it.

It's only a house, he thought. *Only a house.*

...

The morning light was crisp and warm through her bedroom window. The house was kissed with peaceful quiet as Lily gently pressed her toes into the carpet, afraid to wake it.

The dolls were tucked neatly into their beds, Lily-Doll in her bedroom, and Mr. Doll in his, with the blankets pulled up to his gray shoulders.

Lily sat down before slowly pulling the two sides of the dollhouse apart, revealing the inside.

The doll's tiny home felt more like her own than the house Lily lived in. She found herself imagining her own tiny porcelain body with shiny white skin, slipping into a pretty doll's dress and crawling into bed within the dollhouse.

Dolls don't have to move, or go to school, or watch their mommies die.

She thought all day about Lily-Doll. About living in her house and her bed and her skin. A house that never changed and a face that never frowned.

Her fingers walked through the small house's front door, straight into the living room. She sat them on the couch and stared into the tiny plastic fireplace on the far wall. It was made of fake red bricks with a tiny mantle on the top. She touched it gently, imagining the fire's warmth on her fingertips.

Without waking the dolls, Lily stepped into her duck-face slippers and crept out of her bedroom, padding down the hall, down the stairs, and into the empty living room. She stood in the center behind the couch, focused on the wall in front of it.

Slowly, quietly, she took gentle steps across the room to where the TV was hung, slightly higher than she had liked. Her father's words repeated in her head.

"Can't you hang it any lower?"

"Afraid not. The bricks start here"—*the moving man slid his fingers over the slightly raised drywall, where it had been covered up*—*"and the TV has to be hung far enough above it that it won't rest on top, or it's gonna be angled up a bit."*

"It's just a little high." Maren breathed the words out, annoyed.

"Well, whoever covered up this fireplace did a piss-poor job—jutting out of the wall like that. We can rehang it once you get a wall mount that extends out a bit, but if you want it hung today, that's the best I can do." He kicked softly against the drywall with his steel-toed boot, leaving a smudge.

Lily tapped the raised part of the wall with a coiled fist.

Thump. Thump. Thump.

"It doesn't match," she whispered.

…

The sound barely reached under the door of Maren's bedroom. A thick *tack* sound that repeated over and over and over, creeping into his ears as he slept.

When he finally awoke, rubbing the sleep from his eyes, the sounds seemed louder and more frantic with each repetition. He jolted up in bed, struggling to place the noise. The clock read 6:27 a.m.

Was it a branch at the window? A ticking clock? An intruder?

An intruder?

Maren swung his legs to the floor, grabbing his handgun from the top drawer of the nightstand and loading the magazine before speeding down the hall. He was halfway down the stairs when the noise became clear, loud, threatening.

Turning the corner, he kept his gun at his side and out of sight. His eyes lasered into the front door, which sat still and silent as the noise persisted at his back. He turned, slowly, eyes wide with horror as they sank into the source of the noise.

The knife was barely penetrating.

Lily had retrieved her dolls from their beds to watch. They sat quietly, side by side on the edge of the couch. Their stares were unmoving from the spot where Lily crouched on hands and knees, face almost buried into the drywall.

She chipped away hurriedly at the crumbling pieces, cracking and falling onto the wood floor below like thick white sand. A new small hole revealed bricks. *Red* bricks.

"*Lily?* What the *hell* are you doing?" Maren's voice cut through the air like a bullet as the butter knife slipped from her grasp and crashed to the floor.

CLANG!

The noise bounced to and from each corner of the great room.

"The-the fireplace," she stuttered. "I knew it was here. I knew it would match." Lily shook the nerves from her voice, steadfast in her decision. Her father's anger was obviously misplaced.

Maren stood tall while disdain stained his face, concealing the cold gun against his spine. He tapped his index finger jaggedly against the side of it, as the fear that he felt for Lily only moments ago morphed into a sour, hot anger.

"Lily." He sucked in a breath, feeling his temper tighten. "*Stop.*"

"But, Dad, it's so cool! You can see the corner of the brick here at the bottom; I almost got it out! If you help me, I bet we could—"

"*Lily!*" His voice boomed, encapsulating her.

Her small hand recoiled its reach to the knife on the ground as hurt spilled over her face like ink on paper. Her lips parted, forming a response that never came, replaced with the sound of drywall crumbling beneath her feet. She kept still with her head hanging low, and the dolls sat silently staring at the mess.

"This . . ." Maren's face softened, his anger dissolving at the sight of her. "This wasn't a good idea, Lily. Why would you do this to our new house? Why didn't you ask me first?"

"I wanted to surprise you." Lily's gaze never left her feet, and her arms hung heavy at her sides as she stood. Tears welled in the corners of her eyes and slipped down her cheeks. "I knew it would match. I wanted you to *see.*"

"See what? I knew it was there already. I didn't *need* to see it." He pinched the bridge of his nose with his finger and thumb. "You can't make these decisions by yourself, Lily. You need an adult. And *knives?* You know they aren't toys!"

"I wasn't by myself!" Her face was red and blotchy as she turned toward the dolls on the couch. Maren sighed.

"They're *not*—" He paused, forcing patience before he continued, and sucked in a deep breath. "I'll call someone out here to fix it later. Just go back to bed while I clean this up." He grabbed a dustpan from the closet, but the broom was nowhere to be found, lost to the chaos of the move.

Lily grabbed her dolls, holding them tightly to her chest. She whispered softly to them as she passed her father, dragging her feet across the floor.

"*I'm sorry.*" Warm, wet tears touched her lips. "*I'm so sorry.*"

Six.

The floor was clean, the gun was unloaded and returned to the nightstand, and the dull knife sat lifelessly in the sink. Maren folded into the couch as he stared burning eyes into the wall—the bottom right corner, where the holes were. The hints of red brick glared back.

He exhaled. Sleep hadn't helped as much as he needed it to, especially being cut short.

Lily had gone back to her bedroom a little while ago, and Maren felt torn on whether checking on her would make things better or worse. He always seemed to make the wrong choice.

The remote was cold against his skin as he flipped on the TV, needing some distraction from the silence that enveloped him. The channels flicked quickly with each tap of the button, not stopping on any of them long enough to see what they had been. He landed on channel eighty-six, with some cheesy '70s horror movie pulsing on the screen.

"No, please! She's just a child!" the frantic mother screamed, keeping hold of a writhing toddler in her arms. The monster crept toward her.

"You think you can protect her?" An evil laugh fell from his lips as he reached one scaly hand toward the little girl. *"You have no power here. And I will kill whoever gets in my way."*

The mother tripped and fell beneath the monster, shutting her eyes and burying her baby girl in her chest to use her own body as a barricade.

The monster revealed his claws and teeth, both razor sharp, and lunged forward.

Click.

Silence returned violently to the room around him as the TV sizzled with escaping energy. The racket wasn't helping, and the beginning of a headache plucked at his temples, pulling at the cords behind his eyes.

Breakfast, he decided. *Breakfast is always a good idea.*

He had yet to make a visit to the store, so options were anything but plenty. Granola bars, a jar of peanut butter, some stale bread, and miscellaneous wrapped things that were strewn throughout the pantry. The fridge was a barren wasteland of empty shelves.

Maren glanced at the large wall clock. 7:12 a.m.

It was too early to go to the grocery store, and leaving Lily alone here seemed like the obviously wrong answer. Peanut butter toast looked to be the safest option.

He chewed his breakfast in silence, while the blaring red corner of the uprooted fireplace mocked him from across the room. It was a problem for another day, he was sure of that. Why Lily would think to attack the wall with a butter knife at 6:00 a.m. on a Sunday was beyond him, especially since she rarely woke up before nine on the weekends.

Nerves maybe, he wondered. *School starts soon, after all.*

His annoyance shuffled with his guilt. He knew that new schools were always hard on his poor daughter, and it appeared that property destruction was her sorry attempt to cope. He had given her one week at the new house to settle in before they both would return to their respective responsibilities—school and work.

He stood, sliding his paper plate across the counter and wiping his mouth with the back of his hand. Checking on her now was surely a good idea. He slid up the stairs and down the hallway to her closed door, wondering if there might be fresh holes in the drywall of her bedroom.

Knock. Knock. Knock.

The other side of the door was quiet. He waited a moment before speaking.

"Lily-pop? Can I come in?" There was no answer.

The room was dark as Maren turned the brass handle, slowly pushing open the door. Lily lay motionless in her bed, and the blankets buried her in a thick wrinkled pile. He glanced around the room.

Clothes slumped off their hangers against the carpet, boxes piled on top of the furniture, and shoes, books, and toys were in every blank space of the room. It was suffocating in here, and eerily dark. The blinds were closed with the curtains shut tightly in front of them, leaving thick streams of morning light unable to breach through. Even the shallow glow from the alarm clock seemed blurred, sucked in by the shroud of black.

Maren was about to turn around and shut the door again, leaving Lily to sleep, when his eyes found their way to the dollhouse. It was the only thing in the room that held energy, as if it drank it straight from the air. The window, the alarm clock, even Lily was left lifeless, wilting, dry. He knelt down slowly in front of it, drawn in by its gravitational pull.

The blonde doll was tucked tightly into bed, with blankets covering everything but her painted expression and unclosing eyes. Her room looked exactly like Lily's, minus the mess. The bed was pulled into the corner, the dresser against the far wall. The closet doors and the two windows lined up as well, a strange coincidence.

Mr. Doll's room was down the hall from hers. It was clean and boring. A bed in the middle of the room, with a dresser and tiny black television resting on top, facing it. The windows and the closet doors . . .

A strange coincidence. The thought marinated. *His room looks just like mine.*

His eyes pruned over the tiny room, imagining the tiny dresser drawers full of tiny versions of his clothes. He imagined the tiny empty bed holding him as he slept . . . *Empty?*

Sure enough, the gray doll's bed was empty. His gaze traveled through the small house to find it, as the uneasy thought of Lily hugging it to her chest as she slept burned through him. It quickly turned to fog as he laid eyes on its sickly gray skin.

Mr. Doll, with his back to Maren, sat sharply upright on the dollhouse couch. In front of him, the wall looked . . . odd. Where the fireplace had been, the wall was jagged, messy—a rectangle of rough, spotted texture smeared with white.

Mr. Doll sat proudly facing it, admiring the handywork and buzzing with ardor while his stone-like face stared endlessly forward.

Maren followed his gaze to the bottom right corner of the fireplace, right above the floor where a tiny red brick poked through holes in the fresh white wall. It was roughly carved and surrounded with chipping pieces of . . . *What exactly was it?*

Maren slowly reached one finger over the shoulder of the gray doll, hovering in the air like touching his gray skin might bring him pain. His hand moved tentatively forward as he kept his eyes on the back of the doll's gray head, half expecting it to turn.

The darkness of Lily's bedroom was closing in around him, watching his finger make contact with the dollhouse wall. A wet, sticky spot of white hugged his skin as he pulled his hand back to examine it.

What is this stuff? His breaths were quickening. *Spackling putty? Printer paper and still-wet glue?*

He pressed his thumb against his wet finger, creating a soft smacking sound as he pulled them back apart. The residue was thick and soft.

Maren turned his eyes back over the doll, feeling the walls of his daughter's room as they breathed down his neck. His chest constricted, and the oxygen drained from the air.

Did you do this? The thought poked at him while Mr. Doll sat like a lifeless statue, taunting him.

He blew out a quick breath, scoffing at his stupidity. It was Lily, of course. He knew that. Still, this doll's aura seemed to crawl beneath his skin.

The heat of its porcelain rose to the ceiling, and life hummed within the dollhouse as his small gray body sat tense in its place. Maren couldn't take his eyes from the back of its head, as if . . . *as if . . .*

Had it moved?

He was sure that the doll had been straight, pointing forward just a moment before. Now its head was ever so slightly angled to the right, its hard gray skin shining delicately between the shadows. Such a slight change that Maren couldn't be sure if it *had* changed. Had it been like that the whole time? Were its nonexistent eyes curved back over its shoulder since the start? How long had he been watching?

Each question swarmed like hornets in his mind.

Am I losing it?

The dark of the room crept into his lungs, his eyes, his nose, his mind. Lily's sleeping body was so frighteningly still. She had always been such a restless sleeper. When she was small and would climb into bed between her parents after a nightmare, she thrashed and kicked and twitched with dreams. Now, motionless on the bed, she looked hollow.

He pressed his gaze deeper into her, willing her to move, his heartbeat becoming rough in his chest. He stayed painfully still, scared to disturb the air of the room, or the life-sized Lily-Doll in her bed. He let out a long and shaking breath, and primal anxiety spiraled within him.

Lily's father rose from his crouch before the dollhouse as time stilled within the room. The twisting knot in his chest sank deep into his lungs. Darkness cracked and expanded around him, evaporating the shape of the room into an endless mass. Silence poured in from all directions like water into a sinking ship, but his ears rang loudly in spite of it. His hand touched the blanket of his daughter's bed gently, melting into its warmth with relief.

Lily stirred, unburying her face from her pillow. Stray blonde hairs waterfalled down her forehead and over her cheeks.

"Dad?" Her voice revived him. His tense muscles loosened as he leaned his hand farther into the mound of blankets.

"Go back to sleep, sweetheart. I'm just checking on you." His heart fluttered at the release of stress. "I'm sorry about earlier. It's only a wall. I shouldn't have yelled." He stroked her warm face with a softly curled hand. The daylight was brighter now, seeping through the curtains in gentle waves.

"It's okay. It matches now." Her words stumbled from her lips with a sleepy droll.

"I see that." He held up his still-white fingertips, examining them. "What's it made out of?" His tone was light and airy, not a hint of the fear that just gripped him.

She didn't answer, rolling over and falling quickly back asleep, ignoring the question entirely. He didn't care, so long as she was safe.

Maren stood and smoothed down the blanket with his one clean hand. He left the door cracked open slightly as he exited, letting the light from the hall sharply illuminate the dollhouse in one thick vertical stripe.

Mr. Doll sat frigidly on the small couch with his head turned slightly to the right. His eyeless gaze coursed through the open hallway.

Seven.

By the time Lily finally crawled back out of bed, starving, it was about 9:45 a.m.

It was a five-minute drive to the grocery store. Takeout and microwave meals were beginning to lose their novelty, so they spent the majority of their morning picking out breakfast foods, snacks, and dinner options for the week. Maren even allowed her to pick out two desserts: a strawberry cheesecake in a thin plastic tray and peppermint ice cream. An odd combo, he thought, but in the week approaching her first day of school and his return to work, he wasn't planning on telling her no if he could help it.

The events of the morning felt like a million miles away. Each step that Maren took away from the gray doll, whom Lily begrudgingly left at home at her father's demand, made him feel lighter and more relaxed. His stress-induced paranoia and lack of sleep over the past four or five days were starting to get to him, but the bright LED grocery store lights and bustling aisles packed with people reminded him that the house was just a house. Just a small white house with an unsettling reputation.

It meant nothing to Maren, of course—at least that's what he told himself. The rumors, the whispers of the moving men, not even the nervousness of the realtor as she walked him through the house. They had barely spent any time in the basement because she so obviously did *not* want to be down there. *Where it happened.*

He regretted his quickness during the tour, but with that nervous woman hovering over him from the middle of the basement staircase, he decided a quick check would suffice. He hadn't even opened the doors of the two small rooms.

He imagined himself, while the realtor loomed from the stairs with makeup smearing on her sweating forehead and lipstick on her teeth, checking every inch of the basement. He would have plucked the dollhouse from the dust-ridden shelf and laid eyes on the creepy gray doll before his daughter could even know that it existed. He would have brought the dollhouse back up the creaky steps, out the back door, down the gravel path to the trash cans, and smashed the wooden frame with his boot before tossing it in and closing the lid. Dolls and all.

I guess the rumors of Maren's new home didn't include the dollhouse. He expected that the realtor would have removed it herself if she had known it was down there. Or maybe she would have hired someone to remove it, since he couldn't imagine her, a woman who quite reminded him of a frightened Chihuahua in heels, walking down there alone to retrieve it.

Maren had gotten most of the tales and fables of his new home from the internet, which proved to be a terrible idea. They were exaggerated as could be, painting it as some sort of *haunted house* where spirits, demons, and disembodied voices roamed freely. But of course no one had any actual experiences with any of them, just wild ideas.

The only truth of the matter was this: John Meyers, the man who owned the house for over twenty-seven years before Maren, was a troubled, guilty, lonely old man. He hung himself from a supporting beam in the basement ceiling.

John's only daughter, Alina, had died years prior to her father's death at just seventeen years old. John left her alone overnight for a business trip, and she was caught in the middle of a home invasion gone wrong. She was shot and killed by some twenty-two-year-old kid who was trying to rob the place and thought no one was home. The boy fled as soon as he realized what he had done, too much of a coward to call the police himself, but a neighbor heard the noise. Only the ambulance arrived too late.

The worst part? The kid didn't even mean to rob John's house. He was too high on whatever drugs he was taking to remember that the real prize was across the street.

They caught him a couple of days later when he turned himself in. The guilt was too much for him after seeing the face of the girl he had just murdered plastered all over the news. He explained everything to the police, including the part about his dealer, who had steered him toward that neighborhood to rob the man whose wife had been exchanging expensive jewelry for drugs. The kid was in debt with his dealer, and was running out of options, but ended up in the wrong house anyway, shooting the wrong girl who wasn't even supposed to be home. He killed himself less than three months after his arrest.

By the time Alina's anguished father returned to their home, hours had passed. He drove as fast as his heavy heart could take him but his young daughter was already gone, wrapped loosely in a black body bag and displayed for identification. He arrived at the hospital at 6:13 a.m., exactly two hours and forty-seven minutes after his daughter was pronounced dead at the scene.

3:26 a.m.

John could never bring himself to move away from the home he once shared with Alina. His overwhelming guilt was both preventing him from leaving and making it impossible to stay. A few agonizing years would pass before he too met his end within the house.

As the stories go, John's grieving spirit still haunts it, watching over it, believing Alina is still lost somewhere inside. Some rumors say that she haunts the house as well, but that one is less popular. It's much more interesting to believe that John still searches for her, waiting for a chance of revenge on the intruder. There were different versions of the story anywhere you looked, but in all of them, John was waiting in the house, angry.

Maren only seemed to believe these stories at night. Not when he saw the house online, not when he viewed it with the realtor. Here, in the blindingly lit grocery store, it was an obvious lie.

The wheels of the grocery cart shrieked against the floor as he pushed it down the aisle. It was piled high with boxes, cans, plastic containers, juice cartons, a gallon of milk, and a large plastic bag full of thin paper plates. They both despised doing more dishes than necessary. Lily once asked if there was such a thing as paper pots and pans to cook with.

Jewel had been the one to cook most nights, one of her many hobbies. It pained him to think that she would never get to teach these things to Lily.

Being a single parent was hard and lonely. After Jewel died of a rare form of blood cancer a couple of years prior, it was just the two of them—Maren and Lily. Maren moved around too much to ever see the remaining family they had—grandparents, aunts, uncles, cousins. Friends were scarce, besides the few that he would make at work for short periods of time whom he never had an opportunity to see. Lily rode the bus from school and would be left alone for sometimes two hours before he would return. He felt guilty enough about that as it was, without adding in time away with his work buddies. It was out of the question.

He and Lily were cursed to be lonely together.

Lily hated babysitters. As soon as she found out that the young women were getting paid to be with her for those few hours, she stopped engaging with them at all. She would hide, cause trouble, and refuse their help. She even left the house to escape them once or twice before.

When Lily reached eleven years old, Maren finally surrendered the fight and let her stay at home alone for a couple of hours each day after school. So long as she never turned on the stove, left the house for any reason, or unlocked the front door unless her father was on the other side of it.

Lily agreed to the terms and it had worked perfectly until now. Now, Maren tapped his fingers on the handle of the shopping cart with his right hand as Lily tossed a colorful box of cereal into the basket. He couldn't stop thinking about Lily being alone in that house, with her basement-born dollhouse and gray porcelain toy. With the ghost of an angry old man stewing somewhere hidden. Waiting.

He blinked the thoughts away as his fingers stilled.

"Do we really need three boxes of cereal, sweetheart?" He eyed the two boxes that already resided in the cart as she loaded up another in the crook of her arm. A sly smile played on her lips.

"They're different kinds for different days. Eating the same cereal gets *booooooring*." She held the last word to emphasize it, sticking out her tongue at her father's responding eye-roll.

"Whatever. Throw it in." He motioned his hand over the cart as she dropped in it with a *thwack*. She always won.

...

Returning home, retrieving the dolls was the first thing that Lily thought to do. They sat side by side on the edge of the granite countertop as she and Maren unveiled the groceries from their bags. The gray doll's faceless stare penetrated across the kitchen and into Maren as he worked, separating the items into piles. Lily plucked each package from the counter, one by one, and delivered them to their rightful places.

"So . . ." Maren eyed the dolls as Lily admired her new cheesecake before displaying it on the middle shelf in the fridge. "Your dolls are pretty good friends, I see. I've never seen them apart." The gray doll and the Lily-Doll sat half an inch from each other on the counter, burning beneath his gaze.

"Well, Lily-Doll is Mr. Doll's daughter. That's why he loves her so much and wants to protect her." She walked to where they sat at the edge and scooped them both up into her arms. She spoke with an undertone of sadness. "He would feel *so* bad if he left her alone again."

"Hm." A pang of emotion welled in Maren's chest. Was it guilt? Fear? Was Lily referring to the doll or to her own father? He wondered which of them, Lily-Doll or Lily, had been left alone *before?* He wasn't sure if he wanted an answer.

"I see," he continued. "That's good that they can both stay in their dollhouse together while you go to school next week, then. So they won't be lonely." He waited nervously for a reaction, staring down at his hands that clasped tightly together.

"They want to come with me." Her voice was matter-of-fact. She always spoke of the dolls as a child would, like they spoke to her. Like she believed them to be real. Lily was much too old to be speaking of dolls like this, Maren thought. The kids at school would surely bully her if she showed up with them. They would berate her and maybe even hurt her. That was precisely why she could *not* bring them with her to school.

It had *nothing* to do with the fact that Maren hated the idea of her attachment to them. Nothing to do with the hurt that dug its nails into him each time *Mr. Doll* comforted his daughter in a way he never could. He watched with sad eyes as she took the dolls up to her bedroom without another word.

Maren leaned farther into the counter, pressing his palms against his eyes with a deep exhale.

They once were very close, when there were three of them instead of two. Before Jewel died, when Lily was younger, they would regularly go out together as a family—trips to the aquarium, hikes in the mountains, restaurants with cheap, greasy food and ice cream that came with lots of toppings. Sometimes, while Jewel was camped out in her office to write books that she would never publish, Lily and Maren would even play board games together.

Maren worried that Lily was starting to forget the better times that she had had with him, and with her mother. She only seemed to recall Jewel as sick, hiding in the office from her daughter as her illness progressed, afraid to show Lily that something was wrong while she still believed that it could be solved. She regretted it, in the end. She knew that Lily would have wanted to see her mother sick rather than not at all.

There was no office in this new house, just an empty room with Jewel's half-written books piled in the closet. She had always preferred to do things by hand rather than on a computer, which left Maren with a stack of unfinished notebooks full of half-baked ideas—mostly of a mother loving her daughter so desperately that it broke her, knowing that she would, one day, need to leave.

Once Jewel died, Maren was lost for a long time. How could he protect his daughter from the same pain that he was drowning in? His wife, along with the beautiful life that he had shared with her, was gone—ravaged by a selfish sickness that drained the soul of the family through a straw. Loneliness plagued the household and seemed to travel with them through any town they chose to move to. Lily suffered at school, struggled to make friends, and the board games they once played together gathered dust in the cabinet.

Family traditions died out slowly, suffocating over the years. Each of their restaurant trips only buzzed with an empty seat. Christmas trees were hung with lights but no ornaments, which sat mockingly in a box that Jewel used to store her collection. The first lonely year that they tried to hang them up, Maren couldn't bear the sight of them. He hid them away in the attic, promising Lily that he would bring them out again when he was ready, if he ever would be.

Weekly trips to the park stopped when Lily was about seven years old. Maren tried taking her by himself after Jewel was gone, but it just wasn't the same to either of them anymore. Lily asked to go less and less until she stopped entirely. He regretted, each day, the time he chose not to spend with her. He also knew that sometimes Lily simply didn't want him around. He wondered if the sickness took not only her mother from her, but also any good relationship she could have had with him. He wondered if she would have been better off if it were him dying in that hospital bed instead.

Maren shook the thought away, refusing to let it stick. Their relationship was strained, yes, but he was still her father.

He still loved her deeply and she must have known that, no matter what. He hoped, at least.

He wasn't always the best at being a father. He rarely spoke even the same language as his daughter, it seemed like. Sometimes all he felt that he could do for her was mess up. Maren was always forced to have to choose between two bad options, rarely knowing what the lesser evil would be.

He sucked in a breath and trudged up the stairs after her.

Knock. Knock. Knock.

"Lily, can we talk, please?" He spoke through the closed door.

It swung open, revealing Lily and her new favorite toy where it perched in her arm. The gray doll scowled at him, even with no face.

"What?" Lily said, softly.

"Look, I know what it's like to start at a new school. I was a kid once too. I know it makes you nervous, but I just don't think it's a good idea to bring your dolls." He spoke fast, trying to get as many words out before Lily decided, again, that the conversation was over. She stared at him blankly.

"I'm just saying, it's going to make it even harder to make friends when you're carrying those around all day. Kids can be mean, especially at school, at your age," he continued, words pouring over his lips. "Maybe you should just leave the dolls at home, so nothing happens to them."

He hid behind the words of a concerned father, when the truth was much harder to admit.

"I don't care about the kids at school. I already have a best friend," Lily retorted. Maren shrank in the doorway as she held the gray doll out toward him, proudly. She smiled, not at Maren, not at her father, but at this fragile, hollow toy.

"Okay." His voice dropped, defeated, soaking into the floor. He melted back into the hall, allowing his daughter to close herself, once more, inside of her bedroom. Maren was not welcomed inside.

He stood in the empty hallway, with the cold floor beneath his feet. His heart stung.

Jealous of a doll . . . is that what he was? Was he so terrible of a father that a gray, faceless, hollow *thing* could replace him?

Or was he afraid—afraid that he was right? The doll was a *bad thing,* and he needed to get rid of it.

Eight.

Maren sat in the leather recliner at the edge of the living room. The glass backyard door faced him openly from across the room, revealing the large green yard. On the side table to his left sat a book. He hadn't had much time lately with the chaos, but with Lily shut away in her bedroom, as she had been most days since they moved here, the quiet of the house blanketed him. It was the perfect opportunity to read.

The book was called *In Waiting*, a hardcover that had been sitting on his bookshelf for about three years, after being gifted to him by Jewel on his forty-second birthday. She knew how much he loved thriller novels, and had attempted to write one for him herself once or twice, but gave up after accepting that drama and fiction were more her style. She settled on picking one out for him at a nearby used bookstore as his birthday approached.

"I saw it on the shelf and fell in love with the pink cover. It was only a cherry on top that the description sounded right up your alley." Her playful words from years ago, as Maren

unwrapped his wife's gift, flashed through his head. He ran a finger down the face of the book.

"*Even the summary creeped me out, so you have to love it.*" He missed her sweet voice, but remembered her smile the most—bright and utterly bewitching.

He had meant to read it many times before. He would put the book on his bedside table, bring it with him to the yard or the park. He would sit down, ready to read, with the book perched patiently in his lap, but then he would imagine the book being finished. The image of turning over the last page and closing the back cover would flash through his mind, and his heart would become heavy in his chest. His wife's last gift to him.

He clutched the book to his chest. Maren despised the idea of reaching the end, leaving it to die on a dusty shelf, with the newness spent. The pages would fold and the edges would curl. The cover wouldn't rest snugly against the pages anymore. Perhaps he would spill his drink as he was reading, or drop it and scuff the corners. What if he was reading outside and it started to rain, warping the paper?

The book grew warm against his chest, and his throat burned with pressure as he held in his tears. Crying wouldn't bring her back.

He gently set the book back down on the table and looked out across the living room, through the large glass doors. The rain was starting to fall and the gentle taps of raindrops scattered into the grass. Maren inhaled deeply, resting his head back against the cushioned headrest of the chair. A hot, salty tear escaped down his cheek as his face hardened to spite it.

The clouds drew in closer above, reeling in the sunlight from the windows. The room softly darkened around him, leaving a delicate orange cast through the air, like a slow embrace.

He would save the book for another time, he decided, closing his eyes.

The bright-red corner of the old fireplace peeked out at him from the exposed drywall as he sank deeply into the memories of his wife.

A dry smile formed on his lips while the sound of the rain slowly filled the room.

...

The dolls were getting bored. Lily was finally cleaning her things off of her new bedroom's floor and putting them away in drawers, closets, or under the bed. She was usually perfectly content with a messy bedroom, but this time was different. This *house* felt different.

Her stuffed animals sat happily on the bed, bright and colorful with wide grins and shining beads for eyes. They were a sharp contrast to the dolls she favored now—hard porcelain with stiff limbs and empty faces. Lily-Doll at least had her painted smile, unlike Mr. Doll's smooth gray canvas.

"I'm almost done," she said to the empty room. The rain was picking up outside, pitter-pattering against her window behind the curtains. Her long blonde hair had been pulled into a low ponytail as she worked, clearing the things from the carpet. The dollhouse was spotless, so she figured her bedroom should be too.

The small house was displayed proudly in the center of the room. Lily had dragged a side table to the middle of the carpet and set the dollhouse on top of it so she could access all sides and angles. She would walk the dolls through their home with her hands, out the backdoor to play in the yard, into the kitchen to cook their meals, up the wooden stairs to their rooms. Now, Lily placed Mr. Doll in his rocking chair in the corner of the living room so he could stare through the large glass doors to the yard and watch the rain.

Lily-Doll was beside him, perched upright on the couch and staring at the blotchy wall that used to be the fireplace. Lily wondered if she was cold, wishing that it was open again and able to be lit. But Lily knew the plastic logs and fake red bricks would crackle and pop beneath a real flame, anyway. Mr. Doll reminded her of that.

Be careful, Al, you don't want to hurt yourself. She imagined him speaking to her, with a nickname that she imagined he would use. *Al.* It was a strange choice, but it felt natural. Like it was short for Lily but with an A in front of it, she supposed.

She would imagine herself as Lily-Doll, with Mr. Doll as her father, looking out for her and calling her nicknames. It made her feel good, loved, not so lonely. Al or Lily-pop, which one did she like better? Where *Lily-pop* made her feel strange, *Al* made her feel seen. Accepted. Needed.

She felt guilty that Lily-Doll was becoming Lily, and Mr. Doll was not becoming her father—not Maren, at least. Sometimes she wondered if her father would rather have no daughter at all. Ever since her mother died, their once-close relationship had ripped at the seams. Lily looked in the mirror and saw her mother's face, and assumed Maren did, too. Maybe that's why he stopped looking.

She knew that her father loved her, and that he tried. She even knew that she was largely at fault for the way their relationship deteriorated, always shutting herself away in whatever new bedroom she might find herself in. Still, she blamed her father.

She blamed him for leaving her by herself when she asked to be, for giving her space when she refused closeness. She blamed him for not seeing through her anger, selfishness, and pain and holding her anyway.

Even if she didn't know it, she was angry at him for leaving her alone. Even though that was what she always seemed to want.

She had been alone for so long, living in houses she didn't belong to, surrounded by people she didn't know. Even standing right in front of her father, she felt unseen, unwanted—a reminder of what and whom he had lost.

Mr. Doll was a vice she didn't know she needed. He felt like electricity in her hands, and a friend in ways she hadn't known in years. Like a father in ways she couldn't grasp. He spoke to her in her head, things she wouldn't normally think by herself—like how she should clean her room, how she shouldn't light the tiny fireplace even though she would have only done it for a second before putting it out. How she should grab a kitchen knife and chip away at the wall in the living room until it revealed deep red bricks.

She didn't know how, but she knew those thoughts had come from Mr. Doll, the same way that she felt his presence in the room through a faceless gray toy. He felt warm to her when she touched him, vibrating with life.

Lily-Doll was different. She was cold, hollow. Mr. Doll was once quite protective over Lily-Doll, but she felt that something had shifted. He was now growing protective over *Lily.* She could feel it in her soul, the same way she might feel hungry, tired, or sad. She was connected to Mr. Doll, and Mr. Doll to her.

Thoughts of living in the dollhouse flooded her brain. The feeling of the blonde doll's pretty dress haunted her skin, and she felt her tiny feet trail down the dollhouse halls. In her dreams the past couple of nights, she would feel her own porcelain skin and sit on the small firm sofa, staring at the exposed red corner of the fireplace. She would be Mr. Doll's daughter, and he would protect her fiercely from anything or anyone that might harm her.

What would hurt me, Mr. Doll? Lily would ask in her head.

He would reply in a thick, gravelly voice.
The bad thing, he would say.
What bad thing? There's no one here but us.
I would never let him hurt you, he would reply. *I would never abandon you, Al.*

The conversation bounced back and forth in her head. The gray doll watched Lily silently, sternly, as they spoke to each other where only they could hear. Lily started to worry about the *bad thing.* Where would it come from? When would it happen?

Mr. Doll spoke of the *thing* as a "him." A man. Lily imagined a man made of shadows, eight feet tall and wider than the wooden frame of her door, pushing his way into the house at night. He would walk with silent footsteps up the stairs and down the hallway to Lily's bedroom and wait for her to open the door. She knew that once she opened it, the bad thing would happen. She knew that she shouldn't open the door.

She worried at night about the shadow man. Sometimes she was afraid to fall asleep, imagining its large shadow-feet appearing in the crack underneath her door. Or maybe she would see the *bad thing* in her head as she slept. It would slither up the stairs of her mind and mumble gibberish in her ears.

Mr. Doll told her not to worry. He would reach into her dreams and make them sweet, comforting. Lily woke up smiling, and Mr. Doll watched.

Lily-Doll stayed in her bed most of the time lately, as Mr. Doll paid all of his attention, now, to Lily. The small blonde doll stayed propped up on the tiny wooden frame and tiny cotton mattress, staring motionlessly out her window. Mr. Doll still loved her, of course, as she was his daughter. But Lily was real. Lily was warm and alive and needed to be protected.

She worried about starting school as it slowly approached. The week of time that Maren had allowed her freedom would soon come to an end. Mr. Doll worried about Lily being away. She could feel the unsettling tension shiver over his gray skin the day that Maren kept him from their trip to the grocery store. This time, Lily promised to bring him with her.

She knew that her father wouldn't like it, but she had no idea why Maren seemed to hate him so much. Mr. Doll didn't seem too fond of her father, either.

He doesn't belong here, he would say.

"What do you mean? This is our house." Lily spoke softly aloud as she held Mr. Doll in her small, frail hands.

This is not his house.

He always answered in her head, even if she spoke aloud to him. She wondered if she could give him a mouth to speak to her with, maybe eyes to see, though he could see her already.

Lily didn't know why Mr. Doll felt so strongly that Maren didn't belong here. It *was* his house, after all, although she supposed Mr. Doll had been here first. He refused to elaborate most of the time, which frustrated her, but she trusted him deeply—with a fire in her chest like a spell.

The gray doll seemed angry, defensive. Lily commonly avoided the topic of her father during their talks, which became more frequent the more time she spent in the house.

It began as a feeling. She knew this doll was different right when she touched it that first day in the basement. She could sense that he was lonely and in pain, like she had been. They were drawn to each other, even before she knew what he was. Connected in their emptiness.

Lily wondered why she wasn't afraid. She told herself that he was her imaginary friend, that he spoke to her in the same way she knew her stuffed animals were sad when she pushed them from the bed as she slept. But this was different. Mr. Doll was *real*.

Soon, the buzzing energy, the warmth, the *feeling* of Mr. Doll's thoughts manifested inside of her. His gravelly voice would creep into her mind and echo off the walls inside her head. He would tell her not to be afraid, that he was here now and he would never leave again. He apologized a lot, for things Lily couldn't understand—for bad things she hadn't seen and pain she hadn't felt. She knew not to argue with him, so she told him that she forgave him—that she wasn't afraid and she wasn't alone. They were together now.

Lily knew that she needed to take him with her to school, even if it were against Maren's orders. She couldn't leave Mr. Doll alone here; he would worry and fill the room with a thick dread. She would come home and sink into it before it dissipated from the air as the gray doll soaked in her presence.

Worse than leaving him alone, she worried about leaving him with Maren, and what he might do to Mr. Doll when Lily wasn't there. More than that, she worried what Mr. Doll might possibly do to Maren.

She wondered about the doll's abilities as well as his limitations. How different he had become in the short time she had known him. When they met, she could barely feel him, just a whisper in her mind. Now his essence grew each day. He soaked in sunlight from the windows, drank Lily's warmth as she slept. Lily's pain only amplified his own, feeding his presence into the house and making it tangible.

Her father was starting to feel it too; she could sense it. She worried that Maren wouldn't understand, and he would be afraid.

People do terrible things when they are afraid, Mr. Doll warned her.

She wouldn't be afraid; she couldn't be. She knew that one day she would need to face the *bad thing*—with or without her father's help.

Nine.

*T*he darkness was suffocating. His lungs clawed for oxygen through his ribs and the still air burned his eyes. Something cold waited in his right hand, the kind of cold that stung and twisted into his skin. He held it tightly.

He was standing in the hallway, darting his gaze in sloppy lines from left to right, waiting for something awful to happen. What the awful thing was, he wasn't sure. He searched desperately for it.

"This wasn't the plan," he mumbled to himself. There must have been some sort of mistake.

His bones shook violently as he attempted gentle steps forward, toward the window. Paranoia licked his skin with sweat where he stood, staring across the street and into the empty neighbor's house. He shouldn't be here.

There was a rustling noise in the bedroom to his left. His panicked fingers clenched tightly to the cold thing in his hands, lifting it quickly into the air. He waved it around *thoughtlessly, whipping his head to all angles of the hallway. Shadows from each direction danced in the corners of his eyes.*

"Fuck! This is wrong. Third house on the right . . . Third house on the right! No, no, no, no, no . . ." His thoughts were jumbling together. A pool of words poured inaudibly from his lips and splashed at his feet. The rustling grew louder. They were coming. Coming to get him.

Whoever was hiding in that room would soon open the door, and they would kill him, he was sure of it. He raised his cold thing in the air and pointed it at the door, breathing rapidly through clenched teeth. His finger waited impatiently on the trigger.

The door opened slowly, carefully, with barely a sound at all. A small figure appeared in the doorway, menacingly drenched in darkness. Fear coursed through his blood, sparking through his frigid limbs. He pointed his gun into the blackened doorway, vibrating with anticipation, while the taste of copper flooded his mouth.

The figure stepped out into the hallway, reaching its hand into the open air. He refused to let it get to him, sure that what came next would be something terrible. Something violent and angry and vengeful. But what came next was the sound.

It tore through the darkness, ripping it wide open with a strike of bright light. His ears were ringing and his hand stung. The figure melted slowly as the bullet pierced its flesh. Her flesh. The menacing figure morphed into a girl, crumpled and bleeding against the smooth white walls.

Maren clutched his chest in pain, shooting up in his bed. The sheets were soaked in sweat and the taste of copper swam over his tongue.

His hands were shaking softly as he pushed the blankets off, pressing a palm to his forehead and leaning deeply into it. His breathing slowed, chasing the nightmare away.

This recurring dream had plagued him for days. The details of it always fell away as he awoke, but the feeling remained, simmering within him.

Terror. Blinding and unwavering terror.

The darkness was alive in the house. It pulsed around him like a heartbeat, breathing softly. He sculpted the room with wary eyes as the edge of each shadow ebbed and flowed with escaping energy.

It was becoming a pattern these days: sleeping for a few hours at a time, then waking up suddenly from a nightmare that he couldn't understand. He had never been the type to dissect his dreams for meaning, but these were strangely different. They felt real, and urgent. Like the fear was necessary.

He swung his restless legs over the edge of his mattress, ready to make his descent into the kitchen below. His dry mouth begged for water.

The kitchen light was dimmed low, delicately caressing each countertop and glowing on Maren's freckled skin. He grabbed a glass from the cabinet and filled it with water, drinking greedily as it dripped down his chin. He stood at the sink, with fingers tapping softly against the empty glass in his hand, and looked out the kitchen window across the grass. The trees and bushes shook in the cool breeze, casting their shadows on the perimeter walls.

Maren wiped his chin with the back of his hand, setting the empty glass into the sink. Sleeplessness buzzed through his body, but his feet led him to the backyard door. He opened it gently, inviting the cold wind into the house and swirling up his legs and beneath his thin cotton shirt. Goosebumps migrated over his skin.

He stepped socked feet onto the chilled concrete floor of the patio, breathing fresh air deeply into his lungs. The house at his back beckoned him with its warmth, but the yard was open, inviting. The starry sky felt like a portal as he stepped farther into the wet grass, dew seeping into his socks while he stood, staring intensely into the blackness above.

He felt the fog of his brain lifting weightlessly into the sky, steaming out from the top of his head. The darkness out here felt different from the darkness inside. The shadows of the yard were hollow, inanimate. The ones in the house, sometimes, seemed to be looking at him. The kinds of shadows that hid behind corners, slipped under the couch. The kind that made him think to look twice.

There was a silence there too—one that felt wrong. Out here the silence was empty—an absence of sound. When he stood in his house at night, it didn't feel empty. It felt alive.

He ran his eyes over the backyard, memorizing it. The walls around him were tall and white, made of many thin slats of old wood. The grass pushed to its edges, filling the entire space with green, and three trees hovered over him with small bushes gathered underneath. The shed stood tall in the corner with one large door at the front and small circular slabs of stone stamped into the ground around it.

Maren soaked in the evening around him, closing his eyes. His toes curled lightly into the grass and his loose shirt floated around his torso in the wind. The crickets sang in his ears along with faraway traffic. He breathed it all in.

Opening his eyes, his chest began to stir. His teeth scraped and his skin stung with the pull of the house, like a string wrapping tightly around his rib cage and reeling itself in. His feet numbed beneath him in the cold, sucking the heat from his body like water down a drain. Maren took one last look at the sky before turning, creeping back into the house, and shutting the door.

Silence enveloped him. The wind stopped curling at his ears and the *crunch* of the cold grass stopped ringing with his steps. The faraway city traffic and the insects and the blood in his ears all halted at once. The house stopped breathing and the shadows glued to the floor.

Maren stood with his back to the closed backyard door and glanced down at his freezing wet feet. He removed his socks with frigid fingers and tossed them to the side against the wall. His tiredness returned all at once, beckoning him up the stairs and into his warm bed. Whatever dreams waited for him there, he didn't care. He was simply exhausted.

Passing his bedroom, his feet led him deeper through the hall to Lily's closed door. Surely she was peacefully asleep, but how could he be sure unless he checked on her? The thought whispered through his head as his hand hovered just above the door's brass handle. He turned it hesitantly, attempting to prevent any sound from escaping. The door gradually opened.

Through the shadows, she slowly came into focus from her position on the bed. She sat motionlessly, straight up on the mattress, digging blank eyes into the wall. Her mouth hung slightly agape, and her glossy eyes held open, empty and unblinking. Her father tipped slightly into the dark room while his wild, terrified eyes adjusted to the deepened blackness.

"Lily?" His words were barely a whisper. A cautious hand clung to the door handle, becoming slick with sweat.

She sat ghostly still, inhumanly silent. She continued to stare.

"Lily-pop?" he said again, slightly louder this time. His legs begrudgingly willed him forward toward the bed, sinking him farther into the darkness.

He was close enough to hear her now, taking shallow breaths. His ears blared and his thoughts stormed as he carefully maneuvered around the dollhouse in the center of the room and closed in around the edge of the bed. Fearful fingers stretched slowly through the air toward Lily, her unyielding dead eyes still digging into the wall ahead.

Her head snapped to the right toward him. Two empty irises stared puncture wounds into Maren's outstretched arm. He fell back, horrified, flailing in the open air and landing on the floor with a loud *thud.*

"Dad?" Lily awoke at the noise, blinking away the gloss from her eyes and relaxing the tension from her small body. "Dad, what's going on?" Her voice was ripe with fear, like she was ripped from a deep sleep and thrown into chaos.

"You . . . you were . . ." He was leaning on his hands on the floor next to the dollhouse, realizing that he missed it by inches as he fell. Glaring in through the miniature windows, he spotted the gray doll lying on the floor of the girl doll's bedroom. Maren silently wished he had crushed it, while words continued fumbling from his tongue.

"You were sleepwalking, I think," he muttered. "I was checking on you, and I guess I tripped."

"Oh . . . I was dreaming." She spoke slowly, unraveling each word like she was waking from a trance. Lily stared down at her hands, curling and flexing her palms and fingers like they were almost unfamiliar to her. She touched her hand to her hair and slowly slid a thick blonde lock through her fingers.

"Dreaming about what, sweetheart?" He felt glued to the floor, at the mercy of his heart beating erratically in his chest. Anxious fingers thrummed deep into the carpet as he searched her face for an answer, but none came.

Lily paused for a moment, considering, with her lips drawn tightly together.

"Nothing."

"Nothing."

Ten.

The nightmares continued. During the few days since the incident with Lily's sleepwalking, Maren's nights were restless. When he did sleep, he dreamt of crowbars and doors, creeping up stairwells and tiptoeing through halls. He dreamt of darting eyes and panicked mumbling and *down the street, third house on the right, upstairs bedroom facing the road.*

When he lay awake, he stewed nervously in his bed, retrieved a glass of water from the kitchen, or retreated to the peace of the backyard for fresh air. Sometimes he roamed the house, usually ending up outside of Lily's door and wondering if he should enter.

Always he thought of Lily. He thought of her glossy, dead eyes and her slightly open jaw. He thought of her empty gaze piercing through the wall in front of her, staring into nothingness.

Lily would sleepwalk often in her childhood. When she was six years old, Maren and Jewel once woke in a panic to a security alarm blaring throughout the house. Maren barreled down the hallway to the back door, pointing his loaded gun straight at Lily where she stood with one hand still on the handle, staring out the open door into the night. She came to with the sirens screaming in her ears from all directions and a gun in her face, rightfully terrified. At first, she didn't even realize it was *her* who opened the door. Whatever dream that led her to it had promptly fizzled away.

She had done a few other strange things over the years at night, mumbling nonsense and walking into rooms without purpose as she slept, but Maren thought these episodes had stopped years ago. He supposed there was no way of knowing for sure if they had, or if he just hadn't noticed them anymore. He wondered how often Lily sat up in her bed, sleeping soundly with a slack jaw and hazy eyes, like a corpse.

The thought made him shudder.

Breakfast sizzled in the pan beneath him. Pancakes with bacon burnt to a crisp, orange juice with no pulp, and a small slice of cheesecake for Lily. Her last piece. Maren figured this special occasion was enough to prompt dessert with breakfast.

"It's the last big breakfast we can have together before you start at your new school." Maren spoke with a half-piece of bacon hanging from his mouth and a glass of juice in each hand. The liquid thrashed in the glasses as he used his full hands to point Lily toward the dining table rather than the kitchen island. "A special occasion deserves a special seat."

"You made breakfast?" Lily was peeking her head around the corner from the stairs watching him cook, Mr. Doll grasped tightly in her hand.

"Yeah, I mean, I figured with you starting school and me starting work, we should celebrate. Our last morning of freedom." He smiled, raising an eyebrow at her and setting the glasses down in front of two full plates of food that waited on the table. It had been so long since Maren cooked a proper breakfast, he went a bit overboard with the portions. It was enough to feed them for days.

"Yeah. Thanks." Lily smiled warily as she slid into the dining chair. She couldn't remember the last time her father had put this much effort into cooking for her. He cooked typical meals—spaghetti, meat and potatoes, things he could easily make after a long day. Things he didn't need to think much about.

Breakfast was usually every man for himself—mostly cereal, toast, or a banana that Lily could grab on her way out the door as she rushed to the school bus. She imagined her father waking up, pulling himself out of bed, and getting all of the ingredients in order. Making pancakes from scratch, not from a box, the way her mother used to. Burning the bacon just how she liked it, even though he preferred it soft and flimsy. She pictured him painstakingly assembling the food on each plate and displaying the leftovers on the kitchen island to show her how hard he had worked. He must have been down here for hours.

She pushed the thoughts down, unsteady in her excitement. He must have made the food for himself, then made extra for her. Maybe the ingredients were due to spoil and he didn't want to waste them. Maybe the bacon was burnt by mistake. She swallowed her hopefulness, dousing it with doubt. Disappointment was normal for her, comforting. Much more sustainable than hope, she had learned.

"You're welcome, Lily-pop. Eat up. There's plenty if you want more." He tousled her long hair and gently rested his hand on the top of her head. Sometimes he forgot that these small moments were so important. He forgot to keep track of them and make sure they came to be. He felt suddenly guilty for the mornings he sat in his chair with a full bowl of cereal, reading a book—moments when he could have made his lonely daughter feel loved and chose not to. His mouth twitched into a forced smile, and Lily turned her head up to stare at him.

"Okay." Her mouth was already full of cheesecake, which was unsurprisingly devoured first. His heart warmed as she flashed a messy smile at him. Maybe he wasn't so bad, he thought. Maybe they could start over.

"So." He pulled his chair out from under the table, lowering himself into it and over his steaming plate of food. "I have time to drive you to school, if you want. I don't have to be in until 8:30." His stomach fluttered nervously, though he wasn't quite sure why.

"It's okay, I can take the bus. The bus stop is right down the street from here." Her face flushed hot. She brought the glass of juice to her lips and downed a mouthful, focusing her eyes into the wood grain of the table.

"Ah, okay." He paused. "That's fine, then."

It was painfully quiet in the house. Silverware clinked against plates as they ate in silence. A curtain of tension was slowly being lowered across the table, perfectly between them.

His heart burned; his veins surged. All he felt he could do these days was *tap tap tap tap tap* . . .

Maren cleared his throat. He pushed his guilt into a ball and swallowed it, continuing on.

"I really would like to take you to school, Lily. It's your first day." His eyes were glued to his plate, bracing for rejection.

He was realizing, lately, that sometimes his own daughter was a stranger to him. Things that should be familiar between a father and daughter were alien to Maren and Lily. Conversations were often short and physical affection was scarce. Something as small as a seven-minute ride to school felt like asking for a piece of her soul. Something that he couldn't be sure if she wanted to share with him.

"Okay." Lily's soft voice floated into his ears. "If you really want to."

Maren's chest swelled with relief. His jaw released enough tension to put him to sleep where he sat, fork in hand. He tried to keep from rising from his seat and crossing the room to Lily to lift her from her chair like he used to do when she was small and just said her first words or took her first steps. Instead, he simply smiled.

"Okay." His first real smile in days.

…

"Lily, we're going to be late!" He called up the stairs to his daughter from his seat on the couch, lacing his boots. He was arguably more nervous to start at his new job than Lily was for her first day of school, even though it was always the same.

He wore a tight-fitting tan shirt under his military jacket, camo pants, and tan boots laced tightly around his ankles. Being in the administrative department, Maren would be stationed each time in increments of two or three years. At first it started as an excuse to travel, between him and Jewel. They would move across the country, even across the world for a couple of years at a time together. They enjoyed guessing where Maren would next be sent. New York? Japan? *The moon?*

That joke got older each of the many times Jewel had used it. Still, it repeated in his head every two years or so.

Jewel had always been a wild card—a bolt of electricity in a sky full of clouds. She dragged him constantly from his comforts, often kicking and screaming. But she was right, of course. It was always worth it.

When they began to settle down and talk about starting a family, it became less glamorous to move so often. They stayed in one place for three or four years before moving, getting lazily settled in their house and their city and their routines. Once Lily was born, their life slowed, almost halted. When Lily was about five years old, her mother finally had had enough.

"She needs to see the world, Maren, not just this city." She dreamt of a certain life for their little girl—a life full of wonders and big, exciting moments. A life full of experiences. "We need to get her out there, like we were. We can't keep her from it or she'll grow old and boring. This house is a prison for little girls." Maren rolled his eyes and wrapped his arms warmly around his wife.

"She's perfectly happy; she's a child," he would say.

"A child who needs to experience the world before she grows up never knowing that it existed." Jewel was eccentric, and oftentimes dramatic. But Maren could rarely tell her no.

From then on, they were moving again every two years—just enough time for Jewel to take her young daughter on hikes and to museums and on camping trips and boat rides before leaving again, finding a new place to explore. Jewel was Mother Nature's biggest fan.

Lily was very young during most of their adventures, but Jewel always thought that even if she didn't remember the things they experienced together, the adventurous spirit would still grow its roots deep into her. She was so excited for her daughter to mature and one day be able to truly experience everything she so desperately wanted to show her. It was never part of her plan to get sick.

Before they knew it, they were stuck in one place again. Adventures became less and less frequent, hikes turned into trips to the park, and trips to the park turned into board games between Maren and Lily while Jewel slowly worsened in her office. Jewel felt like she needed to hide from her daughter to keep her from the pain of watching her mother die. The guilt ate away at her as she watched her only child sit in the house all day, abandoned.

"I'm robbing her of her childhood, Maren," Jewel said softly through tears. Her weakened hands curled desperately around her husband's, clinging to his strength. "It's not fair to Lily."

"Stop it, Jewel. Don't say that." Maren stroked her face delicately, afraid to touch her too hard—afraid that she might break into pieces under any sort of pressure. "Please, don't," he begged.

Jewel curved against the inside of the bathtub with soaking towels and bath pillows propped underneath her hips and neck to keep her weakened bones from rubbing against the porcelain. Maren helped her bathe at the end. She was too weak.

"Promise me you'll keep going." Tears were streaming down her face now. Her bright-blue eyes looked dulled as she pleaded with her husband, an impossible request. "Show her the world and all the things she can do in this life. My beautiful, stubborn, adventurous girl. You have to show her there's more to it . . . more than *this*." She motioned to the world around her with a frail hand, and warm water from the bath splashed to the tile. She hated her weakness, her grand defeat. Tears welled in Maren's eyes.

"This is *not* your fault," he insisted. "Lily would *never*—"

"Maren." Jewel's eyes were full of sorrow, weeping with regret. "*Promise me.*"

He slipped his arms around his wife. Soapy water thrashed around them with their embrace, soaking his dry clothes and pouring from the lip of the tub onto the floor. Jewel collapsed into his warmth and his comfort, burying herself in the strength of his arms as she cried. Sobs came as heavy as her weakened body would allow.

"I promise," Maren whispered against her ear, holding her tightly. He feared that once he let go, she might disappear forever. "I promise."

"Dad?"

Maren snapped back to the present. His thoughts were pooling tightly in his eyes. Blinking them away, he turned to his daughter where she stood at the bottom of the stairs behind him. Her backpack was slung over one shoulder.

"Hey, Lily-pop." He slapped a smile to his face. "Are you ready for your first day?"

Lily stared at her father, unsure of what to say. A tear had slipped from his eyes and tumbled down his cheek to his chin, which he quickly swiped away with the back of his hand.

"What's wrong, Dad?" Lily's eyes were deep caverns of thought. She searched him for a warning, a *bad thing*.

"Nothing. Nothing's wrong. I'm fine, just . . ." He stood from the center of the couch where he had been waiting. "Nothing." He forced a weak smile again, wrapping desperate arms around his daughter. The daughter he failed.

They stood, motionless, at the bottom of the staircase. She hesitantly brought her arms up and over her father's neck as he held her, breathing her in. Mr. Doll was still grasped in her hand, dangling lifelessly down Maren's back.

Maren wasn't thinking about the creepy gray doll. He wasn't thinking about the nightmares or the loneliness or the small wooden dollhouse. He was thinking of his wife, and his daughter, and the promise he couldn't keep.

How could he show her the world that took Jewel from him? How could he teach Lily happiness when he had none left to give her? Maren could hardly look at her sometimes without breaking. A million bits of Jewel cascaded down her face, cutting into him each time he thought of her. How could he possibly carry on? Just one more of his precious wife's dying traditions, a fish out of water choking slowly in his hands. He was failing his daughter, and failing Jewel.

He released her from his grasp, grabbing the keys from the hook on the wall.

"Let's go." He looked down at her, motioning out the door and to the truck, and locked up the house behind them.

...

The ride to school was quiet. Mr. Doll sat in Lily's lap with her hand draped over him like a seatbelt. Tension painted the car in thick coats, and the doll's presence burned a hole in the space between them.

Maren had given up the fight to keep it at home. Lily-Doll was abandoned inside of the dollhouse, while the creepy gray doll had become the pinnacle of his daughter's obsession. She brought it along despite Maren's best efforts to convince her to leave it behind, and the uneasy feeling that accompanied it was soaking into the leather.

The brakes squealed as the car entered the packed parking lot. Maren rounded the corner to the front of the cafeteria, examining his daughter's new school. It looked dull.

"Do you know where to go?" She always did. He asked, anyway, to fill the gaping space.

"Yeah. I can always go to the office and ask for help." She never did. She would find it eventually by herself. Lily figured her father might feel better if he knew that she could though.

The emotions of the morning were fading away, leaving empty spaces of uncomfortable silence in their wake. Maren left the engine running while he opened the car door, circling to Lily's side and hugging her gently to his chest.

"Good luck, Lily-pop. Have a good first day." He spoke tenderly, resting a strong hand on the back of her head. "I love you."

"Bye. Love you too," she said softly, pressing Mr. Doll to her chest. She slipped the backpack over her shoulder before shutting the car door and heading out toward her new school. The cold air sucked her in.

Maren retreated back to the warmth of the truck and watched her walk through the parking lot, over the sidewalk, and disappear past the tall gates. The fog of her breath formed a cloud around her head, and the gray porcelain doll was still tucked tightly against her body.

The space around the truck was pounding with vitality—students scrambling from their parents' cars and crossing guards directing waves of children into the school. Bells were ringing loudly from speakers in the courtyard, and laughter and loud voices bounced off the tinted windows of his truck.

Maren, still, felt completely alone.

Eleven.

His thick boots stamped prints into the mud as he walked, touring the Detroit military base. It had the same boring buildings and the same flocks of camo-clad men and women with slicked, pristine hair. The same polished boots and colorful pins and wet gray gravel beneath his feet. Nothing ever changed, from base to base across the country or even across the sea. All unwelcomingly familiar.

Still, he preferred it to the discomfort of change. Without his late wife guiding him, he would still be in the same place in the same house for as long as his profession would allow. That's what comforted him about the military—predictability. During his time training in boot camp, many years ago, the only things that kept him sane were his routines.

The Detroit base was surrounded at the outskirts with tall, thick trees. Dewy branches swayed in the wind and the light rain. It always seemed to rain in Michigan, but Maren didn't mind. It comforted him.

Small droplets caressed his skin as he walked, steadily soaking into the collar of his jacket. The clouds were smudged into the sky like oil paint, and the air was clean and cold, displaying his exhales in a thin fog around his head.

At work, he had a simple job: do as he was told by his superiors—fill out paperwork, plan and attend meetings, assist soldiers or their families with questions or an assortment of issues that might arise. It was a safe job—one that never had an end to its tasks—and it paid the bills. He wasn't particularly happy, but he wasn't miserable either. He enjoyed feeling useful and needed and knowledgeable. He took pride in the kind of work that people thanked him for, no matter how rarely it happened.

By about 2:00 p.m., Maren's eyes were heavy with exhaustion. He decided to come home early, to be there when Lily was dropped off by the bus. His first day had mostly been touring, viewing, and shaking hands with people whose names he had already forgotten. Leaving early, he figured, wouldn't hurt.

Approaching the empty house, he braced for the heavy feeling that accompanied it. There was no other house quite like this one. Between the ghost stories, the ominous dollhouse, and the recent recurring nightmares, the house was a blight in his mind. It sat on the edge of the road like an open wound.

Maren pulled his truck into the empty driveway. Everything from the move that hadn't yet found a place inside the house was living in the garage. The cramped space was bursting at its seams with boxes, leaving it mostly unusable.

He poked and prodded the tall exterior walls of the home with his eyes as he stepped out onto the concrete, interrogating it.

The bricks seemed calm, keeping the aura within packed tightly beneath them. From outside, it almost seemed like any other house on this quiet, peaceful street. He turned, staring at the small home directly opposite his.

Down the street, third house on the right, upstairs bedroom facing the road.

The words rang through his mind in a voice that didn't belong to him. The ghosts of his dreams were starting to haunt his waking hours as well. He walked to the front door, imagining the crowbar he had used in the dream to break it open, how the cold metal felt in his hands.

The house was different in his dreams. The door was a soft yellow color with white trim, where it now was a solid deep brown. The door handle, though kissed with age, was the same dull brass. He slid the key into the lock, jiggling the handle until it clicked into place as the key turned, opening the door. He had never thought before why the lock was tricky, or what could have caused it to be.

Maybe a crowbar, he thought, crossing the threshold of the doorway.

The living room was bright, full of shining windows with open blinds. His boots squeaked on the floor as he rounded the corner to the stairwell, peeking up to the second floor. In his dreams, the walls were hung with photographs and art pieces. Here, the walls were empty, blank, void of personality.

He trudged up the stairs, his tired legs bowing under his weight as he climbed. He envisioned the body from his dreams that wasn't his, sneaking up the stairs beside him, with its wild eyes and erratic movements. He saw the carpet squishing under its shoes where, now, was only hard wood. He stopped halfway up the stairs and turned, peering down to the first floor. At the far wall of the living room, his mind's eye could see each of the warm red bricks of the fireplace.

Maren's jaw clenched and his tongue scraped the sides of his dry mouth. He shoved his paranoia deep into the blackened corners of his mind as hard as he could, but the thoughts blossomed anyway. He could feel the crowbar rattle in his grasp as he snapped the doorframe. He could feel his hesitant steps up the carpeted stairs and the sweat trickling down his spine. He could feel the cold thing in his hands as he pointed it toward the open door of a bedroom. Toward a shadow. Toward a girl.

He shuddered violently, clawing at the thoughts to get them out. Standing at the top of the stairs, seeing the door handle of Lily's bedroom from around the corner, he froze. His feet had betrayed him, taking him absentmindedly up the stairs as he drowned in his mind. He glanced to the window at his left, framing the street and the houses perched at its edge. The neighbor's house across the road was in full, perfect view from where he stood.

Cash and jewelry. Thousands of dollars' worth. The strange man's ideas cracked through his head.

It was only a dream, of course; Maren knew that. A dream that felt disturbingly real. The yellow door, the photos on the wall, the darting eyes and jagged voice—these things had nothing to do with him. These things weren't real. The human mind is a curious and powerful thing, Maren thought, but it can't see into the *past*.

It was such a ridiculous notion. He had no reason to believe that these dreams had been real—flashes into the history of this house as if memories were contagious, seeping into his brain from the air.

No. Not from the air.

"Shut up," he whispered to the empty hall, bringing a coiled fist to his lips.

From him. From John.

"Shut up," he said again.

He refused to acknowledge the small parts of himself that gave in to the rumors, the whispers of the ghosts.

His stubborn inner voice toyed with him. The Maren who feared the rumors liked to fight with the Maren who renounced them. It was a constant battle as his uneasiness grew. New seeds were planted each day, lately. New roots sprouted from each corner of the house as it watched. Waited.

He pushed forward toward the door of Lily's bedroom, ignoring his newfound obsession over stories of the old man.

Stories. That's all they were.

His hand rested gently on the cool doorknob, burning his skin with the feeling of the cold thing from his dreams. He remembered it, sizzling in the air as it pointed toward this very spot, where the girl bled against the floorboards.

John's daughter. Alina.

"*Stop,*" he mumbled angrily, his forehead pressed tightly against the smooth wooden door. His naïveté disgusted him. He was a man—a strong, intelligent, military man who didn't believe in things as trivial as ghosts. He didn't fear things like dreams and dolls. Children did.

Maren turned the knob, swinging the door into the empty room. He was shocked to find it spotless, not a single thing out of place—which, for Lily, was unheard of.

The floor was completely visible, no piles of clothes for his feet to avoid as he toed his way inside. No wrappers or empty cups littering the desk or the side table. No shoes that were kicked off thoughtlessly and sent across the room in either direction. Even a freshly made bed with fluffed pillows.

Just . . . *perfect.*

The dollhouse glared at him from the center of the room, where it was carefully perched on a small table that used to sit next to Lily's bed. The silence of the small space was thick with vitality, streaming from the dollhouse like bugs circling a streetlight. His fingers buzzed as he touched both sides of the wood, pulling it apart on its hinges.

The inside was almost more pristine than Lily's bedroom. Dust, grime, and fingerprints were completely foreign to its interior. The floors appeared freshly wiped, the beds both neatly made. The blonde doll was placed carefully on the smooth cushion of the living room couch, gazing blankly forward into the fireplace.

Maren searched the house with hungry eyes.

Looking for what? he wondered. He wasn't sure.

The furniture was arranged with an intense attention to detail. It was a miniature version of his home, down to the tiniest detail—the layout of the rooms, the color of the cabinets, the blank white walls, and the rug under the dining room table. Even the blankets from his bed were same in color as the ones laid over the gray doll's. They were tucked in at each corner under the mattress, same as his. Everything matched.

The dry feeling in his mouth began to burn down his throat and into his stomach as the realization boiled in his chest. He snatched the Lily-Doll from her spot on the small couch, examining her—her bright porcelain skin, her smooth yellow dress, her piercingly lifeless blue eyes. Maren slid his thumb and forefinger down the length of her thick blonde hair, which stopped just below her shoulders, a bit shorter than Lily's.

He imagined his daughter, obsessively cleaning the dollhouse in the confines of her room as her beautiful blonde hair streamed far down her back. He imagined Mr. Doll, possessively watching her.

In Maren's mind, the gray doll had eyes—deep black eyes that gouged holes through his innocent daughter. It had ears, listening intensely as Lily spoke. It had a mouth, as well, he imagined, with a voice that came as a low growl, poisoning his daughter with dampened words. It was sinking its blackened teeth farther into her throat with each calculated word.

The house around Maren was slowly swallowing itself. It was a snake, devouring its own tail. Soon the energy of it would burst, popping each seam as it snapped its giant hinges and sucked Lily into its black hole.

"*Shut up!*" He slammed his fists into his temples while his delusion ricocheted in his skull. The Lily-Doll fell flat onto the carpet beside him, unbothered by the commotion. He squeezed his eyes tightly shut.

A low creaking noise interrupted him from the spot where Lily stood, ripping through the weight of the moment. Her fearful eyes stung deep into her father's skin.

Maren's eyelids fluttered open. He released his fists from the sides of his head and stood clumsily before the open doorway.

"Lily, I . . . I wasn't talking to you." He shrunk at the sight of her. His words dripped of shame as each one sank into the carpet between them, barely a whisper. "I'm sorry, I . . . It wasn't . . ." His thoughts couldn't find their footing, stumbling around on his tongue. Lily glared through him and down to the doll at his feet.

"I'm sorry. I dropped her." He knelt down to retrieve the blonde doll, gently lying her on her side over the small couch where she sat before. He turned swiftly back to his daughter, waiting in silence while the gray doll's head peeked eerily from the lip of her backpack.

"What's going on?" Her mouth turned down slightly with concern and her eyebrows curved up at their edges. Was it fear? Anger?

"Nothing's going on, sweetheart. I didn't mean to scare you. I was just in here cleaning things up a little before you got home. I didn't expect it to already be so . . . spotless." Maren forced a soft laugh from his tightly wound chest. "I didn't hear you come in."

They both stood extremely still, afraid to spook the other.

"Why did you yell?" Lily didn't laugh or smile. She simply stared.

"The . . . birds," he said. "They were so loud, just a minute ago . . ." Maren's hand loosely motioned toward the window as a nervous smile stretched above his chin. "I guess my yelling did the trick. They're pretty quiet now, huh?"

"Yeah." Lily's expression softened slightly, almost empathetically, before flattening once again. She took a deep, slow breath in, running her eyes over her bedroom. Her hand moved to the strap of her backpack, slipping it from her shoulder and landing it carefully at her feet. She gently unzipped the large pocket where Mr. Doll was nestled inside.

Wrapping both hands around him, Lily drew the doll into her chest and allowed him to soak in his surroundings. Maren, the dollhouse, and Lily-Doll, who was tipped on her side atop the couch, all stared back at him. The gray doll had no reaction, just an overwhelmingly blank expression as its heat filled the room. It poured from invisible holes in its dull porcelain flesh, soaking everything that it touched. The air turned to smoke.

Quiet pounded in Maren's ears, and his skin pinched under fingernails that he dug roughly into his palms. Hot anger swelled from the deep pit in his stomach at the sight of the gray doll, its glower boring into him like a lion might prey on a mouse. Maren plunged his sharp eyes through its empty gray skull, envisioning the way it might *crack* against his fist.

"What's wrong?" Lily bent slightly forward to meet Maren's eyes. She looked so old in this moment, mature past her years—much older than she had before, even this morning.

"It's been a long day, I'm sorry. I just . . . don't feel very good," he said unconvincingly.

She shrank from the doorway, allowing him to leave. Lily and Mr. Doll watched him drag himself into the hall before stopping and turning back toward his daughter.

"Did your first day go well, Lily-pop?" The words squeezed their way out of him.

She nodded, silently willing him away.

"Good. That's good." He waited for something else, a word or even a look, but none came.

Before retreating down the hall to his room, he gently bent forward, embracing her with hesitant arms before he could talk himself out of it. He hugged his daughter desperately, burying his face into her long hair and inaudibly begging for her arms to wrap around him in return. Her small hands tightened, instead, around Mr. Doll.

He released her, wordlessly stepping farther into the hall and freeing her stiff frame from his arms. She melted back into the fog of her room and shut herself inside with the doll.

Maren escaped back down the hallway, closing and locking his bedroom door behind him. His weakened body collapsed onto the bed, agonizingly aware of the choice his daughter had just made. Her tiny fingers, grasping the doll, tangled around and around inside of his brain. They knotted his spine and his lungs and his heart. They pulled tightly, slowly killing him, inch by inch.

...

He stared at the ceiling for hours. Thoughts pooled around him on the bed and soaked into the sheets, which he gripped tightly between white-knuckled fingers.

I'm going crazy.

The idea repeated in his mind, the same way that flies smashed their tiny skulls into glass windows, searching for a way out. Over and over and over.

He had always been such a levelheaded man. Jewel used to run to him for comfort, for sharp logic and warm words. He was always rational, always unmovable. What had he become, here in this house?

This fucking house.

Fear bubbled into hatred, panic into resolve. Men didn't cower in their beds; they ripped the problem out by its roots. Men plucked the seeds from the soil so they couldn't grow at all. Men held power.

Maren felt powerless.

Whatever power he had here, in this house, over his daughter and over his own thoughts, was running out. He blamed himself—his nightmares for making him paranoid, and his insecurities for making him weak. What kind of father blames a doll for his failing relationship with his daughter? What kind of man lets old wives' tales infect his sanity?

Lily deserved better than this. He needed to fix it.

He jolted forward, launching himself out of bed. It was nearly dinnertime, and he expected she would be hungry, but cooking for her wasn't good enough.

He thought about their life before the tragedy. Before the doll, before the nightmares, back to before Jewel passed away. When they were a *real* family. He imagined the hikes and the adventures, the restaurants with greasy food and ice cream with so many toppings. He remembered how Lily looked when she was happy.

Maren quickly slipped on his shoes, smoothed his shirt down with the palms of his hands, and headed down the hallway toward his daughter's closed door. Nerves ate at him while his hand curled into a gentle fist, knocking softly against the thin white wood.

"Lily?" Her name floated from his tongue like florets from a dandelion. His gentle tone like a web, hoping to catch a fly.

He heard a soft voice from the other side of the door, mumbling secrets. The voice grew louder. "Yeah?" she replied, clearly.

Maren cracked open the door, peeking inside at his daughter. She sat cross-legged on the carpet before the dollhouse, which was open on its hinges. Mr. Doll and Lily-Doll sat on tiny barstools that were pulled from the tiny kitchen to face her. She turned toward him, blank-faced, like he had just interrupted something. Maren swallowed hard, pushing on.

"Why don't we go do something together, just the two of us?" He spoke with intent, with a hidden desperation.

Lily cocked her head slightly sideways, her blue eyes widening at his words. She misheard him, she thought. She stared at him, silently puzzled by the request, unsure if she should reply.

"Like . . . go somewhere?" She sounded so much like a child now. Her matured face had been wiped away to reveal his young daughter, only eleven years old, staring innocently toward him. His heart swelled.

"Yeah, I was thinking . . ." He paused, studying her face as he spoke. "Maybe we could go out like we used to. Get some dinner, go somewhere exciting." His voice grew stronger with each word, childish excitement rushing through his veins with each erratic heartbeat. He hadn't realized just how separate they had become, that something as simple as leaving the house together could make him nervous.

It had been much too long since they bonded like a father and daughter should, he knew that. He was grieving selfishly over the loss of his wife, idolizing his solitude and neglecting the most important thing that he had left. Lily was too young when she lost her mother to properly express her pain and her needs, and Maren was too self-absorbed to recognize them. He hated himself for a long time, but only now did he fully understand why. The pain he felt each day in remembering his wife, Lily also felt for her mother. Only she was just a child, alone, forced to cope by talking to dolls that she viewed to be as lonely as she was.

Maren *knew* that doll was empty. That this *house* was empty. That the dreams and the stories were infecting him with malice toward this stupid toy his daughter was forced to connect with. Maren had given her no choice; it was his own fault. *This* was the reason for her sleepwalking and his delusions and their increasingly strong disconnection.

It had to be it.

"So, what do you say? Just you and me." Maren broke the pressing silence, motioning toward the dolls with his eyes as a message: *Leave them behind.* "I miss you." The words were heavy, nearly cracking his voice.

Lily looked back and forth between her father and Mr. Doll. Her head scrambled with thoughts that pushed and pulled each other through her mind. The doll or her father?

Mr. Doll sizzled in his small chair, like hot oil popping in a pan. His empty face was nearly bursting with intensity. Lily clasped her hands tightly in her lap, desperate to believe her father's sincerity. This moment was important, she could feel it. She could see it scrawled over Maren's tight face and frigid jaw, in the way that his fingers tapped the doorframe where he grasped it, like he needed help staying upright.

Just you and me. The words repeated in her head.

The emotions welling in Lily's chest were unrelenting, unrecognizable. She didn't know, until this moment, that her father's words were what she had been craving for so long. That the look on his face would prove to her what she had convinced herself wouldn't come back. That he loved her. He *missed* her.

She tore her eyes from the small gray doll, leaving him alone in his chair as she stood. She smiled widely, with innocent, blue eyes.

"That sounds fun," she said. She missed him too.

Twelve.

Lily slipped on a bright-yellow blouse along with dark jeans and blue sneakers with white flowers on them, her favorite shoes. Her long blonde hair was held back from her face with small clips, proudly displaying her pale skin, rosy cheeks, and freckled nose. Mr. Doll watched silently as she cracked the door of her bedroom, toes pointed toward the hall. Her face burned.

Looking back into the dollhouse, guilt consumed her.

Don't, the deep, sulking voice said, infiltrating her mind.

She continued, her feet clipping the floorboards as she walked away, and the gray doll's aura followed closely behind. It bounced from the walls and clouded from the vents around her as she moved down the hallway to the stairs. Each light followed her with a subtle flicker as she passed it, popping with warmth. The ceiling bowed softly toward her, like an extended hand.

She ignored it, skipping steps on her way down the stairs to escape the second floor. The mouth of the stairwell opened for her at the bottom, and thick waves of energy stretched toward her like a tongue finding food in its teeth. She stood steadily, overflowing with resolve.

I'm going, she said sternly in her head. *Just for a little while.*

Heat receded from the doorway like the warning before a tsunami, promising to return, as Lily pushed past it and into the living room. The invisible strings that Mr. Doll had wrapped around Lily's wrists slowly thinned away with each step she took toward the door, and toward her father.

The house was brimming with the spirit of the gray doll. Each word, each touch, each look that Lily bestowed upon him only breathed his presence deeper into the walls—into each crack, each empty space, each darkened corner. He watched her from every angle as she abandoned him.

Maren stood, leaning against the doorframe, waiting. Lily jumped from the second step and landed on the hardwood, her shoes squeaking against the floor. She rounded the corner, stopping a few steps away from her father where he stared at her, displaying a smile that reached his eyes.

He was reminded suddenly of just how beautiful his daughter was, as if seeing her for the very first time. She looked just like Jewel.

"Where are we going?" Lily could hardly contain her excitement, but she shoved it down into its box anyway, afraid the moment might disappear.

"Well, if you're hungry, why don't we start with dinner? You can pick whatever you want." He stood nervously away from her, like an awkward young boy afraid of rejection. His hands found their way into the pockets of his jeans. He had changed into his nicest pair, with his nicest green button-up shirt and only pair of clean shoes to match.

Lily smiled and nodded, trying to choose between the only three restaurants she knew off the top of her head, wondering if they could even find them in Detroit.

Maren reached toward the doorknob, touching it lightly with the tips of his fingers, before snapping his arm back in fear.

"What the . . ." He rubbed his hands together, furrowing his eyebrows at the door. "It shocked me."

Lily stared angrily forward, piercing the bronze handle with her gaze.

Stop it.

She watched with wide eyes as her father's hand moved, once again, toward the handle. He gripped it this time without drawing back. Lily swallowed hard.

"That was strange. Pretty strong shock, like a fence." He laughed, opening the door and glancing up to the gray clouds. "Must be the weather."

He didn't understand. Lily couldn't tell him.

She turned back to face the house, soaking its air into her skin. The tension was boiling beneath her feet, and shadows crept forward from all corners, then halted before her. The house stilled, holding its breath.

It's okay, she whispered wordlessly. *I'm sorry.*

"You okay?" Maren's voice rang from behind her as he held open the door. "You ready to go?"

"Yeah. I'm ready," she said to the house, turning her back on it and walking out into the cool air behind her father.

. . .

The restaurant was bustling with people. A chorus of loud voices thrummed in her ears, and bright lights flashed around her in a haze. It was jarring, perfect.

Lily grabbed the tall burger from the plate in front of her with both hands, trying to maneuver her jaw into biting it. Burgers must be larger inside the restaurant than they are if you order them to go, she thought.

She eyed the pink strawberry milkshake in the middle of the table. It was her favorite flavor. She could hardly wait to drink it, but decided the burger should go first. She didn't want to risk upsetting her father when things were going so strangely well.

Maren sat opposite her in the bright-red booth, an equally large burger held to his mouth. He had already figured out how to bite it.

"You gotta smash it," Maren said, barely audible through the food that he was still chewing. He grinned, setting his burger against the plastic tray and miming a smashing motion with his fist over the top of it, grinning.

Lily giggled, redness flashing over her cheeks. She set her burger down and began slowly squishing her flattened fingers against the top bun, mashing the burger together. Grease and ketchup ran down the sides. She felt silly, but her father smiled at her, so she didn't care.

She held it to her mouth once more, easily biting into it and ripping off a large chunk with her teeth. She laughed, chewing her food and kicking her feet against the bottom of the booth.

This moment seemed to be infinite. Maren and Lily had forgotten all about the last three or four years, if only for ten minutes, while they chewed their squished burgers and laughed together. Maren pushed the strawberry milkshake across the table toward his daughter, inviting her to take a sip.

"I'll be right back. You sit here and enjoy your milkshake, okay?" Maren's heart was so full it might pop. He rose from the table while she nodded, wiping her hands into her napkin to grab the shake.

The bathroom was completely empty, even though the entirety of the restaurant seemed to be packed with people. It was quiet too, Maren thought, washing his hands. Time slowed while he rinsed the frothy soap from his fingers and stared at himself in the bathroom mirror. The reflection seemed gray.

He leaned forward slightly, getting a better look. He *was* gray. The lighting in the room was odd, casting his skin with the soft, even color—his face, his arms, his eyes, even his lips. He looked down away from the mirror and brought his wet hand closer to his face to inspect it. The color glistened behind the water that was dripping from his fingers and down his arm. Gray.

Suddenly, the lights flickered from the ceiling. One by one they illuminated and dulled. The buzzing sounds of the lightbulbs were audibly clear as the noise from the restaurant fell away. The bathroom was so silent, he wondered if it had detached from the building and floated away.

An eeriness settled into the bathroom, falling like snowflakes that stuck to each corner and melted into his clothes. Maren felt a familiar fear slink up his spine and tighten around his throat, strangling his thoughts. His stomach twinged like a fist, curling stiff fingers through his insides.

The sound of the water fell into his ears, still running from the tap where he had left it, and flashed him back to reality. He turned it off, staring at the brushed metal and catching his reflection in it—distorted but clean. He cocked his head, returning his gaze to the mirror.

All at once, the sounds of the busy restaurant returned to the empty bathroom. His skin was no longer gray, the lights no longer flickering. He wondered how long he had been there, staring blankly into the glass.

He quickly dried his hands with a towel, tossing it into the trash and swinging the door open to leave. He shook away the awful feeling from the bathroom as he walked but it clung to him, lingering like a sour stench.

Approaching the booth, he eyed Lily where she sat with her back to him. She was stiffened, staring forward with her arms resting motionlessly at her sides.

Maren slid into the seat across from her, noticing her burger with only two bites missing. The milkshake beside it was almost completely full.

He slowly raised his eyes to meet hers, expecting the sadness to have returned to her face—expecting rejection, or an expression that meant he, again, failed.

Instead, her eyes were glossy and unfocused, pointed over his shoulder where he sat. Her head leaned forward slightly, held up by her frigid shoulders and straight spine. Her jaw, still with a smudge of ketchup near her bottom lip, hung open.

Like a corpse.

He shook his head at the thought, shoving it away again. She was tired, that's all. She was exhausted after her first day of school. That was it.

His explanation gave him no comfort. He froze, staring at his daughter's wide, empty eyes that looked past him and dug into the wall. The image of Lily sitting up in her bed and cloaked in the thick darkness of her bedroom projected from his mind.

Lily's pale face looked hollow, with two lifeless eyes staring back at him. The only thing holding his scream inside of his throat was the soft sound of his daughter's shallow breaths crawling from her lungs. Otherwise, she looked empty. She looked *dead.*

He wondered how something so terrifying, something that shook Maren's bones beneath his skin, went seemingly unnoticed in this busy room. Waiters continued walking with their trays full of food. Customers loudly kept up their conversations. No one noticed the lights as they softly flickered, or the sudden weight of the air. No one even seemed to notice his daughter sitting blankly across from him like a fragile eggshell, ready to crack.

"Lily?" he finally said. He whispered it, like he needed to be quiet, as if the noise around them wasn't stabbing and clawing at his ears. Lily didn't notice.

"Lily?" He forced her name out louder this time. His paranoia was returning all at once, squirming inside of him like a tapeworm. His hands curled around the edges of the table.

Tap tap tap tap tap.

His eyes were wide and wild. He felt frozen, helpless. He stared into the gaping hole of Lily's mouth as it hung open.

Tap tap tap tap tap.

Panic vibrated his skin as he pounded his fingertips against the wooden underside of the booth. The sound filled his ears.

"Sir?" A young man appeared at the edge of Maren's seat with a cold pitcher of water. Condensation dripped down its sides into the patterned carpet beneath his shoes.

Maren blinked, ripping his eyes from his daughter's blank face and snapping his head toward the waiter.

"Would you like a refill?" The man smiled wryly, tipping the pitcher forward and pouring it into Maren's half-empty cup before walking away. Maren eyed the man in shock, amazed that the world around him hadn't stopped. He had expected the waiter to see his daughter and his face to become pale. He imagined him screaming at the sight, dropping the full pitcher onto the carpet and leaving it to soak. In the minute or two since Maren had returned to his seat, a million years had passed. And no one had even noticed.

He swung his eyes back to his daughter.

Lily sat, milkshake in hand, sucking a thick piece of cut strawberry through the plastic straw. She glanced up at him, blinking her eyes like she was waking from a deep sleep. Maren stared in utter shock and confusion.

"Lily?" He could barely breathe. "What happened?"

His lungs were crumpled inside of his chest between his ribs. He tore through his thoughts for a clue, for any indication that what he had just seen was real. It couldn't have been.

"I just feel kind of sleepy all of a sudden. I guess I zoned out for a minute." She was unmistakably calm. Maren watched the spot below her lip where the ketchup was still smudged as she spoke.

It was real. I saw it.

He ran a hand roughly over his face and into his hair. His food patiently waited on the plate in front of him, though he was no longer hungry. He mulled over what to say, or if he should say anything at all. Maybe he *was* going crazy. Maybe he was seeing things that weren't real.

But I saw it all—the bathroom, the lights, Lily's slack jaw.

He shook his head gently, his head bowed toward his lap. *No,* he thought. *I imagined it.*

The ketchup. He raised his chin to stare at it while his thoughts argued in his mind.

"You've got . . . ketchup. There," he said, pointing. Lily raised an arm to her mouth, wiping it with the back of her hand, while her father stayed focused on her face in disbelief.

He needed this to go well, now more than ever he believed that. Fear rose in him like bile, threatening to explode. Lily was here, right in front of him, but the feeling that plagued him was just as powerful as it had been when she was gone, locked away in her room with her dolls—the feeling that she was quickly slipping away.

He raised the overflowing cup to his lips, taking a large gulp. The cold would clear his mind, he thought. Lily was fine, after all. She looked completely unaware of whatever Maren's eyes had just witnessed.

Lily finished her burger and loudly slurped up the remaining drops of the empty milkshake. It was a warming sight, knowing that his daughter was happy. Even if it was just for one moment, he hadn't completely failed. He imagined Jewel in the booth beside him, smiling at their daughter. It was enough to keep his unrelenting paranoia at bay.

Lily clasped her hands in her lap when she finished, stretching and wiggling her fingers. Her mind wandered as she stared at her warm, soft skin.

...

The car door slammed shut, shaking the old pickup truck. Maren and Lily sat side by side in the front seat. A takeout box with Maren's half-eaten burger rested on the leather between them. His stomach twisted.

"Where to?" Maren asked, curling his fingers around the steering wheel while the engine gasped to life.

"We're not going home?" Lily was starting to think about Mr. Doll. Maybe he was worried about her. Maybe he was angry.

"I figured we could go somewhere fun, now that we've eaten. It's barely six o'clock." He pulled a smile to his face, turning his head toward her.

"What about Mr. Doll?" she asked. She felt guilty for saying it as soon as the words left her mouth. Maren's smile shattered as he turned back toward the windshield.

"If you don't want to, that's fine, Lily-pop. I just thought I'd ask." He reached toward the gearshift, defeated.

Quiet stretched out between them like a blanket. Lily thought hard, pulling and pushing each option through her mind.

"Well . . ." Lily whispered hesitantly, fiddling nervous fingers in her lap. "We could go to the aquarium. I heard some of the kids at school talking about it today. It just opened a few months ago." Her eyes pushed to their corners toward Maren while keeping her head pointed forward. "You can pet the stingrays."

Her father exhaled softly through his nose, the tips of his mouth twitching up. "Yeah." He breathed. "Let's go to the aquarium, then."

The car moved swiftly down the road. Cars, trees, and people on the sidewalk flashed outside of Lily's window as they passed. For once it wasn't raining, allowing the clouds to part and the sunlight to pool into the truck. The people outside held their closed umbrellas at their sides as they walked.

Lily leaned her head against the glass, fogging it with her breath. She thought about the giant tanks of water that would hold all the fish. She thought about the stingrays, how they might feel against the tips of her fingers. She thought about Mr. Doll, what he might be thinking . . . or *doing*.

Mr. Doll was protective. He was paranoid and possessive and afraid.

People do terrible things when they are afraid. His words scraped through her head. What terrible thing might he do?

She often wondered where he came from, and why he was there. At first, the doll was imaginary. She would talk to him in her head, alone and desperate for connection. She was never good at making friends, and felt alienated by her grieving father. The gray doll was an escape from reality.

She would pretend to be Lily-Doll, walking through the dollhouse, seeing through her unclosing eyes. She would sit with her gray father at the dining room table, eating imaginary home-cooked meals. They would crouch on the floor together and play games, or ask each other questions.

She told Mr. Doll all of her secrets, all of her desires—her fears, her wants, her needs, and just how deep her loneliness went. He listened intensely, like he couldn't get enough, like he had been waiting for her for a very long time.

Pretty soon, the voice she had used in her head to make him speak had morphed into his own voice. It was gravelly, deep, harsh. Instead of talking about the dollhouse or playing pretend, they would talk about Lily. He would ask in his own voice where she had been all this time. She was not sure how to answer.

He asked her when her hair had gotten so long and when she had taken down her pretty artwork. She would just say that she didn't know, unsure of what he meant. She couldn't remember having any artwork before.

He started showing her things in her dreams. He would show her what it was like inside of the dollhouse, inside the porcelain skin. He showed her what it was like to never be alone, to never have to want to be seen. He saw her.

He saw inside of her head, inside of her dreams. He reached into the deep caves of her emptiness and filled it with promises, devouring her fear and her pain. As her connection to Mr. Doll grew, so did his connection to the house and his presence inside of it. She began to feel him in every dark corner and every empty space. He spoke softly to her in her head more and more, and Lily welcomed him. She was tired of the emptiness, the loneliness. Tired of the silence.

She never feared him or wondered what came next. She only floated in his acceptance and in his *love*. That's what he called it. He often told her he loved her, even when she had done nothing to deserve it. He told her he missed her, even when she was right there. In the house, his warmth blanketed her. Here in the truck, away from him for the first time since they met, she felt cold.

Maren glanced at her as they drove, sitting silently beside one another. Lily wondered for a moment if she *needed* Mr. Doll, or if he needed her—and what might happen when one day, they left this house, too.

Thirteen.

Maren stared up at the bright neon sign.

"Tails of Wonder. Clever name," he scoffed, turning into the parking lot of the aquarium.

The brakes squealed as they pulled into an empty space. Lily's eyes brightened at the letters plastered on the front of the colorful building.

"I think it's cute," Lily said as she smiled, climbing out of the truck and closing the passenger door with a *thud*.

The inside was just as colorful as the bright-blue exterior. The building was full of people staring into tanks, holding hands, or chasing after their young children as they ran past the exhibits.

After purchasing tickets, Maren and Lily headed down the hall into the heart of the aquarium. A giant domed ceiling hovered high above them, with iridescent drawings of sea creatures and freckles of light peppering each of the walls. Small tanks, filled with many different kinds of tiny fish, were scattered across the room. They continued farther inside to a stretching hallway, soaking everything in. The air was clean, with a subtle smell of salt water.

All around them, vibrant pinks, blues, and purples saturated the walls. The lights were dimmed deeply, leaving the large tanks of water to illuminate the long vaulted spaces. Each tank was nearly floor to ceiling, with only a couple of feet at the top and bottom for the walls. Bright LEDs flashed inside of the tanks, displaying each color of the rainbow in turns. The multi-colored fish swam in all directions, some as large as sharks.

Lily eyed a family to her right, a bit farther down the winding hallway, standing before a giant, clear tank. Inside, three large fish swam in slow circles in the water. The two smiling parents with their young son in between them all stared wide-eyed at the creatures.

The little boy, two or three years old, held one of his parents' hands in each of his own. His tiny fingers were too small to grip them, so he held tightly to a finger or two instead. The couple took turns looking down at him while he babbled happily at the fish, before glancing at each other and smiling deeply. Lily could feel this small family's connection and love from across the room, and it tightened around her throat. She often tried to remember times like this, times that she must have had with her own parents. She hoped that they were still there somewhere, buried deep inside of her memories. For now, none came to mind.

The room quieted around her as families slowly trickled down the hall. The couple and their smiling son disappeared into other sections of the aquarium.

Lily swallowed the sour taste from her tongue as she approached one of the many walls of glass, toeing forward hesitantly. A large group of bluish fish swam in circles together near the bottom of the tank, thrashing through the illuminated water. Soft green lights pulsed behind them near the back of the enclosure, glossing their colorful scales with its reflection.

As soon as Lily got within two feet of the fish, they scattered in every direction. Some ran into each other in their panic before disappearing into the endless blue behind the colorful plastic reef. Lily frowned, with both hands pressed against the glass, and stared into the empty water.

"Lily? Are you okay?"

She jolted from her daze, turning toward her father as he spoke. Concern filled his eyes under furrowed brows.

"Yeah. I'm fine." She focused her gaze over his face, blinking away the fog.

"I lost you there for a minute," he said. He spoke softly, like he was afraid to scare her. "Are you sure you're okay?" He almost lifted a hand to touch her forehead but froze in place instead.

"I think I'm just tired . . ." She shifted her focus back to the tank, toward the lights and their gently changing colors.

Maren pressed a hand onto the cool glass, sliding his thumb across it and leaving a smudge. He took a deep breath, releasing it slowly as he slid his hand back down into his pocket.

"This place is pretty cool, don't you think?" He moved toward the next tank, where pinkish-orange fish roamed their makeshift ocean. They swam slowly in front of him, so close he could touch them if it weren't for the glass. He tapped the tip of his finger against it, causing the fish to twitch.

Lily approached her father, directing her attention toward the vibrant orange fish, and Maren slid to the side allowing her closer. Once more, the fish swarmed to the back of the tank, leaving Lily to stare into the emptiness.

"Why don't they like me?" Lily soured, rhythmically tapping her knuckle against the glass, hoping to call them back.

Maren smiled. "I don't think fish *dislike* anyone. I think they just got a little spooked."

"I'm not scary," she whined, looking down at her shoes.

"No, Lily-pop, you're not scary at all." Maren patted her blonde head with a gentle hand. "These fish are just . . . a little dumb," he said, letting out a soft laugh.

Lily looked up at her father while her lips curled into a grin.

"Yeah, fish are stupid." She giggled, sticking her tongue out at the barren tank. The fish inside still waited in a tight bundle in the corner for their imaginary predator to be gone.

They walked past dozens of tanks filled with hundreds of colorful fish and sea creatures. Lily loved the starfish and the snails that cupped the glass, and the jellyfish as they floated like giant white bubbles in the water. Maren followed her closely behind as she explored the aquarium with an innocent, childlike wonder. She was nervous in her excitement, coasting from tank to tank as her father watched, smiling.

The hallway opened up to a wide circular room. There was a large marble fountain at its center, with a giant round skylight in the ceiling above. Sunlight pooled into the room, dripping down each edge of the fountain and stretching across the glossy floor. At the curved edges around the space, there were several highlighted exhibits. At one end sat a vibrant coral reef, with tiny motorized boats for the children to captain. At the other, a gift shop packed with people that were holding giant stuffed crabs or ridiculous fish hats. Lily was immediately drawn to the far end of the room, where the giant "Pet the Stingrays!" sign was gleaming above a pool of thrashing water.

The stingrays swam in a long, wide white enclosure that rested on the ground, with a floor-to-ceiling wall of mirror behind it. The top was open, letting the creatures happily splash and slide up the sides of the walls, poking their wet heads out of the water. The surrounding edges were only about two feet tall, with slick, wet floors below. Smaller signs read, "Slipping Hazard" and, "Watch Your Step" on every open surface.

Lily walked carefully along the outside of the extending tank, peeking over the short walls and watching the stingrays roam in the water. Every so often, they would flap their fins and spray cold droplets in all directions, or swim too close to the edge and send a tiny wave over the lip of the enclosure, pooling onto the ground. Lily leaned her legs against the middle of the tank, letting the water soak into her jeans as she reached her fingertips down into the cool water. Maren waited a few strides behind her, watching her explore through the mirror.

Lily circled her wrist, casting ripples into the gentle waves. Around the tank, the stingrays swam at the edges, gathering on each side. Other children and their parents approached the outskirts of the enclosure, reaching their hands into the water to feel the slick gray backs of the stingrays. The friendly creatures swam against the children's flat hands and wriggled under their excited fingers, splashing at their clothes and their shoes. The kids giggled and pulled their arms away, just to plunge them back into the water again when another stingray made its rounds of the tank.

Lily looked around watching the other children, then dropped her gaze to her own arm where it hung lonely in the deserted water below. A cold, empty feeling rose in her chest. She looked up at herself in the mirror, wet with splashing droplets, and tightened her jaw.

A small table behind the exhibit caught her eye when she glanced back at her father, "Stingray Food" displayed from a fold-up sign at its edge.

The woman behind the table smiled at Lily as she approached, motioning her hand toward the trays that were lined at the edge. Tiny silver fish sat lifelessly against the cold metal, which lay on a bed of ice. Lily reached into the tray, gripping her fingers around their slimy, cold bodies, and picked them up one by one to lay in her palm.

She counted five of them, running a curious finger over their small gray scales and making her way back to her spot at the tank. She plucked one fish from her palm and dropped it into the tank, watching as it sank to the shallow bottom, untouched. The stingrays still refused to approach.

Lily frowned, snatching two more and tossing them in a small semicircle around her. Each fish, rippling the water when it struck the surface, sank straight to the floor.

She shot a frustrated look into the mirror toward her father, who leaned against a supporting beam closely behind, then scattered the remaining food from her palm into the water. Of all of the fish that were strewn across the bottom of the small section of the pool, none were disturbed. The stingrays eyed their food from opposite corners, unmoving.

Lily angrily wiped her wet hands on her jeans, darkening them, before turning on her heels away from the edge of the tank. Maren followed her to the other side of the enclosure to watch the stingrays suddenly erupt into movement toward the now-empty end of the pool where Lily once stood. The tiny fish, one by one, disappeared from the bottom of the water.

"I hate the aquarium," she groaned through gritted teeth, crossing her wet arms over her yellow blouse.

"I'm sorry, sweetheart. Maybe they're just shy." Maren ran his hand over her head, smoothing down her stray blonde hairs. He rarely knew how to comfort his daughter, but always found ways to blame himself for her unhappiness. He wished he had taken her somewhere else, somewhere better.

"No, they hate me. They're all scared of me!" She pointed an angry finger toward the stingrays, surrounded by smiling children with their arms dipped halfway to the bottom of the pool. Their hands stroked the slimy gray skin of the creatures.

Loneliness and hurt welled deep in Lily's chest, rising to her throat, her ears, and her eyes. She tightened her empty hands into fists at her sides, holding back tears.

Maren spoke gently, with words she couldn't hear. Her head was full of static and thoughts of the doll that waited for her at home. Mr. Doll's voice was thick in her mind, squirming through her ears like worms and blocking out the noise from the busy aquarium around her.

Come home, she heard him say in his deep, thorned voice. *Where you belong.*

Maren's words cut abruptly from his tongue, rolling down his chin. He froze, stabbing his eyes at the ceiling as darkness punched out each light. They flickered back and forth like Morse code, threatening those below to leave.

Around the large room, each of the tanks turned black. The light was sucked into the air as it escaped down the flickering halls, leaving the stingrays in darkness and the motorized boats to float aimlessly.

Children fearfully pulled their arms from the water and their parents grabbed their hands to pull them close. The gift shop dulled to black and the fountain halted, water dripping slowly down its sides. The skylight in the middle of the ceiling was the only thing remaining to illuminate the silent room.

Maren turned from the ceiling and back to Lily. Her head was rocked back on her shoulders, pointing her chin straight up into the air. Her mouth hung open, and wide glossy eyes stared at nothing. Her arms hung loosely, limp fingers curling against her thighs. Maren gawked at his daughter in horror, darting his eyes around the room and wordlessly pleading for help from anyone who might be close.

His terrified gaze landed at the mirror against the far wall behind the darkened stingray tank. His reflection, blurred by darkness and bloodshot eyes, stood frozen at its center, with his hollow daughter perched next to him. Behind them, almost to the back wall, stood a large figure. A man. His hard, faceless stare punctured into Maren from behind.

The man was strangely tall, with stretching legs and arms. His eyes, along with the rest of his features, were too soaked in the blackness of the room to be visible. His skin, his clothes, all looked to be a sickly gray.

Maren squinted into the mirror, searching for the figure's face. His heart was pounding so hard in his chest that it vibrated his ribs. He whipped his head around away from the mirror, shooting them against the far wall to find him.

The man, with his shiny gray skin and his hollow, empty features, now stood inches from Maren's nose. Up close, it was hauntingly clear that the gray man's face was barren. No eyes, nose, or mouth, just a slick and flawless emptiness. Maren could feel the cold of its gray body through the air, and the heat of its eyeless glare gouging into his skull. He could feel it burning.

It happened too fast for Maren to do anything but stare wildly into its blankness while the blood drained from his own face. Malice and despair was flooding from the gray man and down Maren's throat, seeping through his ghostly pale skin.

The lights erupted around them, illuminating the room in a sudden, bright flash. Maren's eyes squinted closed, shielding from the light, and when he opened them again, the man was gone. Where he once stood now felt like a gaping hole in the room. He couldn't feel the cold against his skin anymore, or the hate in his chest, but he could feel its energy, its gravitational pull.

Maren's lungs burned and his skin was slick with sweat. He turned back to Lily, holding his breath. Voices and footsteps returned loudly around the room and the employees burst from all directions rushing to check the breakers or to assure their customers that everything was fine.

Several people stopped to stare at Maren, who collapsed into the floor in a breathless panic as he tried to shake his daughter back to consciousness. Her eyes were gently closed as she lay motionless against the patterned carpet.

...

The Henry Ford Emergency Room was packed tightly with worried people, but none as fearful as Maren. He couldn't get the feeling of his lifeless daughter, resting limply in his arms as he ran through the dark hallways of the aquarium, out of his head. Even as she sat calmly next to him in the stiff hospital bed, he couldn't scrape the image of the gray man from his mind. It was a delusion, of course. Just another trick that his upset mind was playing on him.

It was dark, he repeated in his mind, begging to believe it. *It could have been anything.*

Maren barely had the strength to speak or tap his fingers against the arm of his seat. Instead, his hands fell weakly into his lap with his eyes pointed at them, hardly focused.

"You should lie down. It might be a while before the doctor comes back," he heard himself say, detached from his own voice.

"I feel fine, I promise." Lily kicked her feet against the paper that draped down the end of the table. He could tell that she was nervous and confused. He had already asked her at least a dozen times if she needed anything and how she was doing, so he resisted the urge to ask again. Instead, he rose from his seat and closed the space between her bed and his chair, sitting next to her on the crunching paper. He put an arm around her shoulders and pulled her closer, gently resting his chin on her head.

Lily's shoulders were tense, and she felt rigid underneath him. He wondered if she was going to push him away, but before he could know for sure, the door swung open. The doctor entered swiftly with a clipboard grasped loosely in his hand.

Maren released his hold on his daughter, falling back into his seat. The doctor, pulling a chair out from under the desk, flipped through the papers on the clipboard and took a seat. The wheels of the chair squealed against the glossy tile.

"It looks like the tests came back normal. There don't seem to be any issues with your daughter's health, Mister Caplin," he said, staring lazily at the papers. "Lily, have you had enough to eat today? Were you feeling weak or tired before you fell?" He pushed his glasses farther up his nose, not making eye contact with either of them. His voice was dull, like the conversation was dragging.

"She didn't *fall*," Maren growled. "She passed out. She had a horrible look before it happened, like . . ." He didn't feel like mentioning the way her head cocked up toward the ceiling.

The way she looked hollow. *Dead.* He didn't feel like mentioning the gray man, whose hard, polished skin glistened in the weakened sunlight as it drifted around in the dark. He was right in front of him, so close that there was no mistaking it. He had no eyes, no mouth, no nose . . . "Like she knew she was about to faint."

Shut up! he shouted in his paranoid mind. *It wasn't real. It was dark.*

"I don't remember it happening. I don't even remember the lights going out," Lily interjected. "I just remember being carried out of the building and sort of having a headache for a little while." She didn't feel afraid of what happened; she just wanted out of this hospital. "But I feel fine now, really. Can we just go home?" Nothing mattered right now except getting back to the house, back to Mr. Doll. She knew that he would be waiting for her, and that he would be worried.

"I don't see any reason to worry unless this happens again. A variety of reasons could explain this—possibly it was even the flashing lights that triggered it. You did say that the lights were flickering before they went dark?" The doctor was impatient, tapping his foot against the floor.

"Yes, but . . ." Maren was growing more agitated after each word the man uttered.

"Go home, give her some food and some water, and let her rest. Maybe take the day off school tomorrow." He let the papers fall closed in his lap. "If this happens again, come see me and we can go from there."

The doctor's arrogance infuriated Maren, but his uselessness only proved his point. They might as well just go home if these people wouldn't help her.

Lily sat restlessly in the passenger seat of the truck as it coasted down the highway. Her father stared dryly out the windshield, defeated, while the gray clouds stretched toward him in the distance. He had needed this day to go perfectly, needed to make Lily *happy.* Now, any wishful thinking he might have had before dinner slipped through his fingers like sand.

The trip home was silent, but the air in the car burned with intensity. Lily watched the trees as they passed, slipping away around each curve of the road. Each roll of the tires against the asphalt brought her closer to home, closer to Mr. Doll.

I'm almost there, she said in her mind. *Almost.*

The old white house approached quickly as they sank into the neighborhood. The air thickened with the familiar surge of its power, seeping into the car as it pulled into the driveway. Maren's exhaustion was only held at bay by his panic, stirring silently within him like a shark at the scent of blood.

He opened the front door, jiggling the tricky handle to unlock it, and was greeted by the swirling essence of the house as it reeled him and Lily deeper inside.

Lily went straight through the door, up the stairs, and into her bedroom, shutting the door with a soft *click.* Maren watched sullenly from the doorway as she dissolved into the house.

She grasped Mr. Doll tightly in her weakened hands, pulling him from the dollhouse and tightly into her chest as she crawled into bed, still wearing her yellow blouse, jeans, and favorite flowery shoes.

"I'm sorry. I'm sorry. I'm so sorry," she whispered against the doll's face, over and over, while tears slipped over her cheeks and soaked into her pillow. Mr. Doll warmed in her hands.

She drifted deeply asleep as the doll reached into her mind, quieting it.

It was nearly 10:00 p.m., and Maren could hardly remember the morning. It felt like years had passed since breakfast.

He kicked off his shoes, leaving them in the middle of the entryway as he dragged his feet over the hardwood toward the living room. He stopped halfway to the seat his body ached so desperately for to glare at the rough white wall beneath the television. His drowsy eyes sank into the fireplace and into the red bricks that peeked through the giant, curving crack that sliced open the drywall. This morning there was only a small carved hole at the bottom right corner, but now it stretched across the entire width of it.

Maren grimaced, sinking into the reclining chair at the edge of the living room and forcing his eyes closed. His thoughts rattled in his head, threatening to break it, but he couldn't keep himself awake any longer. He didn't have the energy to dissect his hallucinations of the gray man, or to think about the giant growing crack in the wall over the fireplace. He couldn't even dream of making it up the stairs to his bedroom. Whatever remaining strength he once held evaporated into the house as it breathed, lulling him to sleep.

I just need one good night's sleep, his mind whispered, *and all of this will go away.*

Fourteen.

*H*er bedroom window was cracked slightly open, letting in the cool breeze. The moonlight streamed through the window in thick streaks as she slept peacefully in her bed, the blankets curled loosely around her. Her short blonde hair fell in wisps over her delicately closed eyes.

It was late, very late, and the house was almost silent—all except for the soft taps of footsteps slowly climbing the stairs.

She jolted up in bed, shaking the drowsiness from her eyes as they poured over her shadowed bedroom. The desk, full of art supplies, sat flush against the wall on her left, with photos and paintings hung above it on the wall. Her closet door was cracked open, revealing the colorfully patterned clothes that hung inside, just as she had left it. No light snuck in from the space underneath her door, an unsettling reminder that her father wasn't home. She was alone, at least she hoped.

She was sure she heard a noise, one that didn't belong. One that didn't sound like the whir of the air conditioner, or the creaks of this forever-settling house. It sounded like footsteps.

She slipped out from beneath the blankets, stretching her bare feet toward the floor, and rose slowly to keep the floorboard from creaking beneath her. She hugged her arms around her waist, desperate for comfort as a gust of wind snuck in from the window and fluttered against her skin.

Closing in on the door, she became painfully aware of the sounds behind it. Goosebumps erupted all over her body, freezing her in place. Her breaths quickened, and each creak of the stairs slowly rising in her ears made the blood harden beneath her skin.

She took a shaky step backward toward the bed, catching her ankle against the leg of a desk and stumbling to the floor. She landed with a thud, shooting her eyes back to the door in terror. Whoever was out there now surely knew exactly where she was.

She felt like a puppet, held down by tight strings that left her unable to move. Her eyes were glued to the door handle as she waited for it to turn. Instead, she heard an unsteady voice from the hallway.

He sounded afraid, and familiar. His voice was ripe with panic, cracking under tears that waited patiently at the back of his throat. She stood slowly as her heart pounded, reaching toward the handle. The man's low whispers slowly became clear.

"Down the street, third house on the left, upstairs bedroom facing the road . . . Down the street, third house on the left, upstairs bedroom facing the road . . . Down the street—"

As the door cracked open to reveal the dark hallway, the man at the end of it came into her vision. He turned abruptly, with two red eyes burning into her as his arms rose high in front of him. He continued to mumble softly to himself, twitching with anticipation. His fingers tightened around the thing in his hands.

Her eyes focused sharply through the dark and over his face, obscured by the shadows that rippled at his throat. Even through the web of blackness, it was clear—his deep-brown eyes, dark hair, and freckled skin.

Maren tightly gripped the gun between his restless fingers. His familiar voice flooded Lily's ears as he pointed the barrel at her, with a fingertip perched tightly against the cold trigger.

"This wasn't the plan . . ." A tear glistened in the moonlight from the window as it rolled down to his chin.

Lily held out a hand toward her father, stepping into the open hall. A tear rolled over her lips, which parted to let out a silent scream.

What came next . . . was the sound.

Lily screamed, sitting frantically up in her bed and sending the muffled noise squeezing through the walls toward Maren. He stood a few strides from her closed door when his eyes began to focus. His daughter's scream rang roughly in his ears, pulling him toward her room to comfort her, but something kept his feet from moving forward.

How did I get here?

He looked around the blackened hallway, catching the window in the corner of his eye. Stars gleamed through the smudged glass panel. He looked down at his feet where they stood at the edge of the staircase, pointed toward his daughter's bedroom. His brain dug for the memory of waking up, of rising from his chair where he slept and ascending the stairs. It never came.

I was sleepwalking.

Chills paraded over his skin. They crawled up his back, around his neck, and down his arms. He never knew himself to sleepwalk, nor did Jewel ever mention that she had seen him do it. Not even as a child did his parents say so. Maren's bones cringed at the thought of his unconscious body drifting through the house, *this* house. How long had this been happening?

He wondered where he was going, why he was here. He wondered if his jaw hung open, if his eyes were glazed . . .

Lily's scream repeated in his mind, shaking his questions loose. His feet sped to her door, and his shaky hands swung it open and flicked on the lights, scattering the darkness away.

"What's wrong? Are you okay?" Maren was nearly out of breath, his lungs twisted. Lily sat straight up in her bed, leaning back against the headboard with the blankets gripped between white knuckles. Mr. Doll was pressed snugly against her chest, her only comfort.

Lily shot a terrified glare at her father as he swept into the room. His presence approached her like a wildfire, and the heat of it twinged at her nose.

"I'm fine." Her voice came out short, almost angry. The limbs of the gray doll threatened to bend in her tight grip.

"Did you have a nightmare?" Maren asked, concerned. He took slow steps farther into the room to study her face, and his eyes flicked down to the doll in her hands, dulling in offense.

Lily sank farther into the blankets, deflecting his gaze. She still felt the fear from her dreams, materializing in the room and magnifying the features of her father's face.

His deep-brown eyes, dark hair, and freckled skin.

"I said I'm fine. I just want to go back to sleep." Mr. Doll wrapped invisible arms around her, soothing her. Maren's words cut through the tension like a sharpened blade.

"I heard you scream. Are you sure you—"

She buried her head beneath the thick covers, drowning out the rest of his reply. Eventually the sentence drifted into the air and blew away as he took two defeated steps back toward the open door.

"Okay. Goodnight, then." The words flattened in his mouth. His daughter's nickname sat at the back of his throat, unable to be spoken. It had no place in this moment.

She stayed quiet, but he knew what she wanted to say. *Get out.*

Maren flicked off the light, inviting back the shadows, and closed the door as he left.

While he sulked down the dimly lit hall, he thought of his wife. He thought of her seeing their only daughter imprisoned behind her bedroom door. He imagined the pain in Jewel's eyes as she looked through Lily's anger, through her fierce independence, and saw a child who was tightly chained to her loneliness. A child who couldn't even rely on her own father to comfort her after a nightmare.

Maren knew that Jewel would hate him now, what he had become. He hated himself just the same. The man he once was, the man she loved and chose to father her daughter, was lost, disintegrated in his grief. Jewel would no longer recognize him.

He used to be her rock. When she was sick, when she was sinking, he was her lighthouse. He was the man she poured her soul into. Now, he was an empty cup.

The door creaked open into his bedroom, revealing the perfectly made bed at its center. He tore the blanket from the mattress, tossing it to the ground in frustration. The cool

October air coasted in from the windows and caressed his hot skin as he removed his pants and favorite button-up shirt, retiring them to the floor. The excitement he had felt while he dressed before dinner had been rung from these clothes like water and dried in the sun.

He slithered into bed, kicking the sheet over the edge. His skin was slick and wet with heat, enveloping him. Hot fists pressed into his eyes and pushed inward, spewing swirling colors against his eyelids.

Each thought knocked loudly at the base of his skull. Jewel's hatred, his daughter's disgust, his smooth gray skin in the bathroom mirror at the restaurant. The images tumbled through him like an avalanche. He saw his daughter's slack jaw, the flickering aquarium lights, and the gray man with a blank face standing inches from him in the dark.

Mr. Doll.

…

His eyes flicked open, met with sunlight that stabbed through the curtains. His bedroom was peaceful and quiet, and the sun was rising at his windowsill. The alarm clock read 7:24 a.m.

Shit.

Maren sprang out of bed, pulling on his uniform and messily draping the blankets back over his mattress. In the chaos of the night before, he had completely forgotten about work, or setting his alarm. At the very least he had gotten some desperately needed sleep.

He rushed to Lily's bedroom, stopping in front of the door. It was cracked slightly open—a clear indication that Lily wouldn't be inside. She clung tightly to privacy lately, Maren had noticed.

His curious eyes peeked inside to the strangely clean room and the increasingly strange dollhouse at its core. Of all the concerning things about Lily recently, this spotless room stuck out clearly in her father's mind.

For years, from house to house, he worried that she might drown in her bedroom. It was always piled high with laundry and trash that she refused to clean, and Maren had no energy to force her. Now, in this place, it was suddenly spotless.

While he squinted at the dollhouse, the sound of clanging dishes floated up the stairs from the kitchen. Maren sucked in a tight breath as it poured into his paranoid ears.

He imagined his daughter fainting again downstairs, smashing her head into the countertop. Maybe she would drop a glass bowl against the tile and shatter it, piercing shards against her soft skin. Maybe he would find her in some other corner of the house, stabbing a sharpened knife into something else for some other reason.

Panic coursed through him as his feet ran down the staircase, frantic in their search for Lily. He landed at the bottom, catching his breath, and watched his daughter tear off a piece of cold pancake and shove it in her mouth before closing the fridge with her hip. Mr. Doll looked comfortable on the counter, watching her. Maren twitched at the sight, choking down his contempt.

"Lily, you should be in bed." His voice was hard, molded by gritted teeth.

She chewed slowly, burying her eyes into the comfort of the doll. Her face dewed with guilt, or pity, or maybe some brand new emotion that Lily was the first to discover—one that she only shared with her doll. She tilted her head to look at Maren with an expression void of any comprehensible feeling.

Something cracked in the corner of Maren's vision, making him flinch. He turned, resting sunken eyes against the fireplace where the drywall crumbled and clattered to the floor. The crack was quickly growing, and the red bricks smiled at him from behind it. He felt no urgency to fix it.

His jaw hardened, and he lifted a hand to massage it with angry fingers. The red corner of the fireplace taunted him from across the room, where the once-small hole now tore open into a giant gash that infected the drywall. The sight of it pulsed in his head, threatening to pop.

Lily swallowed, finally speaking.

"I'm going to school. I have to eat breakfast." She had never cared about school—never enough to demand to go after *fainting* the afternoon prior. Usually, staying home to rest would be a relief.

"Lily, you passed out yesterday." He hesitated to speak his next words. "You need to stay home." The longer he soaked in the idea of Lily staying here, *alone,* the more he realized he didn't want to fight her for it. Maybe he would rather her be at school, where a teacher would call him in an emergency—where she would be *watched.*

Surely he couldn't miss his second day of work to look after her. It was too important, he thought, and he had a reputation to uphold. He refused to admit that the real reason, which was buried deep in his mind, was that he felt like he could only breathe when he was away from this godforsaken house.

Lily knew that already; she knew that he wouldn't stay. She didn't want him to, anyway. She also knew that he wouldn't want her here alone, that he didn't trust her. At least at school no one cared, and no one was expected to. She could be invisible in the crowd and pretend that life was normal. She could carry Mr. Doll through the campus without the sting of her father's vindictive eyes at her back.

"I'm fine. It's just school," she said, challenging him to force her to stay, challenging him to fight. She held his gaze for a moment while he held his breath.

"Alright, then," he muttered. He didn't fight; he never did. "Would you at least like a ride to school?" His gaze lay cowardly on the ground.

"No, I'll take the bus. It's right around the corner." She stood, silently regarding Maren where he still waited from across the room. Waiting for . . . she wasn't sure. But it never came.

She grabbed her backpack from the floor, slipping it over her shoulder, and brought another piece of leftover pancake to her mouth. Her eyes dropped to the doll on the counter where he waited knowingly. Lily's empty hands clasped around his small gray body and embraced him. Maren's face flushed hot.

"Bye," she said to the open room, quickly glancing at her father as she passed. He followed quickly behind her toward the front door.

"Call me if you need anything. Or go to the nurse if you don't feel well." He spoke calmly, detached. His heart ached somewhere deep, somewhere hidden.

"Okay." She paused, her hand on the door handle. "I have to go; the bus will be here soon."

"Okay. Have a good day. I love you," he said softly.

She cleared her throat. "Love you too." The words dripped from her tongue, burning against the hardwood at her feet and filling the room with smoke.

The door softly clicked behind her as he watched from the window while his daughter walked away.

Fifteen.

The bus moved clumsily down the uneven road. Lily shook in her seat with each turn, hugging tightly to the warm gray doll. She stared out the window, fogging the glass with her breath as she watched the sidewalks roll by.

The chilled air seeped into the leather seat beneath her and against her back. She pulled her jacket tightly to her body.

Mr. Doll stared at her, with eyes only she could see, and wrapped invisible arms of heat around her shoulders. She felt the weight of it settle into her skin and pour like water down her neck and her chest. In return, she swept a gentle thumb over his smooth porcelain, a silent gratitude.

A cloud of emotions rained over her head while she stared deeply into his empty gray face.

Over the past few years, Lily was realizing, she had been blind. Blind to her pain, to her anger, to her neglect. How could she know what she was missing without first having a taste?

Before her mother was sick, life was perfect. But what is perfect worth to a child? A child who only lives in the present, which was only perfect before it morphed into *this*. Only perfect when she was too young to form it as a memory. She was a child, alone, forced to learn slowly that goodness, love, and even presence were all fleeting. Scarce.

She was so young when her mother's health declined that anything before that couldn't stick. Memories floated aimlessly around in her head before they sank down a swirling drain. The foundation around her was built gradually with the only thing she could recall—being alone. Alone while her father held her dying mother, while they hid their pain from her. Alone while Maren grieved, too *strong* to let his daughter see him broken. Alone to face the loss of her mother, and slowly of her father, too.

Now she was realizing just how unhappy she had truly been. With the warmth and the presence of Mr. Doll in her hands, with the possessive protection he offered her, she knew what it meant to be lonely. She knew that, now, she had another choice. With every inch that the bus stretched her from Maren, she felt freer. And Mr. Doll, with his roots dug deeply into her, was no longer chained to the house—or to the heart of it that beat within the dollhouse.

...

The school was a whirlpool of noise. Leaves crunched under her shoes while she walked, holding Mr. Doll's tiny body at her ribs. He soaked in the world around him through his hard gray flesh. He watched the other children as they pushed past Lily in the halls, digging their judging eyes into her.

Lily had grown used to the treatment she received at school. She knew she would be a target, an easy kill. She always was.

She knew she wouldn't be welcomed, and that the world within each school was always the same. Kids would have picked their friends far before she arrived in the middle of the year. They would have picked their seats, their science partners, their hallway companions. They would have their usual spots at lunch and their shared inside jokes. Most of all, they would laugh together at the new kid, who stumbled around the campus unsure of where to find her classes. The lonely new *freak* who had no one to talk to. She could feel sharp eyes around every corner.

Approaching her classroom, she squeezed through a pool of kids in the hall. An elbow swung from a passing student and into Lily's shoulder, knocking her backpack down her arm. Lily stumbled slightly, catching herself, and pulled the strap back to its place as the girl continued walking. She scowled over her shoulder at Lily for getting in her way.

Animals, the doll's jagged voice echoed within her. Anger peeled from his tone.

Lily ignored him, continuing toward her class and retreating to the desk. The classroom around her was packed with many children as well as their loud voices and ridiculous conversations. She slid into her seat, flushed, as her face warmed at the thought of Mr. Doll protecting her—even if she felt wary of his temper.

Crawling like maggots . . . his dark drone continued.

"Ignore them," Lily whispered out loud to him. She often talked him down, even when his anger and his threats fluttered in her lungs like butterflies. She didn't want him to hurt anybody; she just wanted a friend.

This is love, she would think, smiling to herself while he promised to protect her, to destroy anyone who might hurt her.

"What did you say?" A young boy appeared at the edge of her desk, leaning over her. His face was crunched into a devious grin.

The classroom was bursting with energy, and the teacher typed away at his computer through the chaos, ignoring it. The bell was set to ring at any minute.

Lily glanced up toward the blond boy's pink face, warm with anticipation. She exhaled, shrinking in her chair.

"Nothing. I wasn't talking to you," she mumbled, barely audible over the noise of the classroom.

"Well, there's no one else you could be talking to. You're sitting here alone," he mocked. "Unless you talk to your toys." The boy reached a hand to Mr. Doll, tapping the curve of his head with a cocky finger.

"Don't touch him!" Lily whined loudly, twisting her body away from the boy to protect the doll. He laughed devilishly.

"*Him?* How old are you, five?" The boy's friends were starting to take notice of their conversation now, turning their heads to stare. Smiles snaked dryly up their faces, but Lily stayed quiet, cupping Mr. Doll against her chest. Her eyes welled with embarrassment.

"What, are you gonna cry?" one of the boys scoffed.

"Maybe she moved here in the middle of the year because she got kicked out of her last school for being so *weird,*" another boy piped in, giggling. "Carrying a creepy doll around every day." His voice was muffled from where he hid behind his accomplices. His dark-brown hair peeked over the small crowd.

Others around the room began to tune in too. They sat in their tightly knit groups and sank into their comfort, leaving Lily to the wolves. Mr. Doll vibrated between her fingers.

Mongrels. All of them. They should be treated as such. He filled her brain with anger. Redness flashed through Lily's mind like a door had been opened between them.

Maggots. Filthy creatures, he continued. Lily could no longer hear the boys as they sneered—just a ringing in her ears as her classmates laughed, closing heavily in around her. She only heard the gray doll's voice. *They're dangerous. Evil. They need to be punished.*

Lily swallowed hard, blinking the redness away. The boys backed away from her as she stared hollowly ahead, unresponsive to their insults. She could barely notice them.

"Sit down," she finally said in a soft, steady voice. She spoke with authority. Control. The tension grew thick in the air around her, separating her from the bustling room.

The boys fell silent, frowning down at her with furrowed brows. They regarded each other silently, wondering what to do next, before the blond boy finally spoke again.

"You can't—" His angry voice was sliced through by a ringing bell, shaking Lily from her trance. She turned, digging cold eyes into the boy as his voice receded. He curled defeatedly into his seat beside her.

Lily's head fell toward her lap, sending her hair curtaining around her face and closing away the mess around her. Lily and her doll sat in their own little world.

She caressed his gray skin, calming him with her touch.

It's okay, she insisted. *They're gone.*

Lily paid no attention to the boys, or the teacher, or the marks on the whiteboard. She simply held Mr. Doll in her hands as his power coursed through her and his passion ignited her bones. She felt strong.

Mr. Doll would have hurt those boys for her, and the thought should have terrified her. Instead, she bit back a smile.

…

The day went by slowly, full of ringing bells, busy classes, and judging stares. All around the school, children glared at her, raising their eyebrows to the doll held tightly in her arms. Lily barely noticed. She felt invincible, cloaked snugly inside of Mr. Doll's fierce possessiveness. All she seemed to notice was that he cared for her, deeply. Everything else was just white noise.

I love you, Al. I'll never leave you. Never again. The gray doll's voice floated through her. She smiled.

Soon it was lunchtime, and children flooded the courtyard. Lily pulled a bag of leftover breakfast foods from her backpack and slid down the side of a wall. No matter what school she had attended, she always chose the same spot for lunch—the farthest wall from the double doors of the packed cafeteria. Here she wouldn't be bombarded with stares or dumb questions or curious looks. The teachers wouldn't ask her if she'd rather sit inside, where she could *make friends.*

Her father always warned the teachers ahead of time of his daughter's shyness, condemning her to the attention she didn't want. What they thought was kindness, she deflected as pity. She would rather sit alone.

The gray doll stewed in her lap as she leaned against the wall, pulling her long blonde hair behind her back as a cushion. Her skin was cold against the concrete, even with the sun peeking through clouds and kissing her face. She ripped a piece of cold bacon from the bag, popping it in her mouth and studying the layout of her new school.

Many beige buildings stood tall in the cool air, surrounded by dull-green grass and benches that peppered the edges of the sidewalks. The courtyard lived in the center, in front of two giant gates with chipping paint. Deep-brown lettering pressed against the wall beside the gate, reading, "Oak Park Elementary."

Lily chewed slowly, rummaging around in her plastic bag for another piece of food, as a figure moved closer in the corner of her vision.

She turned, squinting in the sunlight, toward the blond-haired boy, the same one from her classroom this morning. His face was hard.

He stopped, hovering over her where she sat on the ground, and planted his shoes inches from her hand where she leaned into the concrete. The boy's eyes narrowed at the doll in her lap.

Lily suddenly became aware of the other boys, two or three of them, closing in behind their angry blond friend.

"What?" Lily asked, already frustrated. She had dealt with her fair share of bullies over the years. Usually, they would start to ignore her if she pretended not to be afraid. This time she truly wasn't.

"What's with that stupid doll?" the tiny ringleader asked. His eyes were squinted, his lips curled.

"Why do you care?" Her voice was quiet but steady. She cocked her head at him before running her eyes over his shoulder to the others in the group. Lily regarded them with a clarity that was much more mature than her own, almost unbelonging to her. She saw these boys for what they were. They were small, stupid, cocky. They were weak.

Old Lily would have cowered in fear of these boys. She would have curled back against the wall and waited for this storm to pass. The new Lily, the Lily she was becoming, would fear nothing—especially not these boys, these *maggots.*

"Because you're annoying. You're talking to a doll like a freak! I don't want to sit next to some kind of psycho who talks to her toys." The group erupted in laughter, pounding in Lily's ears.

"*Shut up,*" Lily spoke like a snake. Her tone was an eerie calm, and her bones buzzed inside of her body. Mr. Doll stung against her skin.

"Or what, are you gonna cry?" another boy called from her left, laughing. A chorus of sneers danced around her.

"No, she's gonna throw her doll at you!"

"Bet she'll tell her mommy!"

Instead of Mr. Doll's voice, this time it was her own.

"*Fucking mongrels,*" she muttered, puncturing her eyes into the blond boy's smug face.

The boy tensed, burning with offense. In one quick movement, he bent over her, snatching the doll from her lap and tossing it to his black-haired friend across the grass.

Lily's eyes caught fire.

She scrambled to her feet as her lunch tumbled to the ground and across the cold concrete. Fury burned from her like a furnace, sending waves in each direction, while her sharpened gaze darted into the black-haired boy. She focused in on his grimy fingers curled around Mr. Doll.

"Give him *back,*" she spoke through tightly gritted teeth. Balled fists formed at her sides, and her fingernails pierced the soft flesh of her palms. "*Now.*"

"Or what?" The boy tossed the doll to his left, into the hands of another.

"Come and get him," that one said. They all laughed.

She could feel the gray doll's aura, heavy in the air and thick with malice. It poured around her like a monsoon. How much of this anger, she wondered, belonged to her? She imagined the blond boy's fingers snapping, releasing Mr. Doll from his grip. She imagined herself leaping across the open space between her and the black-haired boy, tackling him to the ground and sinking her teeth deep into his arm. She felt feral, unhinged. She felt powerful.

Of all of the dark thoughts sliding up her neck and into her ears, which were her own? She couldn't be sure. In this moment, she didn't care, either.

"Does the baby want her doll back?" The blond boy's words crept out from behind her while she watched his *monkeys* toss Mr. Doll. She whipped around to face him, taking a wide step in his direction, while her hands raised like claws before her. They led her to his throat.

Ten twitching fingers clasped around his neck, shoving him hard into the wall at his back. He sputtered, widening his mouth with silent horror while she tightened around him. Untapped rage surged from within her, swirling through each vein and out each pore. She looked down at her hands as they sank into the boy's skin, and she barely recognized them. She watched herself from the air above her body as she disappeared into a welcoming darkness.

The blond boy's red eyes bulged from his head as his arms flailed around her, reaching to her wrists in an attempt to pry them off. He scraped at her skin with his nails, digging them into her flesh.

The boy's accomplices coughed out screams as they reacted, dropping the doll's body into the grass and bolting toward the wall where he struggled. Lily's fingers continued to constrict, just enough to hurt, as power flooded her—hot, arrogant power. She leaned against his cheek where she held him.

"*I told you to stop,*" she growled, warming his ear with her breath. At the edges of the courtyard, the teachers were beginning to take notice.

One of the kids gripped a handful of her hair, tearing her away from the blond boy and throwing her to the ground. Her back smacked the hard concrete, knocking the breath from her lungs while the blond-haired boy crumpled against the wall, sobbing.

Lily rose slowly from the ground on her elbows, looking around at where the boys once stood tossing her only friend like a *toy.* To her left, the doll lay motionlessly on his side, his gray porcelain smudged with dirt. She snatched him with a shaking hand and embraced him desperately.

I'm sorry. I'm sorry. I'm sorry. I'm sorry, she repeated in her mind over and over. Her panic choked her.

You did so well, Al, she heard him say. Lily smiled, pushing back her guilt, just before a crowd of teachers and students closed in around her at all sides. The frantic boys were still loud in her ears.

She turned back to face them, catching her breath, and caught a glimpse of the blond boy. "Cody" they were calling him. Cody looked dazed, overcome with shock. His eyes made her sad.

Lily slowly became aware of the teacher in her face, shouting angrily. She was pulled to her feet by her wrist and led across the campus into a large beige building. The cries of Cody's friends gradually quieted as she walked.

Mr. Doll pressed firmly into her chest, comforting his daughter.

Sixteen.

"**Y**our father will be arriving soon," the man said flatly.

Lily nervously tapped her foot against the leg of the chair while her teeth ripped at the inside of her bottom lip. She sat against the wall in one of the few uncomfortable chairs that lined it, facing the man behind the desk. Mr. Doll was laid on his side in the center of it at the heart of the room, facing her with invisible eyes and inspecting her skin. Even from ten feet away, she could feel his warmth. His anticipation pulsed against the four walls around her.

The man behind the desk clicked his pen rhythmically, filling the room with sharp noise. It tapped against the base of Lily's skull as she tried not to imagine her father's face, or the look that he might have when he arrived.

The principal was a small, shriveled old man. He looked tired, with sunken eyes that accented the purple bags lying beneath them. His hair was graying rapidly, making him look slightly older than he was—a decaying cherry atop his cold, dead gaze.

He was pretending to type something important, staring mindlessly at his computer screen. Lily could tell she was making him uncomfortable, but she continued to stare through him out of spite. He had taken the doll from her when she entered, and she wanted him back. Her skin crawled with impatience.

"Can I have him back now?" She cocked her head at the doll, glancing up to meet the man's shy eyes. He lightly shook his head.

"No, not quite yet," he mumbled. "Let's wait for your father to arrive. He should be here any minute."

"It's been a long time . . ." Lily sighed. "Maybe he isn't coming." Her fingers tapped slightly against the armrest of her chair. She swallowed hard.

"He *is* coming, Lily." He incessantly clicked his pen, staring into the computer screen thoughtlessly. "I'm sure he's just busy with work."

She rolled her eyes.

Part of her hoped that her *show* today, as Principal Hamel called it, would get her expelled from the school. She hated it here so far, much more than most other schools she had attended. Another part of her hoped that she wouldn't be. She worried that changing schools, somehow, would take her away from the house. That her father might punish her further by moving away, somewhere far and hidden. That couldn't happen.

Lily sat in uncomfortable silence, rolling the thoughts of what had happened through her mind for however long she had been kept in this room. She had lost track a while ago, but it felt like hours. The thoughts sloshed in her head, over and over. The rush that she had gotten in her veins, the faces of the boys as they harassed her. The feeling of Cody's throat beneath her palms. She wasn't sure what to make of any of it. Lily had never hurt anyone before.

It was clear that Maren would be angry, that he would punish her, and she worried what he might do. She wondered if he would notice that the boys pulled her hair or threw her down. If he would know that they insulted her, or that they took her doll. The image flashed through her mind of her father, sitting in the chair beside her in this small, cramped office and telling her that she was bad. She saw him thinking to himself that he was right all along. She *was* crazy.

It was a bad idea. She knew that. She shouldn't have hurt that boy. She didn't want her father to hate her; she just wanted control. The control that had coursed through her body as she rushed to the blond boy and gripped his pale neck in her hands. The control that she felt as he feared her, clawing at her arms. As much as she knew that it was bad, the satisfaction of it was thick in her mind. And so was the guilt.

Mr. Doll's voice in her head was calming, soft. He told her he loved her over and over from where he rested in the center of the principal's desk. His words usually made her feel warm, but now they made her feel strange. She couldn't get her feelings straight in her mind, and it scared her. She just wanted to escape.

Lily turned her hands over in her lap, staring down at her fingers. She imagined doll-like skin made of porcelain, wrapped tightly around the blond boy's throat. She imagined the gray doll being proud of her as he brought her back home to the dollhouse. She saw him in her dreams, with two eyes, a nose, and a mouth, smiling down at her. Two long arms that embraced her warmly.

The door at her left swung open into the office, startling her. Maren appeared suddenly in the doorway, filling the small room with the sound of his labored breathing.

"Lily?" He sounded scared. Scared *for* her, she wondered, or *of* her? She met his eyes tentatively before flicking her gaze away and back at her hands, now clasped tightly together in her lap.

Principal Hamel cleared his throat as he set his pen down against the wood of the desk. He stood from his chair, curiously inspecting Lily's father.

"Hello, Mister Caplin, I'm Principle Hamel. I don't believe we've met." He extended an open palm in the air, slicing through the tension with each finger.

Maren straightened his back, stepping deeper into the room past his daughter and toward the desk to return the gesture. He smoothed down his shirt with his free hand while they greeted each other tensely. Lily bit hard against the inside of her cheek, tasting blood.

"Yes, nice to meet you. I'm sorry, I . . . What exactly is this all about?" Maren stood with his back to Lily before glancing over his shoulder to glare at her. "Some kind of . . . incident?"

Lily's eyes retreated to the floor as her father pulled a small wooden chair out from under the desk, falling into it.

The shriveled man cleared his throat once more before sinking back into his own worn chair and taking a short breath in.

"Yes, um, an incident of sorts." He paused, fiddling with his tie. His next words came out low, like a secret. "It seems that Lily got into an argument during lunch with some of her classmates, which ended in your daughter . . . assaulting one of the boys." The words seeped out slowly, like dark sap. Principal Hamel swallowed hard, meeting Maren's eyes.

"She . . . what?" Lily's father shook his head, processing the words as they marched into his ears. His eyebrows contorted above two narrowing eyes, which shot a shocked look back at his daughter. She refused to lift her head, staring holes into the carpet.

"Lily has *never*—"

"I know this may come as a shock, Mister Caplin," the principal interrupted, "but all of the boys who were involved, along with several other witnesses including the staff, all said the same thing. Your daughter was the first to start the fight." He licked his lips, softening his next words.

"After they took her toy and threw it around for a minute, Lily grabbed one of the boys' throats," Principal Hamel whispered, leaning over the desk and pressing his hands against the wood, hoping Lily wouldn't catch his next comment. "She *choked* him. They had to tear her off." His voice was hardly louder than Lily's heart, beating inside of her constricting chest.

Maren slumped into the back of his chair, rubbing the nape of his neck with a rough hand. His silence allowed the principal's words to settle slowly from the air, coating the room.

"I don't understand." Maren swiveled in his seat, landing desperate eyes on his daughter. "Lily, explain to Principal Hamel that there's been some kind of mistake." His words struck her, aching into her bones. She parted her lips to speak, but no words came. Her father swung back to the gray-haired man behind the desk, stabbing him with piercing eyes.

"Unfortunately, there is no mistake," he stated, twirling his checkered tie between nervous fingers before smoothing it against his crisp white shirt. His soft words returned. "This is a very serious matter, Mister Caplin. You're lucky that the boy's parents agreed not to press charges, which took quite a bit of talking down." He took a deep breath in. "We may need to remove your daughter from the school."

"Lily, explain." Maren pulled the second chair out from the desk and pointed at it, glaring into his daughter. She rose from her seat against the wall and dragged her feet toward the desk, collapsing into the soft cushion beside it.

"They were bullying me," she whispered, focusing on Mr. Doll who still lay sideways on the table. The only thing that calmed her was his presence. "They were calling me names and laughing at me, then they took Mr. Doll and started throwing—"

"*Lily.*" Maren's tongue cut her name into tiny pieces. He pressed a firm palm against the desk, turning toward her. "You choked a little boy over your *doll?* You could get expelled, you could have seriously hurt him, and you're telling me this is all because of your creepy little *doll?*" He could hardly contain his anger, spitting words like acid at his daughter before feeling the principal's cold glare falling over him. He leaned back against his chair rubbing his face while Lily's frown sagged deeper toward the carpet.

She felt the beating heart of the doll in her chest, cradling her own as it cracked. Just as she anticipated, her father hardly seemed to care. He didn't care that the boys had yelled at her, or that they called her names. He didn't care that they snatched her only friend from her lap and tossed him around like trash. He didn't care how lonely and *miserable* she felt in this moment. Or that she was consumed by a slowly burning guilt.

She stayed quiet, staring at the doll as a tear rolled down her cheek.

"Lily, if you could please wait in the hallway, I'd like to speak with your father alone." The principal motioned to the door, kindly releasing her from the imprisonment of this tiny room. He lifted the gray doll from the table as Lily stood, gifting it back to her. She wrapped gentle fingers around his smooth porcelain flesh and embraced him desperately. Maren's chest burned.

Finally back in her arms, Mr. Doll filled her with a flood of relief. She slipped out the door and into the bright, open hall.

...

Lily waited in the hallway in one of the many stiff chairs for quite a while. She kicked her feet into the air, listening to the muffled voices from the other side of the door as they debated incessantly, rising and falling like a solemn wave. She could barely keep still in her seat, tensing with anticipation. The doll fed her with his energy, winding it around her skull and into each crevasse of her mind.

She couldn't keep herself from picturing her father's stone face, with his two burning brown eyes staring through her. She couldn't shake the awful feeling that he might hate her, that he might be afraid of her now.

He can't take you away. The gray doll's growling thoughts invaded her. *Not again.*

Lily never knew what he meant by that, but she had learned not to argue. She trusted him.

He won't take me away. He'll only take me home, she replied silently to him, cradling him in her small pale hands.

We need to be together, always. I love you, his cold tone replied. *We need each other, Al.*

Lily warmed at each of his words, soaking in the feeling of being wanted, needed. Being seen the way he saw her, right down to her core. He knew each crack and cavern in her mind, every dark thought and hidden corner. He knew the sides of her that Maren had never met, or didn't even want to.

We'll always be together, she replied. *I promise.*

Her heart fluttered. The unspoken words dripped like sweet honey down her throat.

What if we can't? The doll's voice deepened, echoing off her skull. *What if he won't let us?*

Her stomach twisted at his tone, hissing like a snake in her head. She wasn't sure how to reply. She hadn't considered it.

"I don't know . . ." she said softly to the empty hallway as she slid a finger down the soft fabric of the gray doll's clothing. He was hot in her hands, slowly reddening her palms. "I don't know."

The door opened beside her, steaming with the remnants of a tense conversation. Lily turned to stare as her father shook the shriveled man's hand tightly between both of his own, stern-faced.

"Thank you, sir." Maren's lips were drawn tightly, barely letting the words escape. His head cracked toward his daughter, meeting her eyes and motioning her to stand with a tick of his head. "Let's go, Lily."

She stood from the chair without a word and grabbed her backpack from the floor, tossing it over her shoulder and against her back. She chewed her bottom lip between her teeth nervously.

Principal Hamel nodded at Lily, pity and concern filling his eyes, before retreating back into his office and shutting the door with a soft *click.*

Lily followed her father down the winding hallway and out the door into the parking lot. School had already ended a couple of hours ago, leaving the pathway empty and quiet. Maren's shoes tapped against the concrete as he walked, Lily trailing closely behind him, struggling to keep his stride.

Climbing into the car, she was careful not to let go of Mr. Doll. She gripped him tightly, closing the door and putting on her seatbelt with her one free hand. The gray doll's words stuck in her mind like hot wax.

What if he won't let us?

She had never considered the idea of her father taking Mr. Doll away. She felt stupid for not seeing it, with the way that Maren despised him. The way that, from the very beginning, he had wanted him gone. Her eyes poured over him as he climbed into the driver's seat and angrily slammed the door.

Maren slid farther down against his seat, releasing all of the air from his lungs. He sat silently, holding the keys in a fist instead of putting them in the ignition. Beside him, Lily stiffened, staring anxiously through the glass of her window. The doll stirred in her hands.

"Lily, what the *hell?*" Her father's words were heavy and thick in her ears. He could barely look at her, resting his head against his palms instead. "You *choked* a kid against a wall. I'd get it if you threw a punch or something, but *this?*" He shook his head, gripping the steering wheel so tightly that she feared it might crack under his fingers. "And over a *doll?* What is going on with you lately?"

The stress was eating away at him. He looked tired and hopeless. More than that, he looked afraid.

He inhaled deeply, continuing on. "This is completely unacceptable. You're suspended for two weeks, and you've only been attending this school for *two days.* You should have been expelled but . . . he felt sorry for you." Maren paused, holding back his next thought. Lily didn't need to know that her father had groveled for her place at this school. She didn't need to know that he told Principal Hamel all about her dead mother, all about her troubled childhood and her constantly uprooted life. He swallowed the words hard.

"I'm sorry." Lily barely choked out an apology, dripping with shame. She couldn't get the boy's eyes out of her mind—bulging, red, ready to pop. The terror that spread across his face as he scratched at her arms.

She looked down at her skin, studying the light-red marks on her wrists where Cody's frantic fingernails had carved into them.

"I didn't mean to," she pleaded. Tears were welling tightly at her eyes before she blinked them away. The doll buzzed in her lap, filling her with warmth and drowning her in conflicting emotions. She flinched.

In her mind, her father hated her for what she had done. That boy, Cody, and his friends surely hated her too. The principal, the teachers, the cold way they all looked at her as she was marched into the office, and the image of her hands curled around Cody's throat pulsated at her temples. It was all too much.

The one thing holding her upright was the doll, and his promises that she had done well. That she was strong. She was *powerful.*

She closed her eyes tightly, stifling a cry. Her head threatened to pop under the pressure of it.

"Let's just go home." Maren turned the key while the engine sputtered to life, filling the quiet truck with noise.

His heart burned for his daughter, and for the pain that she felt, but he was clueless as to a solution or any words he could say that might comfort her. He reached out his hand to the top of her head to smooth the stray blonde hairs from her forehead, but his arm stopped dead in the air. It hung nervously, afraid to make contact.

His emotions bubbled through each vein as his hand retreated back down to the steering wheel. They sat like that in silence while the truck rolled out of the empty parking lot and away from the school.

He couldn't stop thinking about what his daughter had done. All her life she had never harmed anything, least of all another child. He kept picturing what her face might have looked like, or how her hands might have felt against the boy's taut skin. He thought about what she must have been thinking as she stood, pushing Cody to the wall with solid arms and choking him against it while he sputtered and cried. He imagined the boy's fear, and his wild eyes.

He was desperate to understand his daughter, to see where this could have come from, but he couldn't think of any one question to ask. Somewhere deep, he knew this was his fault. Who else could be to blame? He had failed her yet again—that much was clear. No child could do this themselves. Especially not Lily, his sweet, young Lily. Not her.

Raindrops thrummed against the windshield softly, stretching against the breeze as they drove, and wet tires twisted against the asphalt beneath the truck. A final thought continued to pound in Maren's head the entirety of the short drive home. He thought about Lily's expulsion, and the commitment he had made to his job. He thought about Lily staying home by herself while he worked for hours and hours each day . . .

I can't leave her alone in that house, he thought to himself. *Not for one second.*

Seventeen.

The seven-minute drive home was nowhere near long enough for Maren to think. They sat in the driveway silently within the car, both of them daring the other to speak first. Lily held tightly to Mr. Doll, with a heart that beat loudly enough for the two of them.

Maren stewed in his thoughts, which throbbed behind his eyes. What would he do about work? About Lily being home by herself for two weeks? What would he do about the godforsaken *gray doll?* His concern and worry were quickly shifting into anger, crawling up his throat and coating his teeth. This doll was nothing but trouble for him, and definitely for Lily.

She had always been a sweet, shy, passive young girl. A girl who caused no trouble and kept to herself. Now in this house, holding this doll, she had become unpredictable. She was angry, violent, and argumentative. She sleepwalked, mumbled to herself in her strangely spotless bedroom, and disappeared from her body in the middle of a crowded aquarium while the lights surged around her before dropping to the floor. Maren's fear had grown steadily within him, devouring everything else. He was scared of his eleven-year-old daughter.

Not only did he fear her, but he feared the doll. A primal fear that gnawed at him relentlessly, even as he doused it in logic.

I am not a superstitious man, he would think to himself. *I will not fear a doll or a house or a dead old man.*

He could feel Lily's nervousness sliding from her skin and into the air. His sweet, young Lily. His troubled daughter who choked a little boy against the wall in the courtyard of her *elementary* school. Maren shivered.

He plucked the keys from the ignition, quieting the truck around them. His lungs gulped a deep breath in while he glanced at Lily, who continued to stare straight ahead toward the white garage. Their car doors swung open and into the cold air outside as the aura of the house pulled them closer.

Maren unlocked the brass handle, cracking the front door open and allowing the two of them to fade into the entryway. He stood in front of the closed door watching his daughter sulk toward the staircase, debating his next words.

"Lily, give me the doll," he demanded. His voice made him sound much surer of himself than he felt, bracing for the impact of his daughter's reaction.

She whipped around to face him, wide-eyed. "What? Why?"

Maren stood firm, digging his eyes into hers.

"You really need to ask me that right now? After the stunt you just pulled?" The more he spoke, the more venom surfaced in his mouth. "Your *obsession* with this doll isn't normal. I've never even seen you hurt a fly, but some stupid kid takes a doll from you at school and you *strangle him?*" His voice was raised now, each word like a knife.

"You don't get it!" Lily yelled at him, startling even herself with the harshness of her tone. "You can't take Mr. Doll away!" She could feel her heart rate jumping.

"You are my daughter! I can't let you hurt other kids and act like a *delinquent* without getting some sort of punishment!" he yelled. "You should have been expelled! I had to beg Principal Hamel to even let you come back at *all!*"

Maren's emotions from the past couple of weeks were all bubbling up his throat, threatening to explode.

"Well, *maybe* I don't want to go back there! Maybe I want to go back to one of the other million schools and million houses that you've dragged me out of!" Her expression morphed into something dark, something hateful. "First you take my friends away, my favorite schools, and my favorite houses. Now you want to take away the only person in the world who loves me?" Tears were stinging at her eyes, but she was too angry to let them fall. She saw the way he flinched at her words, and she liked it. She wanted him to feel each one.

Maren stared down at his shoes, choking down pain. His rotting heart sank deeply into his chest, burning with decay.

"That's not fair, Lily." Her father's strong voice began to crack. "You know I love you, and I try to do what's best for you, but it's not always easy. This doll is not a person, it is a toy, and I am your *father.* Now, give it to me." He held out a shaky hand, opening his palm. His chest felt tight.

Lily clutched the doll with white knuckles, securing him against her chest. Her blue eyes dug into the floor.

"I don't want you to be my father," Lily whispered, her sharp tongue flicking in her mouth. "I just want Mommy back."

She turned and walked up the stairs, ignoring her father's desperate request. Her words hung in the air where she left them, unwilling to try to take them back.

Maren stood frozen, watching his daughter disappear into the fog of the house as the cracks in his chest widened. The darkness sucked the rest of his soul inside.

...

The floorboards vibrated beneath the thick carpet, buzzing at Lily's skin. The lights were off, the door was tightly closed and locked behind her, and not even the birds outside threatened to interrupt.

"You were right," Lily mumbled out a whine, disrupting the heavy silence of her bedroom. The gray doll in her hands surged with power. "You're always right . . . about everything." The tears began to slip slowly from her eyes as she sank into the comfort of the dollhouse.

She was curled against the side of the small table that displayed it at the center of her room while the carpet hugged her legs. Inside of its thin wooden walls, Lily-Doll was resting on the small couch, staring into the cracked drywall over the fireplace. It was slowly crumbling away.

Lily-Doll was always there lately. She hardly left the dollhouse at all. Mr. Doll had seemingly forgotten about her.

"Why do you leave Lily-Doll alone all day?" Lily asked him in a soft whisper. She wondered if Lily-Doll was sad, like Lily used to be. She wondered why Mr. Doll had stopped caring, or if he missed her.

His aura cloaked her in heat, infiltrating her bones and penetrating to her core. He sank into each crevasse of Lily's being like a drug, and she breathed him in like an addict.

That doll is hollow, he replied in her mind, soft but haunting. Lily stared at the pretty, blonde, porcelain doll while he spoke. *My daughter is here.*

Lily's eyes melted downward through drying tears and settled on the doll in her lap. She remembered her words to her father from moments ago. They swirled deep inside of her chest like a raging storm.

I don't want you to be my father.

She cringed at the memory, and the way the words had tasted as she spoke. The tart aftertaste still burned at the back of her throat. The powerful feeling she felt while she spoke, the commanding tone of her voice, it had all completely dissolved. Now she felt heinous. Her face stung with regret.

She tried to remember where her mind had gone when she said those hateful words, or when she gripped the blond boy's throat. She recalled her unwavering resolve to hurt him. To *punish* him.

Cody. The poor boy's name rang in her mind.

Who was she in those moments? She hadn't recognized herself. She could barely straighten her thoughts enough to remember them. Suddenly, she felt afraid.

You are perfect, Al. The cavernous voice of the doll echoed within her. *They deserved this. They hurt you, my daughter,* he repeated, like a spell.

Something stirred in Lily's blood at his words. Something deep and ravenous, like it was waking from within her. Something fed by her pain and her yearning, by her unrelenting desire to be seen. But more than that, it was fed by the house. By the depth of it that she had welcomed within her. It grew each day.

"Daughter?" she breathed the word out, equally a plea and a question. Lily's mind floated off, drifting peacefully in the reality he had bestowed on her. The sting of the words she spat at her father, the pain, the regret, and the haunting feeling of her hands around the boy's neck, it all rapidly receded. She only saw gray.

Yes, he purred. *My daughter. My Alina.*

...

Maren collapsed onto the couch and stayed there for some time, his head buried in his hands. His palms were slick with tears that steadily escaped his eyes, no matter how hard he tried to trap them. His entire body was heavy with grief, like it had been since Jewel died, but this grief was different, cold. This grief was fresh at the loss of his daughter, and at the loss of the man whom Jewel once loved.

Throughout Lily's childhood, he had been too focused on being a husband that he never truly learned how to be a father. Jewel was always there to cradle Lily, to love her and soothe her and protect her. Maren was there for *Jewel,* to shield her from the world outside, to cradle her pregnant belly, to love her and soothe her through the early stages of their daughter's life.

They were two sides of a coin, he and his wife, that served different purposes. Maren loved Lily as an extension of his love for Jewel. His passion for his wife had blossomed through Lily's blue eyes, her blonde hair, her pale skin—in all of the ways she reminded him of Jewel.

Jewel was born to be a mother; she had always been. Mothering Lily was like breathing to her, and Maren admired her deeply for it. Any instance of frustration he had felt as a father was always quickly swept away by his patient wife. His perfect, loving, passionate wife.

When Jewel fell sick, Maren couldn't bear it. He felt his own body deteriorating beside hers as she slowly drifted away.

Lily's young face grew into a constant reminder of the way Jewel had changed. The way her skin now shriveled against her bones, the way her hair thinned and her bright eyes dulled. She was becoming an empty mold of her once-overflowing self. She was *dying*.

Maren tried to protect, to provide, to be strong. He couldn't protect his wife from the illness, or his daughter from the loss. He could provide no comfort, as he had no strength left. Lily watched her father fade and her mother waste away.

Before he knew it, Maren was so empty he could barely open his eyes. He could barely speak with his daughter, or love her in the way she so desperately needed him to. He hated himself for it—for destroying his daughter, failing his wife, and breaking his most important promise.

Lately he felt that the more he tried to be better, the more things around him fell apart. The breakfast, the dinner, the aquarium . . . his connection to Lily was slowly burning to the ground. His ideas all jumbled together into an incoherent mess, arguing in circles with each other inside of him.

I'll take the doll, hide it . . . No, I'll throw it away.

But Lily would never forgive me. I'll keep it, only for a little while, and give her time to calm down.

I'll hide it in my bedroom, or maybe down in the basement, and she will forget all about it.

He desperately swarmed through his mind for a lifeline, a way out of this swirling black hole. Grasping at straws was all he seemed to know how to do.

Maybe she can come with me to work, or I can hire a nanny.

With what money? Nannies are expensive . . . I can stay home with her for two weeks.

And say what? That my daughter is a lunatic who chokes kids who steal her toys? That she can't be trusted at home alone? That will go over well with my superiors . . .

Maybe if I take the doll away and bring it with me to the base, she will be fine here by herself. She has always been fine before this.

"*Shit!*" The tension poured out of his mouth like a faucet, spilling all over the floor. He slammed his fists against the cushion of the couch, sliding the entire thing backward on the hardwood at the force. It shrieked against the floor.

He had no choice. His work was his lifeboat, saving *both* of them from the depths. He could not afford the risk of jeopardizing it over something so foolish.

He shot forward from the couch, shoving down his pain, his guilt, his grief, his misery, deep into its box like he had done many times before. He stomped up the stairs before his brain could catch up, before the thoughts came flooding back and knocked him back off his axis. He stormed all the way to Lily's closed bedroom door.

Knock. Knock. Knock.

"Lily, open the door." His voice was harsh but steady—the voice of a man unafraid of the choice he was making. It felt strange on his tongue.

Lily didn't answer, and the space behind the door stayed quiet. The energy was dull.

Knock. Knock. Knock.

"Lily. Open the door now," he demanded again. The responding silence grew even louder in his ears.

An eerie feeling crawled beneath his skin, sliding up his back and through his hair. He reached for the door handle as a scowl crossed his lips, preparing himself for whatever awaited him on the other side. His fingers curled in the air, stretching toward the knob and waiting for the cold to seep into his skin.

Instead, a jolt of electricity leapt from the metal, sinking sharp teeth into Maren's flesh. He pulled back his hand, shocked by the pain that flooded it, and stared in horror at the door. It was still buzzing like an electric fence.

He looked down at his palm, watching the redness flood across his skin.

Eighteen.

My daughter. My Alina.

Mr. Doll's words caressed the sides of Lily's face, burning at her nose. She barely even seemed to notice that he hadn't said her name.

"Your daughter?" She gleamed. Her eyes brightened at the sentiment. She had been desperately searching for this, wildly craving the acceptance that was now being handed freely to her on a silver platter. She imagined her dreams and the warmth of the dollhouse—the feel of the porcelain encasing her, the love that Mr. Doll had offered her. It was all close enough to touch, but she worried it might slip away before she could have it. She would do anything to keep it.

I've missed you, my precious girl, he continued.

This moment terrified her. She felt the joy of it breathe deep in her flesh, the hopefulness cracking her hardened shell. She desperately clung to the fleeting feeling as her defenses fell uselessly at her feet.

"Alina?" Lily blurted out, wishing she could stuff the word back in as soon as it passed her lips. She felt the opportunity rapidly slipping away at her hesitation.

You are mine. My Alina. My daughter. His tone deepened, sucking her in. *Your hair, Al. It's so long.*

"My hair?" She wouldn't ask again about the name. It didn't matter, nothing did. He *loved* her. Her name was insignificant.

It is so much longer than before. It was beautiful. His words were haunting, like a siren luring its prey.

Lily drew a lock of her hair between her fingers, dragging at the length of it all the way down her back. Her hair *was* long, she thought. *Too* long.

She stood, walking to the desk where it waited against the wall and the mirror that was hung behind it. It softly gleamed her reflection back at her. She stood before it, holding the doll to her hip with one hand and letting his gray skin snake against her body.

She met her own eyes in the mirror, seeing their bright, piercing blue. She saw the long blonde hair streaming down past her shoulders. She looked closer into the glass and saw her hard porcelain skin, and where the light from the windows bounced off it.

You are mine. We can be together again, he hummed the words sweetly into her mind. *Inside of the dollhouse.*

Lily looked back toward the dollhouse over her shoulder. She saw through the small window where Lily-Doll sat, with her bright-blue eyes and her short blonde hair that hung just above her shoulders. Lily melted into the gray doll's soothing voice, allowing her mind to wander. She gently set the doll on the desk.

She pulled a pair of scissors from the top drawer and gripped them with a steady hand. Her slow fingers plucked a thick lock of hair, lifting it into the open air in front of her and cutting it just above her shoulder, like Mr. Doll wanted.

Slowly, she took each lock, chopping her hair with the thick scissors and dropping blonde bundles to the floor in a circle at her feet. Mr. Doll watched quietly from the edge of the wooden desk. His power surged around the room, blowing through Lily like a breeze through a tree.

When she was finished, she stared at herself in the mirror, smiling. She could feel the gray doll's satisfaction as it coursed through her own veins. Her hair fell just above her shoulders, now unevenly cut at each end.

You look so beautiful, Al, Mr. Doll praised, tightening his strings around her bones with each word.

"We can be together now," she begged, "just like you said." Her hands yearned for reassurance as she reached out to touch him.

Not yet. His voice was callous, almost disappointed. His demeanor slowly changed, sending tidal waves of discomfort winding through Lily's chest.

He's going to take me away, the gray doll continued. *We can't let that happen.*

A tower of emotion fell toward Lily where she stood, the sharp scissors still perched at her fingers. She nodded, willing him to continue, to tell her what she needed to do.

In the silence hanging between them, she felt his reply. The cold metal of the scissors warmed slowly in her hand.

I put myself in this doll, Al, he said. *I did it for you, so I could find you wherever you had gone.*

Lily hung on each word, clinging to the sound of his thick voice in her head. She held her breath as he spoke, lungs burning.

Now that I found you, you can come with me. My daughter, my sweet girl.

"How?" She stared at herself in the mirror, memorizing each feature. She soaked in the feeling of the short hair dangling above her shoulders, and the cold rush of the porcelain encasing her flesh. Her body shimmered in the light pouring in from the windows. Her pale face was clear and smooth, with none of her father's freckles on the tip of her nose.

You know, Mr. Doll whispered, carefully.

Lily's eyes blurred and she felt as though she was looking down at herself from the ceiling. She saw herself holding the scissors, and the doll watching her closely from atop the desk. She saw her reflection in the mirror, with glossy, unfocused eyes and a slack jaw.

"Won't it hurt?" she asked, unfolding the blade from the scissors and perching the sharp edge of the metal against the skin of her forearm. Delicate, soft, shiny flesh.

It's not real, Al. You're a doll, just like me, he assured her. Lily stared into her arm as it shimmered in the light. *You won't feel a thing.*

Lily was mesmerized by his words. She fell in and out of a dream as her fingers tightened.

"Won't I bleed?" she asked. The edge dug against her wrist and felt no pain. He was right: This *wasn't* real.

No, sweet girl. Dolls don't bleed.

Lily slid the scissors slowly against the glossy white skin of her forearm and felt nothing. No marks appeared on her body, no blood ran down her arm. There was only clean, shining porcelain. She smiled, humming dreamily.

She lifted the blade once more, eagerly dragging its sharpened edge into her flesh. Nothing was happening.

Lily's mind floated high above her body, bouncing along the edges of the ceiling as she happily pictured the life that awaited her within the dollhouse. Mr. Doll's words stuck to her like honey, coating each thought in a sweet, thick shell.

Knock. Knock. Knock.

The muffled sound interrupted the moment, causing her mind to fall an inch from the sky.

You're almost there, Al. My precious girl. The gray doll burned, throwing heat around the room. His voice stayed a quiet calm. *Almost.*

Lily gripped the scissors, ready to slice at her skin once more, but the sound came again.

Knock. Knock. Knock.

She heard a voice this time, growing louder as she focused on it. A voice that sounded like Maren's, like her father's.

The room was pounding with energy, sizzling off each wall like a hot grill. Electricity vibrated through her bones. Her eyes suddenly focused, meeting her reflection in the mirror as her mind crashed back down into her body.

She looked down at the scissors still perched against her skin and the thick, oozing blood that trickled from two slashes in her wrist. The scissors clattered loudly to the floor.

Maren was pounding on the door now, yelling to her through the wood. His voice was clear and crisp, terrified.

"Open the door now!" His voice rattled inside of her. She stared with widened eyes at the blood that was pooling from her arm and dripping into the carpet. Her breathing quickened, sending panic blooming in each corner of her lungs as she held her right hand against the slippery red liquid. Her legs gave out from beneath her, letting her fall against the carpet while she held tightly to her bleeding arm. The gray doll's presence gradually slipped away from the room, reeling slowly back inside of him.

Suddenly, the door *cracked* open by the brute force of her father, sending it slamming loudly against the wall. Maren poured into the room, almost hysterical, laying eyes on his only daughter as she bled into the carpet. He rushed to where she lay against the floor.

"*Lily!*" he snapped, blanketing over her.

No tears fell from her eyes, just an empty gaze that mindlessly stared forward. She held a hand tightly against her wrist, with shallow, quick breaths passing her lips. The doll watched the scene unfold from the desk, unmoving.

"Lily, what happened?" His words were catching up to his mind as it raced, soaking in the situation around him. His heart hammered into his ribs, almost bursting as he looked down at his daughter. His eyes stabbed at the blood that poured from her, soaking into the lightly colored carpet, but he pushed himself forward.

"Sweetheart, you're going into shock." Maren's instincts took control of his body as he spoke, struggling to stay calm. "It's all right. I got you, okay? We have to go. We have to call an ambulance." His words were more for himself than for her, demanding himself to act fast in spite of his blinding terror.

He shook his cell phone free from his pocket while he lifted his silent daughter against him with a strong arm. He brought the ringing phone to his ear.

"I . . . I need an ambulance." His words were clear, practiced, but his voice trembled. "My daughter is badly hurt, losing a lot of blood. I live at 1657 East Elmhurst Street. Please hurry."

Lily didn't speak. She barely even breathed as Maren sprinted down the stairs, out of the house, and toward the car. He couldn't wait for the ambulance. He had no way of knowing if they would get there in time.

His daughter's warm blood stuck to his clothes, to his hands and his arms and the screen of his cell phone. So. Much. Blood. Maren laid his daughter as carefully as he could into the seat of the truck, peeling out into the street and heading toward the main road. He held himself together with everything he had.

"I'm in a dark-blue Ford pickup, heading eastbound toward I-94," he continued into the phone. "We are heading in the direction of the hospital. I need the ambulance to meet me on the road." The first responder spoke with a calming tone, one that Maren's ringing ears could barely hear. He frantically flicked his eyes between the road and his daughter as she slumped against the window with red seeping into her clothes. His gaze fell on her hair for just a moment and the choppy blonde strands that framed her blank face.

Lily's eyes drifted aimlessly around the truck while she gripped her bleeding arm against her body. She felt cold, but sweat matted her hair against the back of her neck. Flashing lights approached in the distance, and the faint sounds of a siren twisted at her ears.

"Sweetheart? *Sweetheart?* The ambulance is coming. Do you hear it?" Maren's words quickened and jumbled with terror. The strength he presented was made of straw, blowing away in the wind.

"Focus on the siren, Lily," he pleaded. "They're almost here and they'll make you feel better. Just focus on the siren, okay?" Maren honked loudly as the ambulance turned the corner toward him, waving his hand out the window of the truck. His foot pressed the pedal into the floor, toes curling against his shoes at the force. His mind was completely blank, ignoring everything else as the ambulance skidded to a stop at the corner. Bright lights flooded the interior of the truck, illuminating their faces.

Two men erupted from the ambulance, rushing toward the pickup truck and around to the passenger door. Maren barely brought the truck to a stop before he leapt from his seat and rushed to his daughter. Panic was setting in.

Lily's eyes were gently closing as she dipped farther against her seat, losing consciousness. The car door swung open at her back, and Maren watched as the two men carefully moved her onto a gurney, flashing a light at her eyes and shaking her softly awake.

"What's her name, sir?" one of the men shot these short words at Maren as he wheeled his daughter toward the ambulance. Maren didn't reply.

"Sir, her name? What's your daughter's name?" the man said again, louder this time. He was putting something around Lily's face. Maren worried they might hurt her. He desperately wanted to put it on her himself.

"It's Lily." Maren choked out. It took everything in him to keep his emotions inside, to not shove these men away from her and save her himself. He needed to be strong for his daughter.

"Okay, good," the man said, turning his attention back to her. "Lily? You have to stay awake for me, Lily, all right? Keep your eyes open, sweetheart." His words were sweet and calm. He spoke quickly but rationally as the gurney rolled across the asphalt and toward the ambulance.

"You're going to be all right, Lily," the second man said. "Just hold on while we get you to the hospital. Just a few more minutes."

They carefully lifted her into the ambulance, securing her inside. Maren started to follow, climbing in through the open doors before the first man stopped him.

"Sir, we're going to need you to follow in your vehicle," the first man said. "We'll take good care of her."

Maren blinked, stepping back down from the ambulance and standing on the asphalt. He dug his eyes past the men and into his daughter while the doors slammed shut in front of him and the men prepared to leave.

He wanted to scream. He wanted to bang on the doors and demand to ride with his daughter. He wanted to rip the mask from her face and put it on more delicately, making sure not to pinch her skin or tangle it in her hair. But he couldn't do any of those things. He could only watch.

He ran back toward his car, which sat abandoned on the side of the freeway, stopping traffic on all sides. Men and women watched anxiously from their cars, staring through their windows as the scene unfolded.

Maren stormed into the truck, its keys still in the ignition, and skidded in the direction of the ambulance. He stared at his hands against the steering wheel, stained with a dark, deep red. His daughter's blood was slowly drying on his fingers and soaking into the leather seat beside him.

So. Much. Blood.

Nineteen.

Maren tapped his fingers against the sides of his chair under the blinding hospital lights. The hallway was bustling with people, crowding around him at every angle and making it impossible for him to breathe. He desperately wanted to escape outside for a lungful of fresh air, but refused to leave his spot. The doctor could return at any moment.

He hadn't seen his daughter in one hour and twenty-seven minutes and counting. The endless stream of paperwork had kept him busy at first, but soon enough all there was left to do was wait.

Tap tap tap tap tap.

He religiously checked his watch, willing time to move faster, or slower, he wasn't sure. He lifted his arm to check the time again, stopping to stare at the clean, freckled skin of his hands. He had washed the blood off shortly after he arrived, but still felt it sticking against his flesh. It still stained his clothes, taunting him.

They took her in immediately from the ambulance, beating Maren by seconds, so he was unable to see her. They had told him three or four times now that she was going to be fine, but that he just couldn't see her quite yet. He hoped they were right—that his daughter was *fine*. They were professionals, after all, but he tapped his fingers anxiously anyway.

How could you let this happen? he asked himself over and over. He tried to drown himself out with the sharp sounds of his fingertips against the hard plastic. It wasn't working.

You're her father. His voice continued in his head, filling him with guilt. *You're supposed to protect her. If nothing else, at least do that.*

Tap tap tap tap tap.

You're pathetic. Useless.

Tap tap tap—

Finally the double doors swung open, and a short old man strolled into the hall. His gray hair coiled at the top of his head, and his shiny new shoes squeaked against the floor. The badge on his jacket read, "Dr. Herring."

"Mister Caplin?" the man asked to the open room. Lily's father stood, silently pleading for good news.

"Yes, how is she?" He kept his tone even and calm, biting back nerves.

"Your daughter is stable. She's resting now," the doctor stated smoothly while Maren's body nearly melted at the relief. "She needed eight stitches, but everything went very well. No permanent damage was done. One of the cuts was a bit deeper than the other, but the shock was the worst of it."

"That's . . . great. Thank you, Doctor." Maren exhaled, leaning against the wall behind him. The choking guilt receded slightly from his mouth.

The old man paused, nodding. He cleared his throat, wary of his next words. "We will need to ask you a few questions about your daughter's incident. Were you present when she . . ."—his voice was low, whispering to Maren hesitantly—"when she hurt herself?"

"No, I—" Maren coughed up each word, sticking between his teeth as he spoke. "I was downstairs . . . I'm not sure what happened. I wasn't there."

Doctor Herring swallowed, clasping his hands together behind his back. "I see. You were lucky to have caught her in time. Things could have been much worse if you hadn't." The hallway suddenly seemed quiet, filling to the brim with tension.

Maren flinched. "Can I see her now?"

"Not yet, I'm afraid," the man replied hesitantly. "We have a series of questions we will need to ask you about the incident, and about Lily's life at home. It would be best to do so while she is still resting."

Maren bit his tongue, nodding.

The doctor led him through the double doors and deeper into the hallway of the hospital, approaching an empty, sterile room. Maren couldn't keep himself from glancing at each of the closed doors that lined the hall, wondering which one his daughter might be waiting behind.

Doctor Herring motioned to the open door at his side, directing Maren inside and letting the door softly close behind him before walking back down the hall, leaving him in solitude.

There were several chairs placed around the room, a small desk against the wall, and sparse decorations with little color. Maren fidgeted in his seat, anxious to leave, when the door opened again.

"Mister Caplin?" A tall thin woman pushed her head in through the cracked doorway, clipboard in hand. She had a messy curled bun at the top of her head and brown waves of hair spilling from it in all directions. Bright-red lips smiled at him from her thin face.

"Yes, I was told I would need to answer some questions about Lily? When can I see her?" Maren pushed. He had no time for useless banter. He knew full well what they thought his daughter had done, and it was unquestionable. Lily would *never* harm herself.

"Oh, you can see her soon, I'm sure. I just have a few questions about your daughter's home life. Her mental state lately as well." The woman pulled the chair from behind the desk and dragged it across the glossy tile. She perched it a few feet away from him, getting as close as she could before lowering herself into it.

"My name is Lydia," she continued, "I work quite a bit with children of Lily's age who suffer from a variety of mental illnesses, or those who have lived through traumatic events."

"All right." Maren spoke softly, shifting in his seat. He already disliked Lydia. He disliked the idea of his daughter's *trauma* that had already settled into this woman's mind. She didn't understand.

"So, tell me about Lily."

The conversation felt like it lasted for hours. Maren told this strange woman all about Lily's new school, their new home, and her *trouble* with Cody—sparing some minor details. He told her about Jewel, her adventures, her illness, and her death. He even told her about their . . . issues, lately. The fact that Lily rarely left her bedroom. Her obsession with a certain doll.

Lydia had a way of drawing out the details that nobody wanted to share with a stranger. She coaxed with kind eyes, nodding a lot while scribbling at her papers with a bright-blue pen and displaying the occasional pitying frown or empathetic gasp.

"I see," she finally replied. "It sounds like Lily is quite the young girl, and also perhaps quite troubled."

She cocked her head, furrowing her eyebrows. Her red lips pursed. "Has she ever made an attempt like this in the past?"

"Of course not," Maren scoffed. "Lily has never done *anything* like this before. I have a hard time even believing she did this on purpose." His words scrambled over his teeth and his heart rate spiked with offense. "She's always been a perfectly normal and happy kid. I just . . ." He inhaled a steadying breath. "This isn't like her."

"I understand." Lydia scrawled another note onto her clipboard. "Sometimes it can be incredibly difficult to notice when someone is contemplating suicide."

Suicide. The word he had been avoiding since he got here. It pulsed in his ears. Maren was beginning to hate this woman.

"Lily would never have done something like this," he insisted. "The face she made when I found her, it looked like she had seen a ghost." Maren let out a shaky breath, remembering the moment. "It wasn't the face of someone who wanted to . . . die. There *has* to be some kind of explanation."

His throat burned. The emotions he had spent all day burying were slowly making themselves known. Of course, he *knew* the explanation already.

"That's actually quite good to hear." The woman flashed a small smile. "Many patients who come in after an attempt seem to be grateful they didn't succeed. Maybe she changed her mind." She continued scribbling.

Maren's knuckles were white in his lap. This woman had no idea what she was talking about. If Lily were so unstable that she were contemplating suicide, surely he would have known about it. Surely she would have told him.

Surely . . .

Tears were sprouting at his eyes. His vision clouded beneath them as he choked back a sob.

My Lily, he thought to himself. *Did you?*

He forcefully wiped at his face before the tears had their chance to fall. He couldn't bear to believe she had done it. Not Lily. Not her. He knew who was at fault—somewhere deep, somewhere primal, he knew.

It was the doll.

"Mister Caplin?" The woman's arm was stretched toward him between their chairs, a tissue draping from her fingers. "I know this is very hard. I just have a few more questions."

. . .

By the time all of the questions were answered, Maren was exhausted. The strange woman led him out into the hall, down and to the left. She sent him to a gray door labeled 204 and let him lead himself inside.

The room was dull and white, with two beds, one on each side, and a small TV hung against the middle of the wall. A beige curtain separated his daughter's bed from another's, which sat empty on the right side. Lily's thin hospital bed was placed near the window, letting warm sunlight seep inside as the sun set. It glowed against her skin and her blueish-white hospital gown. The room was completely silent, like all of the noise had been sucked out.

Maren approached slowly, resting his feet softly on the tiled floor with each step. He sat down in the firm chair next to his daughter's bed, examining her. His eyes roamed over her skin, taking in all of her soft features and closed eyes.

He interrogated each of the machines that buzzed at her sides, displaying her vitals. Each box softly beeped with a mechanical melody, flashing lights and lines across the screen. Maren watched his daughter's heart rate closely, soaking in each beat.

He couldn't keep his eyes off of her bandages. They were perfectly white and clean, expertly dressed. She slept peacefully, wrapped in the thin white hospital sheets. It was like none of the events from earlier had truly happened, like it had all been some sort of sick, twisted nightmare.

Lily looked perfect. Like a porcelain doll.

...

Almost four hours had passed, and Maren hadn't left his chair. Moonlight slipped into the room from the window, replacing the warm sun from before and glazing the emptiness around him. His bones ached against the frigid seat and his insides twisted with hunger. Neither of them had eaten since breakfast.

He had passed a vending machine in the hall when he entered, but the thought of Lily waking up alone cemented him to his seat. Even the connected restroom felt too far away. His stomach curled.

He was almost dozing off against the windowsill when Lily finally opened her eyes.

"Hey, Lily-pop," Maren breathed, scratching his dry throat. The room was so quiet, and his daughter suddenly looked so frail. He worried his words might harm her.

Lily wandered her eyes over the walls, digesting the sterile room that tightly held her. Worry bloomed on her cheeks, and her eyes widened as it set in where she was.

"Dad?" She began to panic, trying to sit up. Maren held a strong hand over her, guiding her back toward the pillow.

"You're fine, sweetheart, just lie down and try to relax." Her father suddenly became excruciatingly aware of the deep-red stains on his shirt and his daughter's eyes digging into them. He covered his torso with a spare pillow from the edge of her bed.

"What happened?" Lily stared at the beeping machines, the bandages around her arm, the blood on her father's shirt. "Is that . . . is that my—"

"There was an accident. You cut yourself on the arm pretty badly, but the doctors fixed you up and put some stitches and bandages on you. They cleaned you up real well." The words poured from his lips before Lily could fear them. He paused. "Do you not remember what happened?" He leaned forward over her, placing four fingers against her forehead to check her warmth.

"No . . . I don't remember anything," Lily mumbled, holding back tears. "Where's Mr. Doll?" She patted both hands over the blankets around her and searched the bedside table. Maren watched suspiciously.

"I'm sure he's at home where you left him, Lily. This is more important. I need to know what happened." He settled the impatience from his voice, smoothing it. "What do you remember, sweetheart?"

"I don't remember anything . . ." Lily's heart rate sped up on the monitor, filling the room with the rapid beeping sound. She slowly formed her thoughts as a new expression flooded her face, sending the worry to fade away. Her next words were slow and careful, as if she were reading from a script.

"I cut my hair so I could . . . Well, I wanted to cut it. Then I cut my arm by accident . . ." Lily paused, thinking. "And then I lost Mr. Doll and I don't know where he is. Then I woke up here." She pulled lightly at the IVs and touched the bandages that wrapped her left arm. Her eyes intensified, stabbing into Maren. "I want to go home now. I need Mr. Doll."

Maren cupped her hands beneath his own, attempting to calm her. He feared she might rip out the cords in her panic.

"Lily, you need to relax, okay? Your doll is fine. He's at home and we will get there as soon as the doctor tells us that you're okay to leave, which he hasn't yet." His tone was soft but stern. He gently held her left arm just above the bandages as he spoke. "Just let me get the doctor and I'll try to get some answers. But you have to wait here, and don't touch anything. Okay?"

Lily nodded and lay back against her pillow, defeated. Maren stood, moving out the door and rounding the corners of the hall down to the front desk. He walked quickly, anxious to get back to his daughter and unsure of what she might do when he wasn't there to watch her.

"Hello. What can I do for you?" A small young woman spoke from her seat behind the desk. It was covered in papers and colorful sticky notes, with small ceramic animals perched on the base of her computer. She smiled widely, seemingly out of place in the center of a hospital. Maren didn't smile back.

"I need to see Doctor Herring. I'm Lily Caplin's father, room 204. I have some questions for him about my daughter."

The woman nodded politely, picking up the desk phone and dialing a short number before pressing the phone to her ear. Just as it began to ring, Doctor Herring exited a room at the end of the hall, staring down at his clipboard.

"Doctor!" Maren jogged down the hall, ignoring the receptionist, and quickly approached the old man where he stood. "Lily just woke up. I would like to know what the status is. If there's anything I need to be doing . . . I'm not sure how long you plan on keeping Lily here to watch her, or—"

"Yes, I will send a nurse in right away," he interjected. "We will need to evaluate her, see how she's feeling." The doctor flipped through his clipboard, roaming his eyes over the pages.

Maren nodded, turning on his heel and back toward his daughter's room with the old man following closely behind. *Questions* weren't what she needed. These people could not help her. She needed to go home.

Home, he thought. He wished he could take her anywhere else but their *home,* but he had no other option—surely not this soulless hospital.

He pushed the door open into Lily's small room, where she sat up in bed staring at her reflection in the smudged glass of the window. Her right hand was lifted to her hair, sliding her fingers down the freshly cut locks that draped over her ears, hovering just above the hospital gown at her shoulders. She stared at herself, smiling and twisting her short blonde hair around in circles.

"Lily, the doctor needs to ask you a few questions, okay?" Maren broke his daughter from her trance into the window. She blinked at her reflection, squinting her blue eyes at it.

"Hi, Lily, my name is Doctor Herring. How are you feeling, my dear?" He dragged a chair to the side of her bed, falling into it as Lily swept her attention away from the glass. The nurse came in behind him and began removing the IV from Lily's arm. Lily watched intently while the kind woman worked.

"I'm feeling okay. I just want to go home," Lily droned. Her voice was heavy.

"Can you tell me what happened, sweetheart?" The doctor spoke tenderly, coaxing her to respond.

Lily thought for a second, staring at her bandaged arm. She touched her hair again with a delicate hand.

"I was cutting my hair, and I must have slipped," she said, pausing. Her gaze never left her bandaged skin, and her blue eyes darkened. The lights flickered softly above her bed. "The scissors were very sharp." Her mouth twitched.

"Yes, it seems they were. Gave yourself two decently sized cuts, huh?" The old man's tone was careful, slow, as he jotted something onto his papers.

Lily continued to stare while the nurse removed the needle from her arm, and a small dot of blood raised from her flesh. Her short hair fell around her face, blocking the doctor's gaze.

"Lily, it's very important that you're honest with us about what happened." Doctor Herring leaned forward, like they were sharing a secret. "It looks like these injuries may have been intentional. We only want to help you."

Maren's thoughts were storming in his skull. His frustration bubbled to his lips. "The other day we were out at the aquarium and Lily passed out. What if she passed out again this time and doesn't know it? Maybe that's why she cut herself. Maybe—"

"I didn't pass out," Lily cut him off, jolting her face upward toward the doctor. The bright lights receded slightly from the ceiling, dulling the colors of the room. "I remember now," she continued. "I just slipped."

The door creaked open from behind where they circled around Lily's bed, and the strange woman from earlier pushed into the room, smiling her red lips again. Her clipboard and bright-blue pen gleamed from beneath her arm.

The doctor leaned toward Maren, speaking quietly. "We will need to do an evaluation on your daughter. It's important we speak with her alone."

"I'm her father," he retorted in defense. "I'm sure it would be fine if I'm present for the evaluation to make sure she's okay."

"With all due respect, Mister Caplin, it is very important that there is no one else present during the assessment." Doctor Herring spoke assuredly, with no indication of flexibility. "Not even direct family."

Maren bit the inside of his cheek, curling his hands into fists. He looked toward his daughter where she sat in her bed, still twirling one finger in her hair. He sucked in a deep breath.

"Lily, I'm going to be just outside, okay? These nice people need to ask you some questions about what happened," he said. Lily glanced up to her father's face, nodding.

"Okay," she mumbled, chewing on her bottom lip.

Maren tightened his jaw, twitching his fingers at his sides. He turned to leave while the doctor tailed him closely behind, catching him at the door.

"It may take some time. We are going to do a full psych evaluation on her," the old man whispered. "We will need to keep her overnight."

Maren's face flushed hot, and he opened his mouth to speak before his words were intercepted.

"You should go home, grab Lily a change of clothes, maybe one for yourself." The old man's eyes flicked to the red stains at Maren's torso. "Any toys or things that might make her feel more comfortable."

Maren licked his lips, his chest constricting. His mouth moved to form the words he might use to tell this man that he would not be going *anywhere,* but Doctor Herring was right. A shirt covered in stains of her own blood would not do Lily any favors. If he couldn't take her home, he could at least make the night more bearable. The last thing that Lily needed was a night in a cramped hospital bed, but it wasn't up to him.

"Yes, of course. I'll go grab some of her things." He smiled weakly at him, reaching toward the door handle.

"Don't forget Mr. Doll!" Maren's muscles stiffened as Lily's request clipped at his ears. He thought for sure she had been too far away to overhear.

The doctor smiled at her, then stared back at Maren, awaiting his reply.

"Yeah. Okay." Her father swallowed hard. "I'll be right back." Maren took one last look at his daughter before heading out the door, down the elevator, and all the way back to the house.

Twenty.

There was still blood soaked into the passenger seat, greeting Maren through the opened car door. He scowled at it, shivering at the memory. It was almost all he was able to focus on during the short drive home, other than the questions that pounded inside of his head.

How could he have let this happen? His sweet young daughter, pouring her own blood over the carpet, slicing into her skin with *scissors*. It wasn't her fault—it couldn't have been. Something very wrong was going on inside this house. This cursed, blood-soaked house.

As the dull white bricks of the house approached through the windshield, blackened in the night, Maren decided that the best thing to do for now was to push the thoughts aside. He needed to hurry.

Pulling the truck to a stop, he jumped out and ran into the kitchen, flicking on the lights. He grabbed an armful of damp towels and returned to the truck, scrubbing the leather seats as quickly as he could. Thankfully the blood lifted easily, disappearing into the damp material as he cleaned.

Once the car was taken care of, he hurried upstairs and removed his soiled clothes, tossing them into the trash rather than the laundry. With all of the cleaning supplies he could find, he then prepared to enter his daughter's bedroom. The image of her pale skin, her body collapsed into the carpet, stung in his mind. He wavered around the corner of the opened door while the shadows from within crept out into the hallway. The thought of his daughter waiting for him at the hospital was the only thing that pushed him over the threshold.

The door still leaned against the wall behind it from when he cracked it open in his panic, but the handle and lock still looked surprisingly intact. He peered around the empty room, void of energy. It was dark, hollow, and cold. Even in the blackness, the darkened spot on the carpet was visible through the shadows. He flicked on the light.

His daughter's blood taunted him from the middle of the floor where it stained the beige carpet, and the scissors glistened through the black. Goosebumps ran over his flesh at the sight of it.

Maren snatched up the scissors, tossing them roughly into the trash bag. He tipped the plastic bottle toward the blight of red, pouring cleaning solvent into the mess. It bubbled and popped into the dried blood before he covered it with a dark towel and dug his shoe over the top. Red seeped into the material.

The blood seemed to all be condensed into one large spot on the carpet, but he ran cautious eyes over the entirety of her bedroom, careful not to miss a single detail. His sharpened glare landed steadily on his daughter's *favorite* toy.

Mr. Doll sat proudly atop the wooden desk, his empty face staring right at the spot she must have stood. Or maybe, if he *did* have eyes, they might be angled downward, sinking into the bloodied carpet. Maybe he would have watched his daughter die.

He stared at the motionless doll while his face sank to a grimace and the thick scent of soap filled the air. It burned at his nose.

His hands twitched at the thought of plucking the doll from the desk and smashing its tender porcelain flesh under his shoes. He imagined the feeling of it, the sharp *crunch* as it shattered, the relief that might flutter over his skin. The only thing keeping him from it was his poor daughter, the daughter who waited for him now.

Maren snapped out of his trance, bending down to scrub the floor now that the stain had loosened. He scrubbed hard, until sweat sprung at his forehead and his arms grew weak. He didn't have much time.

Soon enough the detergent had all been soaked up and only a dull red remained on the carpet. All the dirty towels, along with the scissors, were tied tightly in a bag to bring to the trash can outside. It was enough, he thought. He grabbed a colorful shirt from Lily's closet, a plain pair of jeans from her drawer, and her favorite shoes. He took one last look around the room, wondering what else he could do for his daughter.

His eyes, again, landed on the doll.

No, Maren thought. *She doesn't need it.*

She asked for it, his voice argued silently in his mind. *She's upset enough already.*

I bet that goddamned doll is the reason she's stuck in there in the first place!

Maren turned on his heel toward the door, but stopped once more in his tracks. His shoulders tensed and his lungs squeezed with pressure.

Steadying himself, he whipped around to snatch the doll from the top of the desk, then hurried back down the stairs.

The gray doll was tossed haphazardly to the floor of the passenger side of his truck, and Lily's clothes were neatly folded on top of the freshly cleaned leather of the seat.

Maren tapped the tips of each finger against the steering wheel, twitching and fidgeting in his seat. The car vibrated with life in the driveway while Maren flicked through each thought in his screaming mind.

Just get rid of it. She'll get over it.

No, I can't do that, he argued with himself. *She's lying in a hospital bed and she asked for her doll. What kind of father would I be?*

What kind of father gives his daughter the very thing that might have put her there?

He couldn't think straight. His skull was thrashing with dark waves like a hurricane. He continued to *tap tap tap tap tap . . .*

It's just a stupid doll! He clung desperately to the idea. *Maybe she's only in there because she put herself there.*

Lily would never do that. I know Lily. I know my daughter.

Do you?

His daughter's words came next, like an echo, crawling up his bones like vines. They poured down into each corner of his being and tightly pulled.

I don't want you to be my father.

He shut his eyes tightly, twisting his fingers around the steering wheel while her words repeated like a blaring alarm.

Maybe, his own voice told him, *if you weren't her father, she wouldn't be in that hospital bed. Maybe the doll is just a doll. Maybe it's you that is haunting her.*

"I'm going crazy," he said out loud to the dark empty cabin of the car. He shifted roughly into gear, pulling from the driveway and heading down the road.

...

The parking lot of the store was fairly crowded for a Tuesday night. He sat in his car, heart pounding, as he stared at the bright fluorescent sign above the doors.

Neighbor's Market.

He hadn't even planned to come here; his intention had been to return to the hospital. He was going to swallow his pride and his guilt and his hatred, and hand his troubled daughter her doll. The doll that was now stuffed tightly under the seat beneath him.

This was a horrible idea; he knew it. He knew it even as he left the car and started walking toward the store. The lights poured out from the glass doors and over the asphalt of the parking lot, spilling over his shoes.

Inside the store, it was loud and full of people. Shrieking wheels of shopping carts echoed from the floor and the lights buzzed over his head as he walked.

He felt out of place here. Like no matter what was happening in his life, these people would remain blissfully unaware. These people were too selfishly focused on their shopping lists, their maddening children, and their useless phone calls; they had no idea that his life was being shattered, that what was left of his family was slowly ripping apart at the seams.

He scowled at each passerby, feeling their judging eyes on his skin. These *stupid* people had no idea what he was going through—no idea of even a fraction of the pain he felt, or the choices he had been forced to make. They couldn't *feel* the weight that he carried. They were weak, useless.

He dragged himself to the quiet aisle at the back of the store. It was bright and cheery, packed with colorful toys that spilled from each of the shelves. Maren ran his hands along the soft material of smiling stuffed animals and the frilly dresses that clothed each of the dolls. None of them looked right.

They were too bright, too happy. Their skin was too pale, their dresses too glittery and pink. Not a single one was gray.

He lifted his hands to his face, rubbing at his skin and eyes until they burned. This would never work, but he had no time to care.

There was a doll to the left, a porcelain boy. It was encased in plastic to protect it, and the doll was dressed in blue. He had black hair and green eyes, with a smile on his small painted lips. He was perfect.

He had little resemblance to the gray doll, which made Maren smile. He looked normal and happy, the type of toy that a normal child might want. One that a normal parent might give as a gift for their child's birthday, or on Christmas. Or perhaps when their child was sick, or in the hospital.

That might work, he thought. *A gift.*

Lily will hate this doll, his negative thoughts retorted. *She might yell and scream and say nasty things like she had done before. She will never accept it.*

I am her father. I know what's best for her.

Maren knew that his daughter would react, but what better place than a hospital? What damage could she possibly do there?

He grabbed the black-haired doll from the shelf, grasping the packaging gently. The doll's eyes shimmered through the thin plastic.

After purchasing the doll, he headed back outside into the dark parking lot. The doll's pale porcelain shone under each streetlight as Maren walked quickly to the car through the cold October air. He pulled his sweater up to his chin with his free hand.

He gripped the car door, creaking it open and gently placing the doll on the seat over his daughter's clothes. The car felt oddly warm and the windows were slightly fogged, even the leather flushed against his cold skin through his shirt as he curled into the seat.

Maren felt the presence of the gray doll beneath his body. It stirred silently from under him before being drowned out by the tumbling of the engine as the key turned in the ignition. He followed the street signs all the way back to the hospital where Lily waited for him. Where she waited for the doll.

...

Maren trailed down the hallway of the hospital, up the elevator, and back to room 204. He stood outside of the door with one hand hovering over the doorknob and the other tightly wrapped around the black-haired doll's plastic packaging.

The door clicked open beneath his palm, and he peeked only his eyes into the room. It was dark and quiet. The lights had been turned off and the TV was black.

He looked deeper inside where his daughter lay motionlessly in her bed. Maren let out a deep sigh of relief—she was sleeping.

It was very late, and he too felt exhausted. He moved to the empty bed, which sat opposite Lily's, and let the door close softly behind him. He placed the wrapped doll on the side table and pulled the curtain that separated the beds farther out along the track, blocking the new toy from his daughter's view. The crisp, sterile sheets that draped the empty bed stared back at him through the shadows.

Maren detested hospitals. He hated the smells, the sounds, and the way the fabrics of the beds felt between his fingers. Hospital beds had always reminded him of Jewel, in a way that he didn't want to remember her.

He sat atop the clean white sheets, wrinkling them beneath him, and found himself staring across the room at his daughter's short choppy hair. It was no longer running down her back the way that his wife's had.

Lily stirred in her bed, turning on her side and kicking the sheet off her legs. She had always been a restless sleeper.

Twenty-One.

He stood in the middle of the room staring at the dollhouse. It had been sitting hollowly in her bedroom for a very long time, taunting him.

He kept the room exactly the way she had left it, after her death. Her clothes, her books, even her old cell phone lay dead on the nightstand. He walked to the corner, running gentle fingers over the artwork that hung from the walls. The desk below them was overflowing with colorful art supplies.

She had been such a happy girl.

An overwhelming darkness burned inside of him, scratching at his chest as he stared at the images of his daughter. The many pictures that scattered over the walls shined her smiling face at him. Alina.

What once was a deep sadness had slowly curdled into anger over the years. A strangling, boiling anger. He abhorred the man who took his perfect young daughter away. But more than that, he hated that he never had the chance to take his own revenge. It ate away at him gradually until each happy *memory of Alina had been erased, replaced with a screaming need to hurt a man who was already dead—the man who had killed himself in his guilt like a coward.*

That was much too easy, he thought. That boy should have suffered.

He lifted the doll from the small wooden dollhouse and held it up to his face, glowering at it. The doll that was supposed to save him. The doll that he couldn't finish.

John had always hoped somehow that his daughter was here, somewhere close. Perhaps she was hidden within the walls of the hallway in which she had died, or wandering the shadowed house after dark searching for her father. He wondered if she was angry with him for leaving her alone, leaving her to die. Sometimes at night he imagined her standing at the end of his bed while he slept, staring.

Maybe, he thought, she was deep inside the dollhouse, living in the bright porcelain skin of the doll that he had made for her. It lay still in the tiny replica of Alina's bedroom, watching him.

That doll was made as a gift when she was just a girl. A beautiful doll for his beautiful child, with blue eyes and blonde hair just like hers. She loved that doll and her small wooden house until her very last day. It remained, surrounded by the rest of her colorful things, as a token of her childhood.

This doll, gripped tightly in his hand, looked nothing like it. It was blank and unfinished, with fresh gray porcelain and an expressionless face. He made it with the hope that it might lead him back to her. He thought that maybe when Al died, she was lost within the house. Maybe if he were to join her, he could find her. He just wanted to see her. Even once.

John gave up any hopes of finding her after creating the gray doll. Staring at the empty vessel in his hands, he realized his foolishness and left the doll to gather dust.

Now, in his desperation, it was his last resort.

He placed the gray doll in its small gray clothes and black shoes before setting it back inside the dollhouse right next to Alina's. He scooped up the thin wooden frame of it with strong arms, walking slowly from the bedroom and all the way down the stairs, deep down into the basement where he had prepared it.

A thick rope hung from the beam that spread along the basement ceiling waiting for him, an old wooden chair placed beneath it. The shelf in the small room in the corner had been cleaned and cleared off, leaving space for the dollhouse. He set it down carefully, like she might be sleeping within, just out of sight of the rope. He didn't want her to watch, but he couldn't do this alone. He couldn't bear to leave without telling her goodbye.

John plucked the blonde-haired doll from the small house, gently bringing her to his lips and grazing a soft kiss on the side of her small face. The cold porcelain stung against his skin.

Placing her back in the bed, he took one last look at her. His beautiful, perfect daughter.

"I love you, my sweet girl," he whispered. "I'm so sorry."

Tears rolled down his face, dropping from his chin and soaking into the dark orange dirt at his feet. The ground drank it greedily, absorbing it. He turned, leaving the small room behind and coming face to face with the rope. It swung slightly side to side, beckoning him.

He let out a shaky breath as he stepped onto the chair, begging it to hold under his weight for just one moment longer. He had just one more second of this life left inside of him.

The noose steadily found its way around John's neck, prickling against his skin, just as the old chair began to crack.

He jumped, tightening the rope as one last image flashed through his mind.

Alina.

Maren's eyes fluttered open as his heart thrummed manically inside of his chest. He shot up in his bed, chasing the dream from his mind and darting his eyes in each direction, soaking in the reality around him.

He was used to his nightmares by now, but this one was different. This one stabbed in his head like barbed wire, penetrating through his skin and down to his bones. This one was *John.*

The sound of his thoughts filled the room, buzzing loudly in his ears as he slowly remembered where he was. The morning light was creeping through the glass and bouncing off the tiled floors, drenching the small hospital room. It looked so peaceful that he almost felt normal, even if just for one moment.

Maren rubbed his dry eyes with rough fingers and slowed his breathing, freeing himself from the trap of the nightmare. The black-haired doll smiled at him from the bedside table where he had left it, shining its green unblinking eyes. He roamed his gaze along the walls, hunting for the clock.

6:29 a.m. It was going to be a long day.

Lily tossed and turned in her bed, warping the sheets and pooling the blankets over the edge of the mattress and onto the floor. Her choppy hair was streaming over her face and across her white pillows. Deep in sleep, she looked so much like herself. So much more so than she had lately. Maren crept his way out of his own bed, careful not to disturb her, and snuck into the hallway.

...

"Your daughter shows no signs of depression, suicidal thoughts, or any inclination of wanting to harm herself," the doctor said. Maren had caught him in the hall, guiding him away to speak in private about Lily's evaluation from the night before. They sat in the same two chairs, in the same empty room that the strange woman from before had questioned him in.

"She misses her mother, of course," Doctor Herring continued. "She mentioned arguing with you several times, and she is having a hard time fitting in at school, but these are all completely normal issues for a girl in her situation." He flipped through his notes. Maren's hungry eyes scoured the pages for a hint, words highlighted in bright yellow or messy circles scraped into the paper, but there was nothing to catch.

"That's great. So . . . what does that mean?" Maren cocked his head, leaning forward in his chair.

"Essentially, your daughter does not seem to be at risk of another attempt—on the surface, at least." The doctor set his clipboard in his lap, intertwining his hands over the top. "She insists that the cuts were an accident, that she slipped and the scissors must have cut her in multiple places, or something like that. She said she wasn't sure exactly what had happened. It's highly unlikely, but not entirely impossible . . ." He took a ponderous breath in. "The lacerations were both very clean, as if they were done quickly and without hesitation. That's quite unusual for a patient who has cut themselves, especially at her young age. They often hesitate due to pain or fear, and the cuts are jagged and. . ."

Maren stared at him with darkened eyes, raising his eyebrows at the details. The doctor swallowed, keeping the rest to himself.

"I'm not saying I believe her story," he continued. "However, under some sort of freak circumstances. . . maybe—"

The story was ridiculous. Deep down, Maren knew it wasn't true. He knew that something more sinister had happened. But at this moment he was desperate to believe him. He nodded slightly, cautiously. The old man spoke again.

"Maybe Lily is fine. Or maybe this *was* an attempt, but the experience made her somehow snap out of whatever emotions that led her to it. She seems to be a normal, functioning, eleven-year-old girl."

"That's . . . good." Maren paused, unsure of what to say. The doctor's words were jumbling around in his mind.

"We will be keeping her for the day for observation, but she will more than likely be discharged this afternoon if there are no further issues. We will speak with her again later today for another evaluation, then discuss the next steps of taking her home," Doctor Herring said, holding out a sheet of paper and a pen, prompting Maren to sign.

Discharged. Maren thought he would be happy at the word. He had been begging to take Lily home from the moment they arrived, but was she safer *here?* Did he actually believe that taking her home was in her best interest, or was he drawn to that house, just as she was? He shook the thought away.

He had barely skimmed the papers before etching his name above the dotted line, desperate for all of this to be over.

The doctor smiled dryly, slipping the signed paper back onto the clipboard and rising from his chair. He held out his hand to Maren, who shook it hesitantly.

Maren had no idea what to think of any of this. Was he crazy for thinking his daughter might have cut herself on purpose? Was Doctor Herring, for believing that she hadn't?

He wondered what Lily might be hiding, or if he knew his own daughter well enough to decide if she was telling the truth.

The next few hours were spent trying to stay sane, and waiting for Lily to wake up. He paced the hallway, ate a painfully dry hospital-cafeteria breakfast, and made several stops at the vending machine. Mostly he lost himself in thought about the gray doll. He pictured it stuffed beneath the seat of his truck overnight, spinning with the energy of a nuclear bomb and waiting for his daughter. *Maren's* daughter.

Sitting in the stiff, sterile hospital bed, he scraped his hands over the dry sheets and stared at the black-haired doll. He wondered how Lily might react to it, or if the hospital staff might want to keep her for another day upon her horrific response to the new toy. Maren could still see her dark face in his mind when he first tried to take the gray doll away from her. It stuck in his brain like sap.

"Dad?" Lily's voice floated across the small room, scattering his thoughts.

"Yeah, Lily-pop?" Maren stood from his wrinkled bed, pulling the curtain slightly forward to make sure the doll was kept out of her sight. "How are you feeling?"

"Where's Mr. Doll?" she replied, ignoring his question entirely.

The room stilled, encapsulating her words as Maren's blood went cold. He stared at his daughter, watching her blue eyes seem to darken.

"Sweetheart . . ." He faltered nervously. "We have to focus on your health first. I can get the doctor, make sure everything is okay before—"

"Give me the doll." Her voice scraped at his eardrums as it slithered through the air. She could feel him, Mr. Doll's thick aura. Maren reeked of it.

He raised an eyebrow at his daughter, shocked by her tone. His young Lily, who had just woken up from her first night in a *hospital* and seemed completely unbothered by it. No regard for the events that had led them here. No regard either for her father, who stayed by her side all night.

"Lily, I don't have your doll. You need to be patient." Maren reached for the black-haired toy with a hesitant hand. Thick fear coursed through him as he cleared his throat. "I got you this present from the store last night. I figured he could keep you company until we get home." He pulled the new doll from behind the curtain, revealing it to her.

Lily's eyes narrowed and her face turned down into a deep grimace. The face of his young daughter looked much older at this moment, and much angrier. He could barely recognize her. She breathed in slowly.

"Bring it to me," she demanded.

Maren moved slowly across the floor to his daughter with the new doll in his hands. Lily's extended arm waited for his gift, hanging in the open air above her bed. He set the pretty package in her flattened palm.

The wrapper tore open loudly, and Lily grasped the pretty boy doll with tense hands. She ran her darkened eyes over each detail of it, touching a finger to the blue clothing and bright porcelain skin.

"Isn't it nice?" Maren's words were heavy and slow as he pulled them out, one by one. "I found it at the store down the road. I hoped it might make you feel better."

Lily didn't reply. She covered the doll's head with the end of her bedsheet, swirling it around its neck and over its black hair.

Maren watched with shaky eyes, unable to move. His expression melted.

"This *isn't* Mr. Doll," she growled, wrapping her palm over the blanket that encased the doll and tightening it. Maren's breath quickened.

"Your obsession with that doll, it isn't right." His entire body was tense and scared. He was terrified of his daughter and the black in her voice. "It's just a doll, Lily."

"*This* is just a doll." Her fingers gripped its head. "*An empty, fragile, stupid doll.*"

Her lip twitched upward as the doll's skull *cracked* under her force. The sheet around its neck shielded her soft skin from the shards as they shattered, raining into her lap. "*See?*" She lifted her head, meeting Maren's sunken eyes.

He stared down at Lily, inches from her distorted, smiling face, as invisible spiders crawled up and down his arms. His skin tinged with fear, and his daughter's once-blue eyes looked empty. Hollow. *Black.*

"Lily . . . *stop,*" he begged. She barely took notice of him anymore.

He took a fearful step back from her bed as she continued to destroy the doll, snapping its leg off and crushing it between the sheets. A sickened grin stained her face.

Maren turned, horrified, and pushed out the door into the bright hallway. He tore through the hospital searching for Doctor Herring, pleading for the nurse or the strange woman with red lips, anyone who might be able to help him, anyone who could tell him what was wrong with his daughter.

He ran to the empty room in which he was questioned, to the receptionist's desk at the end of the hall. There was no one to save him. He stood in the middle of the empty hallway, darting his eyes over the walls and the doors. He felt stuck, cemented to the tile. His lungs crushed and his throat swelled; his heart beat in his brain.

Doctor Herring suddenly emerged from a room far down the hall and began walking in the direction of Lily's room. Maren swallowed his panic, desperately following the doctor through the blinding white lights. He reached him just outside of the room, struggling to breathe.

"Mister Caplin, I was just looking for you. Is Lily awake?" The old man was calm and collected, almost cheery. Maren choked out his words.

"Yes. She's awake . . . she's . . ."

"Great, I'm just going to check in on her before we send her some breakfast, okay?" His hand moved quickly to the door handle before Maren could stop him.

"Wait, I—" His words fell to the tile as the door creaked slowly open, revealing his daughter's room. Darkness seeped from the entryway and poured into the hall. Maren braced for whatever came next.

"Good morning, Lily. How are you feeling today?" The Doctor swept into the room smiling, his clipboard perched to his chest. He disappeared from Maren's vision, leaving only the sound of their voices.

"I dropped my doll." Lily's sweet tone rang in the air like a bell. "My daddy bought it for me. Now it's broken." She cried like a child.

Maren leaned into the doorframe, winding himself around it and stabbing his eyes through the fog around his head. His tired eyes widened.

The black-haired doll lay shattered against the floor. The smashed pieces of its head were intricately placed around its body, as if it had fallen from a height and exploded against the tile.

"Oh dear, that's not very good," the doctor replied, soaking in the sight of the doll. "How did that happen?"

"I was just playing with it . . . and it dropped on the ground and broke." She sniffled, sitting up in her bed with the white sheets tidily folded over her legs. Her blue eyes glistened with sadness.

Doctor Herring crouched before her bed, carefully gathering each of the shards in his hands.

"Let's get this cleaned up. We don't want you hurting yourself on these sharp pieces," the old man said, comforting her kindly.

"Thank you," she whined. "I'm just glad I have my other doll at home at least. That one's my *favorite*." Lily's voice darkened at the last word as she wiped her fake tears away with the back of her hand. "If anything happened to him, I'd be *really* upset." She turned her eyes up at her father as she spoke, with a small voice that Maren barely recognized.

He stood in the doorway, struggling to process the scene. His daughter's blank face stared through him, and the roots of her words wrapped around his neck.

"Yes I'm sure you would be!" the doctor replied. "I'm glad your favorite doll is safe at home. You should be able to see him today, if all goes to plan."

Doctor Herring poured the many pieces of the broken doll into the trash can and swept the floor clean with a rag. Maren's jaw was so tense that he feared it might crack.

"Yay!" Lily smiled widely, never tearing her eyes from her father. His face twitched.

Twenty-Two.

Lily was discharged at about 6:00 p.m.

The day passed slowly and without incident. Lily was a bright, cheerful, normal eleven-year-old girl—at least to the hospital staff. Whenever Maren found himself alone with her, she was different.

She barely spoke, and often stared—out the window, at the wall, or at Maren. She stared like she was listening intently to whatever voices were speaking inside of her head.

Where are you, Mr. Doll? she would ask in her mind. *I feel you. Are you here?*

She heard no response. She searched and searched in her head for his voice, but it never came. She was growing impatient.

He had spoken to her last night inside of her dreams, when the feel of him was fresh on Maren's skin. It drifted into the room and blanketed Lily, keeping her warm. The doll had told her to be careful, that whatever her father was planning, she needed to be ready for it.

Now, after a day of pretending for these strange people, answering the doctor's *stupid* questions and keeping herself in line, she felt ready.

She changed from the hospital gown into the clothes her father brought her, slipping on her favorite flowery shoes. The bandages on her arm felt strange and tight against her skin. She didn't believe these people when they said she had cut herself. After all, she had seen it with her own eyes. There were no marks, no blood.

Dolls don't bleed, Mr. Doll had told her. Lily looked down at her perfect porcelain flesh and smiled.

She was wrong to be scared yesterday like she was; she knew that now. They were *all* wrong. Lily scolded herself for disappointing Mr. Doll, for failing him in her fear.

He would never harm her. He protected her and loved her fiercely, more than Maren ever could. Whatever Maren said was *wrong.* Whatever he was planning, he wouldn't get away with it. That's what the gray doll told her.

They left the hospital, sinking into the gloomy afternoon as they slipped outside through the sliding glass doors. Lily's hospital band was loose on her wrist, and the thick bandages wrapped around her other arm. She turned the band around in circles as they walked.

The crisp air swirled deep into her lungs while she watched the setting sun glow against her shining skin. She trailed behind Maren, all the way back to the truck.

The closer she got to the car, the more she could feel him. The gray doll's voice gradually grew inside of her, spreading across her body and flowing through each of her veins. She felt the rush in her lungs and blood like morphine. She could see the truck bubbling with his power, about to burst.

As soon as Maren cracked open the car door for her, Mr. Doll's vibrating aura swarmed out, almost pushing her over with its weight. She smiled, letting the warmth melt into her flesh.

Lily saw the clean leather seat of the truck, bright and perfect like she knew it would be. There was no blood, no stain. Her cheeks flushed pink.

I knew it, she said silently to the doll. *They were wrong.*

She climbed into the truck and settled into the seat as Maren shut the door behind her, leaving her alone while he walked around the edge to the driver's side. He gave her just enough time to reach under the seat and touch the doll with excited fingers.

Wait, Mr. Doll warned in his low raspy voice, right before her hands met his skin. *Don't make him do something rash.*

Lily frowned, withdrawing her hand from beneath her father's seat. She wasn't sure what he could mean by that.

Rash? she wondered. *Like what?*

Maren swung open his door, meeting his daughter's eyes with a hesitant smile. His lips were moving, but all she could hear was the doll.

Be patient, his voice continued. *Don't tell him that you know where I am. Don't give him a reason.*

A reason for what? she prodded.

"Lily?" Maren's voice found a way to cut through to her. He stared from the driver's seat with a sharp brow and narrowed eyes.

"I'm fine. I'm just tired," she said. His expression let her know that this was the right thing to say, though she hadn't heard his question. It was all he ever asked her anymore, anyway. *Are you okay?*

The doll was quiet for the rest of the drive home, stuffed under the seat. Lily pressed both hands to the leather, feeling his vibrating heat pulse at her palms. It calmed her.

Soon enough, her home came into view from the windshield. It buzzed at the edge of the street, throwing sparks of its energy into the air above. Lily felt the embrace of the white bricks and the power of its bones as the truck pulled into the empty driveway. The house had missed her.

Mr. Doll grew stronger here, in the presence of his home. Lily felt his voice deepen and his strings tighten around her, reeling her farther into the house. She welcomed it. This house was a part of him, and now a part of her as well.

Maren slid his key into the tricky door handle, wiggling and pushing until it clicked open. The house flooded their bodies with heat as they entered and disappeared past the threshold.

...

"Are you hungry?" Maren asked. They both had already eaten dinner at the hospital, but the silence was palpable. He couldn't think of anything else to ask.

"No," she replied. Her responses were short today, and quiet. Lily sat on the couch completely still. She looked impatient, as though she was waiting for something to happen.

Maren awkwardly shifted in his spot behind the kitchen island. He couldn't shake the looming feeling from the hospital, or the deranged look that hung from his daughter's face as she crushed the doll's skull in her hands. The foreign voice at her lips still echoed in his mind.

He had been waiting all day for her to ask where the gray doll was, bracing for the impact of her words, but they never came. Her horrid desperation from the morning to get him back couldn't have faded that fast, he thought. He wondered what she was planning, or if she had simply given up.

He couldn't seem to admit that he was growing terrified of his daughter, always scared of what she might say or what she might do. At the same time though, he was also scared *for* her. He was constantly bouncing back and forth between trying to protect her from this house, from the doll, and wondering if what she truly needed was protection from *him,* from her own father.

Maybe he *was* crazy.

He wondered what was more believable, a haunted house and a possessed doll, or a failing father leaving his daughter to rot in her loneliness, turning her sour.

He wasn't sure, but either way, Maren hoped that the problem would be solved once the dolls were out of their lives for good.

Lily suddenly straightened in her seat on the couch, turning toward the front door slightly at the sound of Mr. Doll's heavy voice. Maren watched her rise without a word and hurry up the stairs like a dog following a scent.

"Lily?" he asked. She moved quickly out of sight toward the second story of the house, unresponsive.

She ran up the stairs, down the hall, and through her open bedroom door, shutting it behind her. She hurried to the window, following the sound of the doll's deepened words.

You must hide it, Al, he growled. *Keep it somewhere safe.*

Hide what? Hide it where? She leaned against the window, staring out at the driveway and through the smudged glass of the truck. Even from a distance, his voice boomed within her mind from every direction. The entire house was flooded with him.

Your doll, sweet girl.

She turned to the dollhouse at the core of her bedroom, cocking her head. Sliding down onto the carpet, she reached a hand in through the window of Lily-Doll's bedroom and curled her small fingers over its cold porcelain body.

You must keep her close, the doll continued. *We will need her soon.*

Lily's eyes widened at the pretty doll, welling with curiosity. She ran a finger down her face and against her soft blonde hair.

"Need her for what?" she whispered softly to the room, staring into Lily-Doll's bright-blue eyes.

Do you trust me, Al? he pleaded. *You know, my girl, that I know what's best?*

"Yes," she replied. It felt like a dream.

You want to be with me, inside the dollhouse? To escape, away from your pain? Your loneliness?

"Yes." She hugged Lily-Doll tightly to her chest, nodding.

Hide her, Mr. Doll insisted. *Quickly.*

The sound of Maren's footsteps echoed from the staircase and down the hall, sweeping beneath the crack of her door. Lily blinked away the trance and stood quickly, clutching Lily-Doll. The footsteps were getting closer.

She scrambled, searching the room for a spot to hide it. Her heart pounded with fear that she might be caught, unsure of what her father might do if she couldn't hide it in time. She couldn't disappoint Mr. Doll, not again.

Quickly, she stuffed the doll deep inside of her pillowcase, flipping it upside down. She pulled the blankets to each edge of the bed, smothering it, right as Maren twisted the knob on her door and swung it wide open.

"Lily-pop?" His voice was shaky with a fear he couldn't hide as his wide eyes dug into Lily where she stood in the center of the room. He caught his breath. "Just . . . checking on you. Making sure everything is all right."

"Yeah." She steadied herself. "Everything's fine."

"Okay. Good, that's good. I just . . . Do you need anything?" Maren was awful at comforting her, or anyone for that matter. Jewel was always so good at it. She would have baked Lily a pie and made her a blanket fort by now. The two of them would have been giggling beneath the sheets playing with colorful toys. Instead, she was standing in the middle of her bedroom alone while Maren helplessly stared at her.

"I'm okay. I'm just tired. I think I'll lie down," Lily said, unmoving.

"Why don't you come lie down on the couch and we can watch some TV?" He tapped anxiously on the door as he leaned against it, one foot through the doorway. His eyes quickly glanced down at the faded stain on the carpet, a very soft red. Lily didn't notice.

She waited for the doll's instructions, but they never came. A small part of her clung to her father's attempt to connect with her while another part pushed it away. She looked down at the empty dollhouse, considering.

Mr. Doll wouldn't like it.

"Where is Mr. Doll?" The words came out before she could stop them. She wondered what her father's plan was, why he was keeping Mr. Doll in the car. She wondered why the gray doll seemed more concerned with Lily-Doll than he was with his own small body, stuffed beneath Maren's leather seat. She couldn't hold in her questions anymore.

Her cold eyes turned to her father where he stood in the doorway. He cowered from her, leaning against the wooden frame with tapping fingers. He felt weak.

Tap tap tap tap tap.

"Lily, I—"

Lily's mind went numb before his response reached her ears. Her vision went black and her mind flew above her body toward the ceiling. She floated, watching herself below where her feet sank into the plush carpet.

Her own voice swam in through her ears, sweet and airy. The space around her felt warm.

"*It's okay, Dad. You're right. It's just a doll,*" she heard herself speak, watching her lips move and her body lightly twitch. She was dreaming now, surely.

She saw her father straighten at the threshold and watched as his eyes widened at her response. His tense shoulders relaxed.

"You . . . you're not upset?" Maren's voice was stretched thin, like the room was underwater. Lily strained to focus on the conversation as she drifted above her body and her mind threatened to float away.

"*No, I love you, Dad.*" Her smile pulled across her face and her words were dragged out. "*The doll is just a toy, of course.*"

Lily couldn't recognize her own voice. She had no control of it, or of her body. She was only able to stare.

"I love you too, Lily-pop." Maren smiled with relief, barely able to believe the sudden change in her. Maybe the doctor was right; she *had* snapped out of it. Maybe things weren't so bad after all.

"Go ahead and get some rest, then," he continued. "I know you've had a long day."

She watched her lips smile and her head nod at her father while he slipped out of the room and closed the door behind him. She watched her body climb into the bed and pull the sheets up to her chin before closing her eyes. All at once, the light fizzled from Lily's vision, throwing black spots over her eyes as she was pulled into a deep sleep.

Twenty-Three.

The light was slowly being pulled from the windows and sucked into the horizon, where the sun fell just below its edge. The silent expanse of the room hummed with anticipation.

Maren reached the bottom step of the staircase, planting his feet on the hardwood and glancing around the large room. He greedily soaked in the peacefulness of the house. It had been so long since he felt it.

The wind was whipping the windows outside, and the light rain thrummed against the glass. Cold October air pushed and pulled the house around him, but the warm floorboards hugged his feet. He could stay in this moment for a long time, staring outside into the sunset. He breathed so deeply that he could taste the calm.

Moving to the kitchen, he fixed himself something quick to eat in an attempt to rinse the aftertaste of dry hospital food from his tongue. Then he sat in his reclining chair, staring out into the growing night sky, chewing slowly.

Once the kitchen was clean, the doors had all been locked, and the sun had disappeared from the edge of the horizon, Maren headed upstairs. He readily welcomed a good, long night of sleep.

It was still early, barely eight o'clock, when Maren poured himself onto his bed. He rolled over the top of it, soaking in the darkness and the quiet of the bedroom and burying his face into the pillow, relaxing into its familiar scent. Just as he began to close his eyes, the book at his nightstand called to him.

Lifting his head, he dragged his eyes to the pink hardcover of his wife's last gift where it rested at his side atop the small table. Her sweet words sang to him from the pages.

Even the summary creeped me out, so you have to love it. Her words flashed through his mind.

He sat up against the headboard, sliding the book from the edge of the nightstand and dropping it gently into his lap.

"*In Waiting* . . ." He read the cover aloud in a breathy voice, running his fingers down the smooth face of the book. He flipped the cover open and finally began to read . . .

Chapter One

The forest was dense and dark. It threatened to swallow him whole as he ran through the brush.

Each of the branches scraped at his legs, ripping at his skin and his clothes as he passed them. His lungs constricted with pain while he struggled to breathe, but his feet continued to carry him forward as quickly as he could go.

He was running out of time; he knew that. Surely, it had her by now. She would be held tightly in its jaw, her bones cracking between its many sharp teeth. She would be struggling to breathe, as he was now.

She would soon be dead.

He pushed his way farther into the woods, following the sounds of her screams.

"Maren! Help me, please!"

Maren tore his attention away from the page, shutting the book. He held his breath, his enormous crazed eyes staring holes through the bright-pink cover.

Maren? His mind crowded with questions. He didn't understand.

Is this why Jewel had bought it for him, because the character shared his name? Did she even know?

He flipped the book over, skimming through the summary, but there was no mention of the name "Maren."

Was this a joke? He tightened his chest, swallowing hard before continuing to read . . .

"Maren! Help me, please!"

The sound of her voice echoed around him, bouncing from each tree and penetrating his skull. He was getting close; he could sense it.

A large hill appeared in the distance, covered in tall grass and sturdy trees. Birds flew through the air as he ran, entering the creature's territory.

From the top of the hill, the expanse of the forest stretched out around him, covering the land in green. Maren searched desperately in each direction for the sound of her voice, but all was quiet, even the birds. He only heard himself gasping for breath.

"Lily!" he screamed into the void of the woods. "Where are you?"

Maren slammed the hardcover closed, locking its contents within. His heart was racing, and his fingers gripped the edges of the book with white knuckles. He lifted the cover once more and peered at the pages, scraping his straining eyes carefully over each word. He read them two, three, four times, making sure they were real.

Maren and Lily. There was no mistake.

He stood from the bed, pacing the room to release the tension building in his bones. His jaw was tightening so hard that a headache was beginning to bloom at his temples.

The story was penetrating him, shaking him deeply. Lily was lost, held by the monster, and Maren couldn't protect her. The fear all came crashing back in giant waves against him, weakening his legs.

The book had been tossed to the bed, waiting in the sheets where the bright-pink cover burned his eyes. He stared at it, turning a thought over and over in his head.

Jewel . . . Did you write this? he pondered. She told him she bought it from the store. She told him . . .

I would have written it myself, but I just can't seem to write thrillers. Her sweet voice suddenly came back to him. *Drama and fiction are way more my style.* He soaked in each of her old words.

Maybe she lied, he thought. *Maybe this is her.*

Of course . . . Jewel had always loved surprises.

Maren's heartbeat slowed and a thin smile replaced the dread from his face as he collapsed back down against the warm sheets. This whole time the words of his Jewel had been waiting for him inside of this book. Waiting for *years.*

He plucked it from the bed with gentle fingers, like he was holding his wife's hand. Emotion welled inside of him, rising to his tired eyes in thick, salty droplets. He wrapped his arms tightly around the book as the tears finally escaped down his face.

He continued to read . . .

The silence of the forest enveloped him where he stood, waiting for a response. A clue, a sound, a signal, anything that might lead him back to her. He took deep, slow breaths in, ignoring the burning pain in his legs from running. He had to keep going.

"Maren!" Her voice stabbed at him.

He darted in the direction of her voice, almost losing his footing against the uneven ground. He heard a chorus of sounds—rustling leaves, twigs breaking, a footstep landing, a struggling small voice. He could almost see it. He ran and ran.

The creature appeared out of nowhere as Maren rounded the corner. It stood, towering over him and blocking the sun with its giant body. The creature was slimy and gray, with a jaw that stretched ear to ear on its enormous face. Teeth the size of Maren's body protruded from the creature's dark gums. Teeth that dripped with red.

"Lily?" he breathed out her name, cowering at the sight of her.

Lily was held tightly in one large hand of the creature, its slimy fingers constricted like a snake around her torso. Blood oozed from her mouth and from the wounds in her side that the creature's sharpened teeth had left. It smiled at him, breathing hot air over Maren's face.

"She's mine." Its voice was a raspy growl, crawling from its throat. "You're too late."

Lily was already dead.

"What the *fuck?*" Maren mumbled.

The color drained from his face as the open book slid from his fingers, falling against the mattress. His jaw fell open, and the warmth from his skin disappeared into the air around him, turning him cold. Any ounce of comfort he once held from the thought of Jewel's words turned to ashes in his mouth. Disgust poured over his face at the thought of his wife, *Lily's mother,* writing these words, even *thinking* these things about him.

Was this how she saw him? Was *this* what she thought of him? Of what he would do for his *daughter?*

He grabbed the book from the bed and threw it angrily across the room where it bounced from the wall and *thudded* against the carpet below. It was all too much.

The darkness had seeped into the room from outside, slithering through the windows and infecting every corner. Shadows closed in around him from every direction as the silence rang and his anger bellowed inside of him. His chest ached.

Why would you do this? he asked her silently. *Why would you say those things?*

She had loved him deeply, he thought. She loved both of them. Was this a sick joke? Something she thought he might find funny? It was nauseating.

He would *never* let that happen to Lily. He would destroy the monster before it ever even touched her. He would rip it apart with his bare hands. He was strong. He was *unmovable.*

His head was spinning with rage and confusion. His body stung with pain at Jewel and these horrific words. His Jewel, his *wife.* The woman he loved more than anything in this world had apparently thought so little of him.

It wasn't true. It *couldn't* be.

Maren stormed downstairs, stomping his way down each step and into the living room. He snatched his keys from the table and darted outside into the night.

The car door swung violently open, sending the warmth from the truck spilling over the driveway and onto his bare feet. A chill ran up his spine.

The doll still buzzed from beneath his seat, teasing him. Even still, while hot anger paraded inside of his body, heavy fear held him in place.

"*Damn it!*" he yelled into the darkness, forcing his body to move.

Quickly, he stuffed his hand under the leather and wrapped his fingers around the gray doll before he could stop himself. He ripped it out, holding its small body only inches away from his face and slamming the car door shut with his free hand. Maren was fuming with rage, gouging his eyes into its faceless gray skull.

"I've had *enough* of this," he hissed, tightening the doll in his grasp. He turned back into the house with a hunger for revenge, a desperate need to hurt a man who was already *dead*.

The monster, the gray doll, *John*.

Twenty-Four.

Maren slammed the small gray doll onto the dining room table. It shocked him that the force alone didn't shatter it into pieces. His breaths came in thrashing waves, heaving his chest at each inhale while he stared wildly at its sickly porcelain skin. He could feel the glare of the doll penetrating his body, even with no eyes.

He stormed into the kitchen of the quiet house, suddenly hyperaware of his impulsiveness. The room settled around him, keeping him still while he wondered if Lily had already heard the commotion. He worried she might come downstairs any minute. He wondered if the neighbors might have heard him yelling outside, or if someone might think to come check on them.

Most of all, he wondered if the doll truly *had* power, and if destroying it might take that power away.

His angry eyes dug into the doll where it sat across the open room, burning into the dining table. Hatred was fizzing and popping over Maren's body, evaporating into the house. The doll was quiet and unmoving, taunting him still.

Maren slid open a wide kitchen drawer, slowly and quietly. He perked up his ears in preparation for hearing his daughter's light footsteps down the stairs. A restless hand rummaged over the many utensils in the drawer that never got any use while his eyes stayed glued to the staircase, anticipating his daughter's cold face appearing at any moment. Steadily, he pulled out a large wooden mallet and held it in front of him, testing its weight and the grip of the handle.

Lily never appeared on the stairs, and her footsteps never caught in his ears. The house stayed completely and hauntingly silent. The only sound that remained was that of the wood sliding down his skin as he sank the handle deeper through his grasp, tightening it just below the head.

His footsteps were slow back to the table while he readied himself in his head.

I would destroy the monster before it ever even touched her.

He raised the mallet high in the air above his body, ready to bring it down hard against the doll's weak, gray, faceless head.

I would rip it apart with my bare hands.

He prepared to hear the crisp crack of the porcelain. He prepared for it all to be over. He imagined the doll exploding under the weight of the mallet, its energy expelling from the air. He felt the house, afterward, settling into the ground. His daughter's face flashed through his mind, running downstairs and witnessing the scene. What would she say? He wondered.

He couldn't let the thought derail him. He couldn't let the doll win. It would dig itself further into the house, into himself, into *Lily.* He wouldn't let it.

Maren took a deep breath in, swinging the mallet down on an exhale.

Tick.

The mallet barely grazed the doll's skin, tapping the edge of its forehead. He held the wooden weapon over the doll's empty face before releasing it, clamoring it against the table. He couldn't do it.

He couldn't risk whatever breakthrough he may have just had with Lily, not over some horrible prank of Jewel's. He couldn't risk hurting her after he finally seemed to have gotten through to her. She was *finally* forgetting about the doll, and hadn't even asked for it back since her outburst at the hospital. The horrible way that she had acted.

She must have regretted it, he thought. *She must feel bad.*

He stared down at the gray doll where it still lay against the dark wood, making the same empty expression it always had. Maren felt ridiculous standing over this doll, ready to shatter it.

How much power could this thing really have, after all? It had done nothing at all to stop its own destruction. It just watched helplessly. It was *empty.*

Perhaps he could just hide the doll somewhere, keep it from Lily until whatever spell it had cast over her dissipated. If she found out that he destroyed it, it might ruin everything all over again. She would hate Maren for taking him away.

Yes, his inner voice whispered to him. *Hiding it away is safer.*

Maren lifted the doll from the table and its warmth settled into his palm. He frowned at the sensation, staring down at it.

He made his way to the large glass doors that led into the backyard, unlocking and sliding them open before stepping out onto the patio and toward the grass. He followed the slabs of stone that stretched around the yard to the large wooden door of the shed.

It was dark outside. Shadows blew in the wind around him and leaves crunched against the ground. He lifted the latch of the door, creaking it open to reveal the cobweb-ridden shed.

There were shadows covering every inch, and the scent of dirt flooded his nose with each inhale. It seemed like no one had been in here for a very long time. Everything inside was covered with a thick layer of dust and grime, made home to spiders and any other creatures that may have found their way inside.

Rusty tools hung from the walls and protruded from each shelf. Boxes of old nails and screws were scattered over the overflowing desk at the corner, and a large cardboard box sat below it, bursting with scrap wood and trash. Maren waved his hand around in the air in search of a light, a chain to pull, a switch to flick, but found nothing. A creeping feeling slid over his skin.

He stepped a bare foot tentatively over the frame of the doorway and onto the dirty floor of the shed, waiting to feel something sharp at his skin. He gripped tightly to the gray doll, continuing to move past the threshold with another step. In here he could barely feel the pull of the house or hear the sounds of the faraway traffic. It felt empty and dull.

Maren felt around through the darkness, reaching his hands into the cardboard box and pushing around the wooden pieces to make room for the doll. Once he had created a spot big enough to hold it, he gently pushed the doll into the mess and balanced the scraps over its body to hide it. Only the top of its gray face remained, peeking out at the door of the shed.

Maren quickly walked back out into the open yard, wiping both hands on his clothes. He shut the door and secured the latch, making sure Mr. Doll was locked inside before turning on his heel back toward the house.

Slipping back through the large glass door, he shook the cold from his skin and wiped his bare feet over the mat. The kitchen was empty, the wooden mallet was quietly returned to its drawer, and the doll had been hidden away. The house was still silent, meaning Lily had stayed asleep.

The night seeped into Maren, along with the lingering uneasy feeling that followed him from the dark old shed. He flicked off the kitchen lights and turned toward the staircase, ready for the embrace of sleep.

Heavy feet tread up each stair, down the hallway, and through his open bedroom door where the bright-pink cover of the book greeted him from the carpet. He scowled at it, shutting the door behind him and crossing the room, lifting it with angry fingers.

Maren turned the book over in his hands, inspecting it. He wished he could somehow ask Jewel why she would have done something like this. His overwhelming emotions had faded, but the disgust and hurt still lingered. His sunken eyes skimmed over the cover.

In Waiting. Written by Reyna Pollemn.

"Quite the prank, Jewel," he scoffed to the empty room, flipping the book over and reading the summary.

Terrence is tightly wound in a gambling addiction. Terrified of destroying his own life and the lives of those around him, he grabs on to a lifeline—the game. Each trial promises power, but at heavy cost, and the deeper he sinks into the game, the more he has to lose. How far will he go to win?

"What?" Maren drew his face tightly together, turning the book back over and opening to the first page. His eyes tore through each word.

No, that's not right.

The whole thing had been changed. There was no Lily, no Maren, no dense forest or slimy gray creature. His daughter was neither lost nor dead. It was only about a man, crying over his horrible life in the middle of some stupid casino.

He flipped through each page in the book, desperately searching for the words that were no longer there. He bent the spine widely, expecting the pages to have been torn out, expecting *something* to have been altered.

He scrambled through the entire book before landing on the very last page.

There she was, Reyna Pollemn, an award-winning author. She smiled at him from the photo above her short bio. It was all about how she had gotten the inspiration for the book from her late father.

Maren's head was spinning. He was *sure* of what he had read. He couldn't have imagined it. It was real. It was *there.* This gift from his wife was being torn apart in front of his eyes. His last piece of her, deteriorating in this house. Or was it because of him?

He stood from the bed, desperate to get the book out of his sight.

I'm insane, he thought, gripping tightly to the hard pink cover as he rushed toward the stairs. *I'm the one who needs help, not Lily.*

I know what I saw, his own voice argued back. *I know what I read.*

I need to sleep. He descended the staircase, heading back down into the kitchen. *Anyone can lose their minds if they don't have any sleep; it's scientifically proven.*

Yeah, sleep. I just need sleep.

Maren slid through the living room and set the book on the countertop in the kitchen, as far away from his bed as he could get it without locking it outside with the damned gray doll. He needed to keep it away before he ruined it, his wife's precious gift.

He crawled back up the stairs, down the hallway, and poured himself into his bed. Pulling at the chain of the lamp, he invited the darkness to soak through the walls and pour over his body, forcing his stinging eyes closed.

I'm sorry, Jewel. I'm so sorry, he pleaded in his head. *I promise I'll read the book another time.*

Twenty-Five.

The air felt cold around him as he snuck around each corner of the house. The darkness nibbled at his ears and licked his skin, taunting him while he moved. Tall shadows swam through the space, lapping at his feet and arms like waves. His breaths were shallow and quick.

Slow feet crept up the stairs beneath him, stopping at the edge of the second floor. The hall was eerily silent as he studied each corner.

He knew what was coming, but he didn't know when, or from which direction. All he knew was that this thing in his hands was his lifeline, and he could not let go of it. He held it so tightly it pinched at the sides of his fingers and the cold stung deep into his flesh.

This is wrong, he thought. Very wrong. Something sinister was here and it was waiting for him, expecting him. It prowled in each empty space and prepared its sharpened teeth. It knew him deeply, and it knew what he was afraid of. It knew *his capabilities and his inadequacies. It knew each step before he could take it.*

A sudden noise sliced through the heavy silence and shivered up his spine. He followed it through the hallway toward the closed door of a bedroom. It sat still, staring back at him as he froze, waiting for it to open.

There it was again, the noise.

Thud. Thud. Thud.

Like slow, creeping footsteps.

His fingers tightened around the gun, and two anxious eyes bored into the wooden door as he stood waiting. Waiting for the monster to appear, flashing its teeth and claws. Waiting for the darkness to wrap its thick arms around him, strangling him.

The door steadily creaked, widening as blackness spewed out and flooded the hallway, eating whatever streaks of light that had made their way through each window. It swallowed him whole.

He pointed his gun toward the doorway, with the cold trigger shaking beneath his fingertip. The split second passed like hours while he waited to be taken, to be swept away by whatever awful thing was seeping from the bedroom. It emerged, reaching a pale, bony hand out toward him.

He couldn't let it get to him; he couldn't let it win. The gun vibrated in his grip, begging him to use it. He slowly curled his finger around the trigger, pulling gently, as the figure moved in the doorway and opened its wide jaw.

Click.

Maren opened his eyes, shaking at the sensation. He brought his gaze to the gun that was still held tightly in his hands, and to the trigger that his finger had just pulled. His whole body was slick with sweat.

His eyes bulged from his head, soaking in the reality at his fingertips. The gun, its barrel pointed toward the open door of his daughter's bedroom. His daughter, standing motionlessly at the threshold. The trigger, tightening beneath his grip.

He quickly dropped his arm down to his side, frantic to keep the weapon from pointing at his daughter any longer. Terror scraped through him as he dragged his fingers over the cold metal in the dark, only to realize that the gun had been unloaded. The magazine remained tucked inside of the drawer in his nightstand where he always left it. His whole body shook.

Ever since Lily was born, he had never left it loaded. Not once.

His eyes crawled back up toward the shadow in the open doorway. Lily swayed gently side to side, like she could barely keep upright. No sound escaped her lips, and she had no reaction to the gun that had just been pointed at her, or the trigger that had just been pulled. Maren slowly set the gun down against the floor, gluing his attention to his daughter, horrified of what she might be thinking, what she might have seen.

The pitch black curtained around him as he delicately approached her. He held his arms out toward her, hands shaking, as if she might run at any moment.

"Lily?" His voice was desperate and panicked, but quiet as a mouse.

Maren reached out to touch her shoulder, but stopped, leaving his hand in the air. He sucked in a deep breath of relief.

She was sleepwalking. They *both* had been.

Her head was rolled slightly forward hanging over her shoulders. Her jaw hung open toward the floor and her arms rested weightlessly at her sides. It was so dark he could barely make out the features of her face, but her eyes looked closed—empty, at least.

He shook his daughter's shoulder gently, attempting to swallow his paralyzing fear for long enough to lead her back to bed without scaring her, without hinting at the fact that he had just come dangerously close to ending her life.

Almost killing her.

Lily stirred slightly, lifting her head with her eyes still gently closed. She mumbled a word that Maren couldn't catch as he directed her back inside of her room and beneath the warm blankets. They smelled like her.

Maren tucked her neatly into bed, watching her fall back asleep as he struggled to be sure this moment was real. He tried to calm himself, forcing his hands to stop trembling. He could hardly tell if he was still breathing or not.

It was unloaded. She's safe. The words repeated in his mind as he attempted to comfort himself. It wasn't working.

Nothing happened. It's okay.

He sat like that for several minutes, wishing he could lock this moment away inside of the night. Wishing that it weren't true.

He kept waiting for his eyes to open, waiting to wake up in his bed tucked between the sheets. He waited for the nightmare to stop. It never did.

After quietly closing the door, he flew to the edge of the staircase, swiping his unloaded gun from the floor and quickly heading downstairs. Leaving the gun unloaded was no longer good enough.

The lights strikingly illuminated the kitchen while Maren scoured each drawer for a screwdriver. He retrieved it, revealing the bright-yellow handle from where it had been hiding inside the packed junk drawer.

As quickly as he could manage, he disassembled the gun into as many small pieces as he could without smashing it to bits with a hammer. Each piece was rendered useless, scattered in every direction. Once he was finished, it lay on the counter completely unusable.

Each scrap of metal was then swept into a large bag and knotted tightly at the top, and the screwdriver was returned to the drawer. He prodded through his memory, making himself absolutely sure that no other firearms were present in the house. This was his only one.

One thought pounded in his brain over and over: This could *not* happen again. These dreams that plagued him were growing too strong.

Maren tossed the tightly tied bag deep into one of the kitchen cabinets beneath the counter, piling the cleaning supplies in front of it. No matter how strong the dream was, it couldn't put his gun back together. It couldn't even load it, that much was clear. He gripped that fact hard, thanking it.

If he *had* loaded it, his daughter would already be dead.

Maren took a glass down from the cabinet above the sink, filling it with water from the tap. Droplets slid down his chin and into his shirt as he drank, downing the entire cup. His mouth had never been so dry in his life.

Knock. Knock. Knock.

The noise interrupted his thoughts.

His head whipped to the window over the sink that overlooked the darkness of the yard as the sound echoed in his mind—a shrill tapping that seemed to be coming from all sides.

He stood painfully still, holding the empty glass to his lips as stray droplets soaked through his t-shirt, and waited for the noise again.

Knock. Knock. Knock.

It repeated, same as before, piercing through the silence and bouncing from the walls inside his skull. It was coming from the window.

Slowly setting down the glass, Maren was careful not to let it make a noise against the counter, afraid the tension of the house might snap. His heart raced in circles as he turned, taking cautious steps across the kitchen toward the glass. It was suddenly too quiet, too dark, even with the bright kitchen lights glowing around the room. The air thickened around him with each breath, choking him.

From inside, the yard beyond the window was almost completely black, like the moon refused to shine on it and the stars had turned their shining heads away. Each tree stood tall to stare at him, and the cold air whispered through the glass against his face as he leaned over the counter, squinting his eyes to look closer through the window.

The space was empty, only swaying blades of grass behind his reflection, which peered back at him with wide, terrified eyes. Maren took a small step back just before the glass began to tremble.

Knock. Knock. Knock.

Maren shivered, flinching at the sharp sounds and cowering behind the edge of the counter. The force of each strike was tangible, shaking the window gently.

He suddenly regretted dismantling the gun, and his twitching fingers yearned for it now. He delicately pressed his face to the glass, cupping his palms around his eyes to see.

The yard was still empty, and the darkness was still thick. There were no branches, twigs, leaves, or rocks—nothing at the window that could have been making this sound.

It could be neighborhood kids throwing pebbles, he thought. *Or a bird running into the window searching for warmth.*

He flicked through each excuse in his head, waiting for one to stick.

This is ridiculous, he thought, bottling his terror.

Maren moved hesitantly toward the back door, sliding a knife from its stand on the countertop and readying it at his side. He threw the door open, refusing to let his fear take over as he passed into the yard, dragging his vision over each corner and back to the barren window. The light from the kitchen pooled from it, illuminating the ground below where yellow autumn leaves sprinkled the patio floor.

There's nothing here, he thought, pleading with himself to calm down before his heart exploded in his chest. His knuckles were white against the knife.

The door waited open at his back, beckoning him inside, but he needed to be sure.

Toeing forward, he slowly approached the window. His bare feet crushed colorful leaves beneath him and the sound comforted him, replacing the eerie silence.

He was being silly, of course. There was nothing there—the knocking had stopped. Even so, the closer he got to the window, the deeper his stomach began to twist. Even through the cold, sweat dripped down his back and wet his skin.

He stood inches from the window, staring into the empty kitchen, while his reflection, again, stared back. Ripe anxiety thrashed inside of him like a warning as he pressed his face to the glass.

Knock. Knock. Knock.

It shook against his skin, freezing his blood in each vein. Maren's eyes bulged as he tore his cheek from the window at the sight of his own distorted reflection.

It had disconnected from his body, reaching a curled fist toward the other side of the glass and knocking from *inside* the house. His own face smiled down at him with a wide and toothy grin, stretching from ear to ear like a mask. It slowly pulled its sickly gray hand back from the window and stood smiling, waiting.

A sound escaped Maren's lips, meant to be a scream but emerging as a silent yelp and catching at the back of his throat. He fell backward, passing the edge of the concrete and landing on his hands in the cold, wet grass. The knife fell from his grasp and clattered against the hard ground.

His breathing stopped as he clutched his chest in an overwhelming panic. His vision went cloudy and his legs fell weak. Jittering hands patted the ground around him, searching desperately for his weapon. He felt around blindly for it, refusing to tear his eyes from the gray reflection above him that still smiled down through the glass. His teeth gritted so hard he felt them crack.

Adrenaline was pumping furiously through his body, throwing him to his feet. His crazed eyes finally tore away, falling to the knife where it lay against the concrete. His face scorched with heat as he scooped it up, sprinting toward the doors and back into the house, pointing the sharp end of the knife at the window.

Once more, nothing was there.

"*Where are you?*" Maren muttered, his voice like a snake. "*You're hiding, aren't you?*"

He circled around the island of the kitchen with the large knife waving in the air, fearfully inspecting the entire room. He waited impatiently for the thing to emerge again.

He would be ready this time.

The air around him was deathly silent. No energy buzzed from its corners; no shadows danced in his vision. Just the feel of the knife vibrating in his shaking hand filled his senses. He couldn't get it to stop.

His terror began to disintegrate, falling around him from the air and puddling against the kitchen tile before hardening again as anger. He desperately wanted to scream, to throw the knife across the room, shattering the glass. He used every ounce of his power to keep the reaction inside, bringing his free hand to his mouth and sinking sharp teeth into his flesh to release the urge. The pain bubbled in his mouth.

"*I'm going crazy,*" he mumbled, teeth chattering. "I'm going *crazy.*"

A shiver settled over him, turning his glare through the open door as the realization infiltrated his face, soaking into his skin and down to his bones.

The doll.

His burning eyes shot to the shed where it hummed from the yard, and the corner of it that peeked out at him through the window. He saw the old door and the latch that hung from it, unlocked.

No.

Maren rushed outside, cutting his feet on sharp rocks and thorny twigs as he ran thoughtlessly to the shed, ignoring the pain. He swung the door open, sending it slamming against the wall as he pushed inside and dug furiously for Mr. Doll through the mess, finally feeling its smooth porcelain in between the thick pieces of wood. He snatched it from the box with an angry fist.

"It's *you,*" he growled against its face. "*You bastard. It's all you.*"

The darkness of the shed was closing in, popping at Maren's ears and pinching his skin. Mr. Doll burned in his grip, reddening his hand like a hot grill.

Maren tore back into the house, drawn to the energy of its walls. It called to him like an escape from the cold and the darkness, an end to the madness.

This doll was *evil. Haunted. Possessed.* Everything that Maren had heard about this house had been proven to him now. Mr. Doll, Lily-Doll, their supernatural dollhouse, it all needed to go. He needed to get rid of it.

Tonight.

He grabbed the heavy wooden mallet from the drawer, still imprisoning the doll with his free hand, and trampled up each step on his way to the second floor.

Twenty-Six.

Maren ripped through the staircase, bumping into walls and slipping his wet feet from the edges. His ears were ringing with noise as he arrived at the top, turning toward Lily's bedroom and slamming each step into the hardwood of the hallway.

Lily shot up in her bed at the sounds, gripping the blankets around her in fear. He flicked on the lights, illuminating the small wooden dollhouse along with his daughter's terrified face. She looked down at Mr. Doll, held tightly in one of her father's strong hands, and the large wooden mallet in the other.

"Dad . . ." She followed his eyes where they had landed, boring into the dollhouse that perched atop the small table in the center of the carpet. "What's going on?" Her voice was stretched thin.

Maren's breaths were staggered, and his expression was overflowing with resolve, anger, and fear. They all jumbled together inside of him, making him twitch.

"Lily. *Where is the doll?*" he growled like a feral dog.

He took two wide strides into the room, landing at the outskirts of the small, frail house where it buzzed beneath the light. He aggressively swung open its hinges, revealing the empty interior. Lily watched fearfully from her bed.

"What are you—"

"*WHERE?*" Maren shouted, causing her to flinch. He couldn't take this much longer. He had spent far too much time horribly attempting to convince himself that he wasn't afraid, that the house was just a house and the doll was just a doll. That the stories were only stories.

He failed.

He had known from the start that something was wrong. The feel of the air, the movement in the house. The dreams . . .

His life, or what was left of it, had fallen completely apart. This house was stealing his sleep, his sanity, his *daughter.* It had to stop.

Lily took in the sight of her father and stared wide eyes toward Mr. Doll, begging him for help.

You were right, she cried to him in her mind. *You're always right.*

"*ANSWER ME!*" Maren bellowed.

"I don't know where she is," she finally willed herself to speak. "I lost her."

Maren lifted his arm, displaying the thick wood of the mallet high above his head. He brought it down with the force of all the anger he had been desperately stuffing inside. Lily screamed.

CRACK!

A giant chunk of the dollhouse weakly crumbled as the blow landed, sending chipped pieces of wood and tiny furniture erupting into the air. Lily pleaded with Mr. Doll to stop him, but his voice was absent from her mind. His blank face shook in Maren's palm as the mallet struck the dollhouse again, taking out the entire right side.

"Stop! *Please!*" Lily clambered from her bed, crying like a child as Maren continued to destroy her prized possession. She scratched at his arms, reaching for the mallet, and he effortlessly shoved her away.

"Give me the doll! *NOW!*" Maren screamed, even louder this time. He was overcome with power as he lifted his weapon again, poised to smash what was left of the dollhouse.

Lily's eyes welled as she waited, begging for the voice of Mr. Doll to come and save her. She couldn't disappoint him, but what *could* she do? He had told her to keep Lily-Doll safe, that she was most important. That they would *need* her.

She swallowed hard. "No."

Maren's eyes turned red, and his whole body flushed with rage. He swung the mallet into the center of the dollhouse, shattering its hinges and demolishing the wood into scrap. He smashed and smashed as Lily cried from where he held her under his arm. Mr. Doll dangled from Maren's hand right beside her.

I did what you said! her thoughts reached for him. *Please!*

My sweet girl, it's almost over, Mr. Doll finally replied.

Lily breathed, squeezing her eyes tightly shut and waiting for the horrible sounds to cease.

After a moment, Maren stilled, catching his breath. Lily opened her eyes, rolling over each sliver of wood as they rained into the carpet. The dollhouse had been completely destroyed.

Maren released his manic daughter, letting her fall against the carpet, heartbroken. He knew what he had done, and he knew that she would surely hate him now. But he wasn't finished.

His most important job above all was to protect her, even if she despised him for it. Even if things would never be the same. He lifted his left hand where Mr. Doll still waited.

Lily's eyes widened. She rose from the floor and ran at her father once more. Her small hands reached hopelessly forward for Mr. Doll while Maren shoved her back onto her bed. She choked down a sob.

"I'm sorry, please! Please, don't! PLEASE!" She could barely speak as his strong hand held her against the mattress, keeping her from reaching the doll. Maren tossed its gray body to the floor, securing the heavy mallet with his only free hand and lifting it again into the air. He aimed at where the doll lay motionlessly against the carpet.

Just as he swung the mallet down, Lily's small hand reached out in front of him, grazing the doll with the tips of her fingers. She was moving much too erratically to contain while also making it impossible to perfect his aim. When he struck the arm of the doll with the wood, he also struck several of Lily's tiny fingers.

She cried out in pain, forcing Maren to tear his attention away, and the mallet clattered against the floor. The gray doll's left leg was broken at the knee, and small porcelain pieces were scattered around the carpet. Two of Lily's fingers were bleeding around the nail bed, and she held them tightly in her right hand. Maren froze in shock at what he had done.

"Lily, sweetie, I'm so sorry," he mumbled. "I didn't mean to—"

Before he could finish the sentence, Lily had grabbed the wooden weapon from the ground, taking full advantage of her father's distraction. She wouldn't let this moment go to waste.

She felt cold blood move through her, manifested by an unrecognized emotion she felt over every inch of her skin. She couldn't process her own thoughts before they caught up with her body. She swung the mallet at her father's shocked face.

Maren moved just before it connected with his lower jaw, tilting his head upward where her short arms couldn't reach. The mallet, instead, connected with his collarbone, filling the room with the sound of it slamming roughly against his chest. The force of it vibrated through the wood and up her arm. Her eyes shut tightly, not wanting to see what she had done.

Al, stop, Mr. Doll spoke in her.

She couldn't hear him. The only thing left in her mind was the small body of the doll, its broken leg lying against the carpet.

Her father was holding his collarbone with both hands, doubled over against the wall. He looked up at her, dazed and confused, just as she reached down with bloody fingers and slipped the doll from the floor. She hugged it quickly to her chest before tearing out of the room and sprinting down the hallway.

"*LILY!*" Her father's voice traveled through the air like thunder, shaking her bones as she ran. She turned the corner, sliding her socked feet against the hardwood and barreling toward the stairs.

Right before she reached the edge, her body skidded to a halt, clutching his small body tightly.

I told you to stop, Mr. Doll hissed.

"I'm sorry, I can't let him—" She stopped, letting a tear slip down her flushed skin. Mr. Doll silenced her words.

He can't hurt me, he growled. *He is weak. Fragile.*

Maren ran from the bedroom after his daughter, approaching her where she stood frozen in front of the stairs.

"Lily, give me the doll. *Now,*" he demanded through jagged breaths.

"Okay," she said, turning slowly toward him. Her body was stiff and straight, and her arm reached far out in front of her, displaying the doll to her father. Her glossy eyes stared at nothing.

Maren frowned at her, confused. He slipped the doll from her fingers while Lily twitched.

He stared down at his daughter while she stood completely still. Her unfocused eyes looked through him, and her arm still hung in the air empty-handed. Something wasn't right.

Maren turned back toward the room to retrieve the mallet, not taking his eyes from his daughter.

Trust me, Al, Mr. Doll spoke within her mind, keeping her still from inside of her.

He's going to hurt you, she fought to reply. *He can't; I won't let him.*

Lily looked down from the ceiling at herself, standing still and allowing Maren to steal her only friend in the world to destroy him.

What if Mr. Doll was wrong? she wondered, so deep inside of her that she hoped he wouldn't hear. *What if Dad can hurt him?*

Lily focused in on the doll as her father walked slowly back to her bedroom. She focused on his skin shining in the light of the hallway and the shattered porcelain halfway down his leg. Lily began to snap.

He can hurt you; he already has, she insisted.

No, Al. Don't. His voice darkened. He was losing his grip.

I can't let him take you away. I can't lose you.

Al . . .

The doll's voice slowly faded as Lily's mind came crashing back into her body, right as her father stepped in through her door from down the hall.

Her glossy eyes blinked back to reality, focusing over her father. Maren's face dropped as Lily scowled, running toward him at full speed. The doll burned in his hand.

Maren escaped into the bedroom and threw the door closed, but Lily was too quick. She pushed her way into the room, reaching for the doll and launching it from his grasp. It fell to the floor against the pile of rubble that once was the dollhouse.

Her father took hold of her, snaking both arms tightly around her waist and pulling her to him, barely keeping her from grabbing Mr. Doll. He was terrified, in awe of Lily's violent meltdown and her insane attachment to this doll. Her outburst had only made him more certain of his decision. He couldn't let her stop him.

Lily thrashed in his arms, attempting to wriggle from his grasp. She tumbled to the floor, forcing him to grab his sobbing daughter with both hands and throw her over his shoulder. He stalked out of the room while screams ripped from her throat. She pounded her small fists against his back while he walked away from Mr. Doll and into the hallway.

"*I hate you! I hate you! I hate you!*" she shrieked. "I never wanted to stay with you. I want Mom!" Each word stabbed like a knife at his chest, but he pressed forward.

"I'll hate you forever if you hurt him! He's my only friend, *please!*" she continued. "I want *him* to be my dad, not you! *I hate you!*"

Maren dropped her softly against the floorboards of the hall, keeping her from the door as he slipped back inside the room and locked it shut behind him.

Lily banged loudly on the door, so hard that it seemed to shake the whole house. She had gone completely feral, but Maren carried on. He must finish what he started. He must protect her.

Each drawer was flung open in his search for the Lily-Doll, pouring out the contents of each one onto the floor. He checked the closet, under the bed, in each slit of the bookshelf, and behind the desk. She was nowhere to be found.

Lily was throwing herself against the door now, and the tricky handle wiggled with each blow. He needed to hurry.

He gave up his search and went for Mr. Doll first, crouching where it lay against the carpet. He plucked it from the floor and brought it to the thick top of her dresser, laying the doll flat on its back.

Maren raised the hammer high in the air, swinging down hard.

Crack.

It landed against its hollow gray skull. A large crack emerged from its cheek, traveling down the left side of its face.

Almost there, he thought. *It's almost over.*

Lily was quieting against the door, growing tired. Her stitches were popping at her arm, letting blood seep into the clean white bandages. She didn't seem to care, or even notice.

Maren lifted his weapon again, connecting it against the doll's head as the mallet fell. Its sickly face began to crumble under the impact.

Maren felt powerful; he felt in control. The only thing that mattered in this moment was protecting his daughter—if it was the only thing that he could do right.

With one final blow, Mr. Doll's head exploded against the thick wood of the desk, sending shards of porcelain sliding over the edges. Maren's fingers loosened, letting the mallet slip to the floor.

Each corner of the house suddenly halted, all at once.

It was so quiet he could hear the blood rushing in his ears. Sweat stung against his skin as it slid down his back, and goosebumps trickled over him. The sound of his daughter's limp body echoed beneath the crack under the door as she slumped against the other side of the wood. Her brain went blank.

Maren's eyes searched around the room cautiously as he held his breath. Not even the air moved. Lily was no longer yelling, or even crying, only terrifyingly silent. A darkness bloomed in the air around him, filling him with dread, and he couldn't understand why. The evil had been destroyed here in front of him. It was over.

At least that's what he thought.

He looked down at the broken doll while an invisible cloud erupted from it, curving through the air. His eyes widened, his body buzzed with anticipation, and he waited for the *bad thing* to happen.

All at once, the energy in the room swelled around him like a closing fist. The lights flickered violently and the pieces of the doll shook on the table as the entire house quaked beneath them. The dark cloud snaked across the room, pulsing with the aura of the *thing*. He felt it slip under the crack of the door like it was being sucked away, like it was finding home in his daughter.

The monster, the gray doll. *John.*

The door of the bedroom burst open, exploding into the room and throwing the wood against the wall. It cracked with the wild strength of the force that had opened it, drawing long slits across its face.

Maren's head whipped toward the opening where Lily slowly stood from the ground. Her head bobbed at her shoulders before springing straight up and locking her unblinking eyes to his.

"*Daddy?*" A warped voice escaped his daughter's lips, dripping from her tongue. Her tone contorted into his ears with a mixture of a dragging, gravelly voice and her own. Her eyes were glossed over, their bright-blue color hiding behind a deepened gray. She smiled a wide, toothy grin, cocking her head at him.

Maren cringed at the sound of her words and the look on her face, taking a step back farther into the room.

"*What's wrong, Daddy?*" Her smile was unfaltering and her aura was thick, choking him. Maren could barely think over the piercing sound of her voice, jamming into his ears and scraping his brain.

"*You were right to get rid of that doll; it was really quite dangerous.*" The warped voice continued from Lily's mouth, mocking him. "*I love you, Daddy.*" It was slowly dropping into a growl as her own voice faded. Her mind was slowly slipping away, being tucked tightly within her.

Maren knew this was a dream; it had to be. Just another one of his hideous nightmares, one he would wake up from at any second. He dug his fingernails into his palm.

"Lily . . . *stop.*" The only words he could seem to form fell from his lips and floated down to the carpet, disappearing. Her eyes continued to darken, almost black.

"*Stop? I can't stop now,*" she whined. "*I'm almost finished.*"

Lily stumbled farther into the room as her father took equal steps backward. Soon his back rested against the wall with nowhere else to go. She stood at the center of the carpet, stepping over the crumbled dollhouse and around to the bed. Maren watched as she slipped her hand between the sheets and into the pillowcase, removing the blonde-haired doll from within.

She brought the doll to her chest, smiling.

"*My sweet girl,*" her deranged voice said.

Twenty-Seven.

Maren could do nothing but watch. He felt frozen in place, his heart pounding erratically against his rib cage. His veins bulged and his bones caved in as panic wrapped tightly around his body. Fear hung around his neck like a collar.

Lily's face had become unfamiliar to him, mangled with a hideous grin. Her blackened eyes were glossy and unfocused like she was asleep, but they stared right through him. His daughter's body moved awkwardly, twitching and cracking as she walked. Her fingers curled tightly around Lily-Doll, convulsing as each finger tightened then released. It was like her body was struggling to follow instructions, or something had control of her but couldn't figure out which buttons to press.

"What are you doing?" Maren asked with a shaky voice. The words barely made a sound, floating from his lips.

Lily held the small blonde doll in her hands, stroking its short hair with a trembling finger. Her smile stretched widely on her face.

"Lily, what—"

"*Shut up,*" she snapped in a sickening voice. She turned to face him, dropping her expression with disgust. Her eyes were reddening as she stared, unblinking. "*That is not her name.*"

She slowly drew closer, like a lion circling in on its prey. Lily-Doll sat snugly in her palm.

"*I know who you are,*" the voice continued. "*I know what you want.*"

The words slicked through his ears, making him cringe. They twisted in his head and dug deeply inside, like each word had claws. He felt himself shrink as she approached.

"What? Lily—"

Her throat tore with a terrible screech, vibrating the walls and shaking the windows. Maren covered both ears with his hands to escape it, but he could still feel it in his bones.

"*I TOLD YOU NOT TO CALL HER THAT!*" the voice boomed like thunder. Maren sank against the wall, sliding down to the floor.

"*You call her nothing. You don't speak to my daughter. You're here to harm her.*" Lily's hollow face contorted, like she was seeing him for the first time, like he didn't belong. Maren sat hollowly, unable to speak.

"*I know who you ARE!*" she continued to scream. The room around them filled with dread, blocking out the light from above with its thick, looming cloud. "*I won't let you hurt her again.*"

She moved toward him so quickly that Maren had no time to think. Suddenly the mallet had been snatched from the floor and her bony fingers tightened around the handle. Maren's face twisted with horror as Lily's hostage body raised its arm, swinging down at him. The mallet barreled toward his head.

He dodged to the side, sending it just past his ear and pounding into the drywall behind him. His eyes bulged in shock at the force of it. This time she swung with more power than before. More strength, more malice, more *intent.*

He reached out, grabbing her left hand where she held the mallet and pulling it down.

"*Ow,*" she whined in a soft, child-like tone. "*That hurts.*"

Maren looked down at her small hand in his grasp, and the bloody fingers that still throbbed where he smashed them under the mallet. He released her, at a complete loss of what to do.

His desperate face shot back up at her and her black eyes met him in a challenging stare. They were inches from his face—two deep swirling pools of darkness. She grimaced, lifting the mallet again.

Maren stood from the floor, protecting his face with his hands and scrambling away from his daughter. The weapon made contact with his shoulder, making him cry out in pain. The strength of the blow shocked him, shooting rapidly through his body.

Red blood was seeping from her fingers where he had damaged them, soaking through the bandages around her arm where her stitches continued to pop. Her hands shook and her eyes burned bright red.

"What are you doing? *STOP!*" Maren begged and pleaded, lost completely to the unrelenting chaos. The swings continued to fly toward him, over and over.

He could overpower her easily, but he was terrified to hurt her again. She was already bleeding and out of her mind. All he could seem to do was watch her as terror wrapped its heavy chains around him, forcing him still. The raw fear drained his energy, leaving him weak, powerless. His trembling hands barely managed to protect his face.

"*You can't have her. NEVER again!*" Lily screeched as the mallet connected with Maren's jaw. He toppled over, falling into the carpet while his lip began to bleed where it split. The blow was so hard that his vision started to spot, graying in each corner. He slunk to the floor, struggling to shake the daze.

Lily dropped the mallet to her side, shaking violently, and directed her attention back toward the blonde doll.

"*Don't you see, sweet girl? I will always protect you.*" Her bloody fingers stroked Lily-Doll's dress, staining it with red. "*I would never let him hurt you again. Do you see?*"

She held the doll out into the air to face Maren where he curled into the carpet, groaning. His face was bleeding into the floor, pooling from his lip. Lily's smile faltered as John allowed her mind to surface.

"What did you do to him?" Lily's tender voice asked, suddenly dripping with concern, a sharp contrast to the voice that had just cracked from her throat. Her face twisted again as he took back the control. John's pride dissolved.

"*I protected you, my daughter,*" he retorted defensively. "*Like I should have before. Don't you see?*" The distorted voice had returned to her lips, soaked with desperation.

Maren lifted his head from the carpet, rolling over his shoulders and jabbing his terrified gaze into Lily's face. He was bleeding and afraid. Tears streamed from his eyes.

"But . . . he was only—" Her sweet voice returned for one second before being sharply cut off, drowning her own words with a garbled growl.

"*You said that you trusted me!*" The blackened voice was growing louder. "*You said that you wanted to be with me. THIS is what it takes!*"

Lily's own words didn't return again to her tongue. Her black eyes deepened, pouring into Maren where he crouched.

"Lily . . ." Maren cried weakly. He was powerless, sobbing like a child. His daughter's shell took several steps toward him, turning her head. Her face pounded with hurt.

"*I love you, Al. It's almost over,*" the voice groaned. John lifted the bloodied mallet from the floor with Lily's hand, clinging to the wood. Every ounce of power that he could squeeze from her small body condensed to her arm, sending the mallet flying against the side of her father's head.

Maren watched it move toward him, too broken and helpless to react. Everything hit him at once. He saw his daughter's body with her empty, unclosing eyes. He saw the hate mangled in her face, and the dread pouring from her skin. He saw her fight when she should be crying. He saw the blood that dripped from her arm down to her mangled fingers that gripped the weapon. He mourned his daughter while she stood right in front of him, empty.

The thick head of the wood connected against his temple and he dropped to the ground, motionless.

Lily's cries were lost inside of her body, unable to surface. She was no longer in control.

Once Maren was quiet, Lily's twitching fingers released the mallet, letting it tumble to the floor. She leaned down on the carpet next to him and whispered a raspy voice into his ear.

"*If you come near my daughter again, I will kill you,*" the sickened voice spat. "*She is mine.*"

Lily's body rose, the blonde doll still in her hand, and moved toward the opened bedroom door. She stopped in her tracks, standing over the face of the wooden desk.

The shattered pieces of Mr. Doll were strewn across the top. John stared Lily's dulled eyes at them, cocking her head. A wide smile inched over her lips as she bent down, swiping the remains into her open palm. She held the large pieces of the doll's gray head, its broken body, and loose gray clothes, curling her fist around them. The pieces stabbed into the flesh of her palm, but she could not feel it. She only grinned.

Maren could barely lift his battered face to watch. His head rang with the horrible sound of John's distorted voice as it wrapped around his daughter's tongue. He saw from the corner of his eye as she turned away from him, leaving her father to suffer on the ground alone.

Blood was soaking through the bandages on Lily's arm, darkening the white material with a thick red. It dripped down her skin and from the tips of her fingers as she walked from the room, leaving a trail of warm blood against the hardwood of the hallway. Lily's right hand tightened around Lily-Doll, making sure to not let her go. Without her, John's plan would not work.

It had been so long since John had skin, bones, and warmth flowing through his veins, he had almost forgotten how to operate them. He moved awkwardly, too fast or too slow. Lily's body jolted and stilled, her limbs bent at awkward angles and her expression was wild and tight on her face. Her joints popped and her teeth grinded; her feet dragged across the floor.

Lily was lost somewhere inside, swirling around in John's head like a feather. She floated down his river of thoughts toward a waterfall, accepting the drop that awaited her. Each time she tried to surface, he would talk her back down, locking her deep inside of his box.

She watched from inside through a window. Voices were quiet; images were blurred. It was like she was sleeping, or submerged deep underwater away from the rest of the world. John kept her hidden, safe, in the dark about what he was going to do next—what he had planned to do from the start.

First he needed to make sure he could never be trapped again. Here in Lily's body, he realized just how powerless he had been inside of the doll. Relying on his daughter for his dirty work had only worked so well. She was only a child, of course, confused by the lies of her *captor.*

"*Maren,*" he hissed from Lily's lips. The man who had ruined his life. The man who had taken his daughter, trapping her away and keeping her from her father. Her *real* father. Maren would suffer, but that had to wait. He needed to finish this first.

John approached the bottom of the stairs, dragging his eyes over the dark room. Even through the thick of the night, he could see that it was hideously white, with barren walls and boring, colorless furniture. Alina had always hated homes like these. He always kept theirs bright and colorful for her. The sight disgusted him.

He dragged Lily's feet to the far wall of the living room where the red bricks were covered in thin white drywall. It disguised one of John's favorite parts of this house—the fireplace his daughter had loved so much.

This wouldn't do.

He moved to the kitchen, setting the blonde doll down on the counter gently and rummaging through each drawer. He pulled out a large black hammer that was hidden inside of the packed junk drawer, gripping it tightly with Lily's pale fingers and making her knuckles turn white. It gleamed in the moonlight from the windows.

He wasn't worried about leaving the doll on the counter close by, not after what he had done to Maren. He wouldn't be coming down here again.

John knew him, deeply. Through Lily's eyes, he had seen inside of Maren's mind and through each thought, into every dark cavern and hidden desire. John knew what she meant to Maren, and the pain he felt each time he looked at her.

John knew she only reminded Maren of what he had lost, how he had failed, and how he always managed to hurt each thing that he loved. He felt Maren's sorrow when he looked into her eyes, and the overwhelming defeat that now poured from him.

It was over now. He *lost*.

John walked to the fireplace, crouching before it and inspected the growing cracks. He stuck Lily's fingers through the hole at the bottom, pulling softly as the drywall crumbled beneath his touch. He pulled and pulled as it ripped, revealing the beautiful red bricks from below. John's soft, genuine smile snuck to Lily's cheeks.

He could almost see his young daughter, his sweet Alina, sitting on the carpet before the fireplace in the middle of winter, letting the fire warm her skin. He could picture her toothy smile as they hung their stockings from the mantle, her beautiful blonde hair and blue eyes. He imagined all of it being ripped away that one fateful night. The night she was murdered by the intruder. By *Maren*.

His smile dropped from Lily's face, pulling her arm back roughly and ripping a large chunk of the drywall away. It crumbled in his grasp and rained against the floor at his feet.

The hammer gripped in Lily's small hand winded back and crushed into the drywall right at the center of the opening. John swung over and over, crushing each piece of the wall while each brick slowly revealed itself to the room. Lily's body became slick with sweat, her arms were tired and weak. Her unblinking eyes were red and burning. But John could not feel it; he only felt rage.

Once all of the pieces had been chipped away, the fireplace sat open toward the living room, blaring with vitality.

Each brick stared at him through Lily's skin, speaking to him softly. Lily's battered body collapsed, sinking into the floor as the blood from her arm soaked steadily into her clothes. It dripped and dripped, turning her skin pale.

John took each of the crushed pieces of Mr. Doll out from Lily's pocket, inspecting each one before he tossed them into the mouth of the fireplace. It ate each shard hungrily.

John stalked back to the kitchen, rummaging around again through the drawers before pulling a long blue lighter from inside. He held it out in front of him, fingering the trigger until a flame bloomed at the top.

Next he tossed in a handful of crumpled papers that had been ripped from a book on the counter and lit the entire mound at once. The orange flames wrapped around the papers, cutting through the dark and embracing the shattered doll, smothering each piece with heat. The embers withered away while John stared wide-eyed, exhaling deeply.

The fire flickered in the reflection of Lily's blackened eyes and warmed her skin. John hadn't felt it in ages.

Twenty-Eight.

Maren pushed himself from the floor slowly while the room around him continued to spin. He could barely breathe, barely think, barely do anything but crumble away. His uselessness plagued him as he sat, paralyzed with fear and grief while his strength oozed from his body and pooled around him on the floor. He felt hollow.

"Lily . . ." he groaned. Tears were wet on his skin, stinging against the cut at his lip. He dragged a hand over his face, slicking it with blood. The clock on the desk gleamed in the corner of his eye.

3:24 a.m.

The sound of his daughter's footsteps lifted to his ears, tapping softly down the stairs. He moved to stand and follow them, but stopped himself.

I need to find Lily. The thought ran through his head, quickly followed by another.

That's not Lily.

He cringed, soaking the words into his skull. He refused to believe them—he *couldn't,* but he needed to.

Maren had always forced himself to be strong. Always the rock, the foundation, the unmovable object. Where had that gotten him?

If he had only admitted to being afraid, none of this would have happened. He had always been afraid of the rumors, afraid of the feel of the house during the tour, afraid of the basement and the dollhouse and the *fucking gray doll.*

He could have walked away from it all. Instead he was here, crying on the floor of his daughter's room while the ghost of an angry dead man paraded around inside of her skin, while he used his daughter as a *puppet.*

His *only* daughter.

Instead of being afraid, he had been a coward. He had let this *bad thing* beat him over and over and over while he sat and ignored that it existed at all. Now, Lily was gone.

Gone, he thought. *She can't be gone.*

The room was still spinning, and his body still felt weak. Lily was still gone and John was still winning. Even so, he pushed to his hands and knees, wincing in pain. He steadied himself against the large desk, rising to his feet.

Lily's footsteps had gone quiet. The only noise that remained in the house was Maren's labored breathing erupting from his throat. The more he blinked, the more the room around him became distorted, pulling him into a waking dream. The lights flickered above before shutting off completely. He was submerged in the dark.

He stood still, waiting for his eyes to adjust as the shadows choked him from every direction. The entire house was deathly silent, forcing him to imagine what might be happening downstairs. Each question shot him through the skull.

What had he done with Lily?
Where was he taking her?
What did he want?

There was no time for questions, only action. Each second that slipped through his fingers, he was losing time.

Maren pushed himself forward through the dark to the edge of the doorway, peeking carefully around the corner. His vision was spotty, foggy, and weak, barely making out the staircase down the hall. From where he stood, it almost looked like a man standing at the top.

Maren leaned against the wooden frame, jutting his head farther out and squinting his eyes.

It *was* a man.

He was young, probably mid-twenties, from what Maren could make out. His brain was so foggy and numb that he wasn't entirely sure it was real. But he heard him mumbling . . .

"*Down the street, third house on the . . . third house on the . . . right . . . Fuck! Fuck, fuck, fuck!*" The man smacked a closed fist against his forehead. His body trembled and his eyes looked barely focused. Even through the shadows, they shined a bright red.

Maren squinted, leaning down and out of sight as the man twitched, continuing to mumble.

"*This is wrong. Third house on the right. Third house on the right! No, no, no, no, no . . .*" He was pacing the hallway now, scratching at his arms. Maren had had enough.

"Get out of my house," Maren growled with a voice as strong and loud as he could muster. He stood tall, moving farther into the hallway toward the strange man as the door creaked behind him.

The man stopped mumbling, suddenly turning toward Maren and raising his arms out in front of his body. The hard metal of the gun gleamed in the moonlight.

Maren's squinted eyes widened, and he wildly scrambled back into Lily's bedroom, dropping low to the floor to protect himself. The man's gun rang loudly, shooting a thick stream of light across the hallway. It missed Maren's body by an inch as he retreated.

The sound stung in the air, filling the small room with pressure. Maren crouched against the wall for cover, breathing rapidly while the hallway returned to a haunting quiet outside of the door. He snapped his head around the curve of the wall, peering through the dark and out into the hallway. There was no sign of a man. There was no gun, no bright light, no bullet in the walls.

He frantically checked himself for injury, calling out to the man again.

"Get out!" he screamed, his lungs curling. "*I'LL KILL YOU MYSELF!*"

There was no reply.

He rose slowly, shaking the nerves from his legs as the soft sound of crying gently lifted to his ears.

Lily. He snapped from the daze. *I need to get to Lily.*

Just outside the door, leaning against the wall to the side, sat his daughter. Her short blonde hair hung around her face as her head drooped toward her lap. Both of her arms were gripped tightly around her waist.

"Lily?" Maren whispered, darting his eyes around the hall. "Sweetheart, tell me what happened. Where is the man? He—"

The girl on the floor violently swung her head toward him, digging cold, dead eyes into his face. He jumped back, horrified.

"*Help me,*" she begged as blood poured from her mouth with each curve of her lips. She was covered in it—a thick red ooze. It seeped down her face and from a gaping hole in her chest, puddling over the floor.

Her shaking hands lifted from around her waist, stained in darkness. This wasn't Lily.

Maren's knees fell weak, making him stumble back against the wall as he gawked in terror. The sight of the blood, the wound, and the young girl's life as it dripped from her, it froze him solid in place. His feet slipped in dark blood as he tried to stand.

"Where is Lily?" he choked the words out as the taste of copper flooded his tongue. A sob was tearing from his throat. "I need to find her . . . I need—"

"*Why did you leave me?*" the girl whispered with a voice that cracked and grinded over her teeth. She cocked her head at him, contorting her face.

"I . . . I don't—"

"*WHY DID YOU LEAVE ME?*" she shrieked, pounding against the floor with closed, bloody fists. Her entire body twitched and flailed in agony as red droplets stained the white walls.

Maren scrambled from the floor, bolting down the hall and tripping over his feet to escape her. He held both hands over his ears to block out her desperate cries, losing his balance and slamming into the side of the staircase.

His weakened body fell against the wall while frantic hands gripped the edge of it to steady himself. Catching his breath, he jabbed his eyes back toward the girl.

What girl?

He searched the open space that once held her, but the hallway lay empty. There was no girl, no pool of blood, no shrieking or crying or blinding gunshot. There was nothing at all.

Maren raised his fists, slamming them into both sides of his temples.

Stop it, he demanded, forcing himself to breathe. He shut his eyes tightly, clearing his mind and calming his heart rate before his insides climbed out of his chest.

It's not real.

It's not real.

It's not real.

These were tricks, mind games meant to keep him from his daughter. He was simply breathing life into them, making them real and wasting precious time. His mind raced so fast he could hardly seem to keep up.

That girl, she looked just like Lily . . .

Alina. That's where she died.

Maybe . . .

Everything was falling into place. The doll, John, Lily, Alina, it all slowly unraveled in his mind.

Lily looks just like Alina.

John wants her back.

My Lily. He can't have her. I won't let him.

The fear evaporated as anger began to sprout. It wasn't over. Not yet.

Maren forced his way down the stairs, making his footsteps soft and quiet. A loud banging sound was ripping through the house now, helping silence his movements. The visions that plagued him must have been keeping the noise from his ears before because now it was impossible to ignore. The whole house shook with each one.

BANG! BANG! BANG!

Over and over, again and again. Maren's heart rose to his throat as he imagined where the sounds might be coming from. They grew louder and louder with each stair he descended.

Approaching the bottom, he peeked his head slightly around the corner, seeing his daughter's body as it dropped the hammer against the floor and collapsed before the wide-open fireplace. Each piece of the white drywall had been smashed away or ripped from the edges. The crumbled pieces now lay scattered across the floor.

The shell of his daughter was covered in her blood, dripping down her arm and over her crushed fingers. It soaked into her clothes in thick red streaks. His heart twisted at the sight, but he could do nothing for her. Not yet.

He watched as John took pieces of the gray doll from Lily's pocket, tossing them in messy handfuls through the gaping hole of the fireplace. The red bricks stung his eyes.

His daughter stood again, and Maren shrank back into the corner, hiding his face. John led Lily's puppet into the kitchen, returning with a lighter and a thick handful of papers. He lit everything inside the fireplace, destroying what was left of the doll before collapsing before the warmth of the fire.

Maren poked his head out into the opening, watching while John stared motionlessly into the flames. He seemed to fall into some sort of trance, slumping over with glossy black eyes as he stared.

Lily's father didn't waste a second, desperately searching for the Lily-Doll. She was important—important enough to hide and keep safe. Important enough for John to bring her with him, and to keep her in his sights at all times.

Maren slunk down the last of the stairs as silently as possible. He gouged his eyes into the back of his daughter's blonde head, willing it to stay still, pointing straight ahead.

John was lost in the flames, with loosened shoulders that drooped at his sides. He sat on Lily's knees, leaning into the heat of the fireplace. He was crying.

A storm was brewing in the air above her body like a sinister dark cloud. It swirled around the room with the intensity of John's thoughts, growing wilder by the second. That fateful night continued to play out inside his head, manifesting in each crevasse of the house.

The sounds escaped the confines of John's mind, piercing through the air. A lock being ripped from the doorframe with a crowbar. Heavy footsteps creeping up the stairs. The same booming gunshot and shrieking cries, repeating over and over. Alina's painfully sharpened voice echoed loudly from each wall.

"*WHY DID YOU LEAVE ME?*" John imagined her screaming, sending her voice blaring through the air. He imagined her anger, her disgust, and the blame she might throw at him.

He was completely still within Lily's body, crouched in front of the fireplace. Tears were streaming from her darkened eyes.

Maren swallowed hard, sweating through his shirt with terror. He had no idea what he was doing, but he needed to get that doll. Without the Lily-Doll, it was over.

He crept slowly around the back of the couch, heading toward the kitchen where the blonde doll sat. He ignored the storm around him, the shrieking voice and the cries and the banging. The doll had been perched at the edge of the counter facing John, facing *Lily.* It sat hollowly, staring forward into nothingness.

Maren was so close, just steps away. He whipped his head back toward John where he still mindlessly stared into the fire, lost deep inside of his mind. The invisible storm continued to blow violently around him.

Maren was right in front of the Lily-Doll now, reaching out a bloodied hand to grab her.

Is she in there already? he wondered.

He had pieced it together by now. John had gotten inside of the gray doll somehow after his suicide. Now he wanted his daughter to join him. Only his daughter wasn't here—she was gone, but John couldn't accept that. Instead, he intended to take Lily.

It was all making sense—the strange attachment she had to it, the dollhouse, the way she had cut her hair. The . . . suicide attempt. John had been trying to take her away, bit by bit. And *this* was the finale.

This doll, Lily-Doll, was somehow the key.

He stared deeply into the doll's blue eyes, searching for his daughter—searching for an energy, a heat, the same one he had felt in the gray doll. The same way that *Lily* had felt it that first day in the basement. This doll still seemed hollow, but he couldn't be sure.

Maren reached out a shaky hand toward the doll, touching her with only the tips of his fingers while the storm around him suddenly halted, falling from the air. A heavy silence coated him, replacing the chaos. Maren felt it constrict.

He turned slowly to face John while he rolled Lily's head over her shoulders, jabbing her blackened eyes across the room and through Maren's skull.

"*You can't touch her,*" John's words crawled from Lily's lips like maggots. "*She's mine.*"

Twenty-Nine.

Lily was lost inside a dream. She floated mindlessly, glimpsing through the fog to the pictures displayed far away. None of them mattered, after all—they weren't real. She was curled deep inside her bed beneath the warm covers, snug between the sheets and watching scenes unfold on a screen.

This dream was different from the ones she had been having lately. The dollhouse was gone, smashed to pieces, and so was Mr. Doll. The house was dark around her as she walked disembodied. Images floated in and out of view.

She heard the voice of her father, and her own, warped and distorted. She heard horrible loud banging, the crackle and pop of a fire.

She caught glimpses of Maren's twisted face, slick with blood. An image of a mallet in her hand and red warmth soaking through her bandaged arm. She saw the fireplace licked with hot flames. Each scene flashed like a flipbook, rolling through her brain too fast to process.

John's ominous voice boomed within her from all sides, shaking and shattering the dream at its edges. A feral storm was rippling through his brain and reaching long fingers into Lily's, shaking her back to reality.

"*She's mine.*" His venomous words broke through the quiet.

Maren stood miles away at the edge of the nightmare as it cracked in her head. She strained hard to see him while the space around her tried desperately to reel her back in.

Her father reached wildly for something, something small with yellow hair. His fingers stretched and his face held a crazed expression. Lily-Doll.

She saw him grip her tightly and run even farther away, out of sight.

Lily was snatched back into the depths of her dream, exhausted. The images of Maren were floating away again as the flipbook turned faster through each page. Mr. Doll wrapped her tightly back into bed, back between the warm sheets of the dream. She closed her eyes.

"She is *not* your daughter." Maren's voice suddenly pounded through her skull, shaking her back awake. She searched for his face.

"*Dad?*" she said softly, inaudibly inside of John. Her eyes drifted through the darkness around her, struggling to make anything out. The shape of the room, a figure in the black, her father. Nothing was clear.

There was a light stuffed far away, barely shining. She squinted at it, fighting to stay awake while John stuffed her back down.

"*I told you that I would kill you. I told you to stay away.*" Mr. Doll's voice came next, rolling over her skin. It gripped her. She felt him move, and the light crawled forward.

"Alina is gone, John. She's *dead.*" Maren's voice was clearer this time. She felt the doll's aura constrict around her, holding her still, but she forced herself to focus.

"*SHUT UP, DEMON!*" John bellowed. His heat was rising, boiling the depths inside of him where Lily was buried. "*I know who you are. I know my daughter.*" Anger roared inside of him like a monster, ready to devour him.

"Your daughter died! Long before we came here!" Maren screamed, walking backward, away from John. "She was killed . . . by an *intruder.* She's not here!"

Lily saw Lily-Doll clenched tightly in her father's fist.

"*I TOLD YOU TO SHUT UP!*" John's mangled voice struck through the room and into Maren's skull. Everything began to shake violently around Lily. Darkness swirled in her vision, turning red as Maren spoke through the chaos.

"*LET MY DAUGHTER GO!*" he shouted from the roots of his body. His words were wet with desperation. "Her name is *Lily Caplin.* She's eleven years old. She was born on April 7th—"

John lifted one of Lily's small hands, sending her father's body flying backward across the room and into the wall behind him. His skull *smacked* into the drywall and the air was ripped from his lungs, stifling the rest of his words. He slid weakly to the tile.

Lily watched from deep inside of John in terror. She hopelessly tried to shake herself free, out to her body, to no avail.

"*YOU CAN'T HAVE HER!*" John screeched from Lily's hollow lips, shaking the glass of each window in the large room and sending cracks up from each of their corners. The entire house filled with a tangible malice, raining like ashes and covering every inch of the room.

Lily was thrown violently from her body, too far to return. The dreams of the dollhouse drowned her, wrapping thick vines around her mind as everything went black in her head. The nightmare continued without her as she floated away.

Maren melted farther into the floor, gripping the Lily-Doll desperately to his chest, frantic to protect it. He couldn't be sure that his daughter hadn't been trapped inside of it already. He couldn't risk hurting her.

He could hardly breath, sputtering for oxygen as his daughter's dark puppet approached. The whole house rattled with each step, and the raw energy popped in his ears.

Maren scrambled to his feet, narrowly avoiding John's next attack. He ran for the back door just as Lily's hand raised again, sending shockwaves through the air and shattering the thick glass of the exit. Maren jumped, sliding across the tile and swiftly changing direction. The basement door buzzed from the far corner of the kitchen, waiting for him.

He swung it open, desperate to escape John, desperate to protect the small doll in his hands—his only hope. He imagined the feeling of the gray doll's skull shattering under the force of the mallet, sending John's angry spirit into his helpless daughter. That couldn't happen again. He couldn't let his stupidity hurt her further; he needed to be careful. He needed to think.

The door slammed behind him, and Maren leaned his full weight into the wood to hold it closed. He felt the door cave against his spine at John's force, over and over, as he threw Lily's small body against it.

BANG! BANG! BANG!

"GIVE HER BACK!" John's distorted voice pounded against the door, squealing in his ears. *"GIVE HER TO ME!"*

Thoughts burned through Maren's mind like a fever, pleading with the basement for a way out or even a moment to think. He darted his terrified eyes around the mouth of the basement, looking for something he could make use of.

Suddenly, the door quieted against his back for a split second. He breathed in.

CRACK!

The wooden door shot open with a force so intense that it flung Maren off the top stair, throwing him down. He knocked each bone in his body on the way to the bottom, sliding deeper into the black pool of the basement. He curled the Lily-Doll in his grasp, desperately shielding her from the drop as his ribs smashed against the stairs. His legs contorted beneath him and his arms bent before he eventually landed with a loud *thud* at the base. He groaned, choking down his pain while he writhed in the dirt.

Dust settled in the air around him, disappearing into the pitch black of the basement. The only light was that of the moon, barely reaching through the doorway of the living room and seeping from the small windows above. It illuminated the room softly.

Lily's body emerged from the open door at the top of the wooden staircase, steaming with anger.

"Give her to me. Give me my daughter." John's booming voice had weakened as Lily's battered body slowly disintegrated around him. She was still losing blood, and her muscles ached from overuse. The overwhelming power of John's blows had drained her from the inside. Her feet dragged beneath her with each slow step down the stairs.

Maren watched in horror, coughing and sputtering, unsure of which Lily he needed to protect. Was she here, within the fragile porcelain in his hands? Was she up there, slowly dying inside of her bleeding body? He held the hollow doll in his grasp, waiting for a sign, a feeling, anything at all.

John stood at the center of the stairs, watching Maren from his daughter's burning red eyes. John knew this weakened body wouldn't last much longer, and he was rapidly running out of time. He couldn't risk hurting the doll, but he also couldn't get to Maren without using force. He stood still, staring.

Maren watched in terror from his spot in the dirt as he struggled to rise from the ground. His whole body throbbed in pain, but the blonde doll was still snug in his grip.

"Lily, I'm sorry," Maren coughed, spewing the bloody words into the darkness. Black swirls swam down from the house above, traveling over the stairs and filling the room with dread as John's storm of emotion followed him into the basement. "I'm here. I'll never let him take you. I'll die before I let that happen."

John's voice was hauntingly soft from Lily's lips. *"Then you will die."*

Creeeeak.

The sound came suddenly, ripping through the air. It came from right above Maren's head.

He shot his trembling gaze around in the dark, squinting. It was horrifyingly silent. Lily's body crouched slowly against the stairs, watching him. Maren could hardly see.

Creeeeak.

The sound tore through his ears again, even louder this time. He whipped his head around to find its source.

At the center of the ceiling, a tall shadowed figure swung from the thick wooden beam. It swayed from side to side slowly. Maren watched frozen in place as the figure dropped to the ground, leaving the empty noose to swing in the air.

The large figure approached, staring through him with eyes that glowed through the darkness. Maren could barely make out its features, besides its large cocked head, bobbing from its broken neck.

John.

Thirty.

The dark figure took wide, slow steps, dragging itself through the dirt toward Maren. Its head twisted down its broken neck, swinging against its shoulder. Maren's entire body shook with horror as he struggled to keep his grip on the doll with his left hand. His right curled steadily into a fist.

The darkness was ripe in his eyes, allowing the figure to seamlessly blend into the curtain of black behind it. Maren could barely make out his daughter's battered shell where she crouched in the middle of the staircase. Her black, unblinking eyes watched intently as the scene unfolded, and John wiped his knowing grin over her face.

The figure was enormous, towering over Maren. It leaked of venom, seeping from its darkened skin and scattering into the air. John's energy soaked into it from all sides, solidifying its body with each quaking step and trapping his storm over its skin like armor. The figure's head continued to sway over its shoulder as it walked.

Maren's breaths halted within his lungs. The air was so thick it tasted like smoke, burning his throat and stinging at his eyes, making it nearly impossible to see. The figure lifted its large arm, swinging it toward Maren's twisted face.

He ducked, sending the powerful blow crashing into the thick beam behind him. It struck the wood hard, shaking the entire room and throwing a fresh coat of dust into the air. Maren coughed, sputtering on the blood that still soured over his tongue.

His body was riddled with cuts and bruises. Bones that may be cracked or broken pulsed with each movement, and a disorienting daze still muddied his head. The room around him gently spun.

Maren refused to let go of the Lily-Doll, making the left side of his body next to useless in this fight against the shadow man. He struggled to shield the doll behind him while also fighting back.

"*GIVE ME THE DOLL!*" John's voice howled from the shadow's hanging head as it swung another dark fist toward Maren's face. Lily's body looked hollow on the stairs, slumping her shoulder into the wall at her side. Her head dipped forward, staring into the floor.

Maren ducked barely in time, feeling the breeze of the next blow at his cheek. The shadow's black fist pummeled into the wall at Maren's back, sending shards of the wooden beams over him like heavy rain.

Maren's body was giving out beneath him, slowing his movements. He fought with all he had but it still wasn't enough. He held barely enough strength to evade each attack, let alone return them. With the doll curled between his fingers, he was rendered completely helpless.

He sucked a deep breath in while the shadow man pulled back its arm, aiming its fist again at Maren's bludgeoned face. He braced, ducking against the dirt.

Instead of making contact with Maren's head, the black fist curved in the air, slipping through his defenses and sinking deep into his left forearm. The bone *cracked* under the force, causing his fingers to loosen. The Lily-Doll slipped from his grasp and fell through the air toward the dirt, landing in the large dark hand of John's shadow.

Maren cried out in pain, cradling his broken arm as the shadow snatched his daughter's doll. He reached twitching fingers forward, desperate to retrieve it, but he was too late.

Without warning, the room pulsed like a pounding heartbeat, shaking the floor beneath him and throwing his body to the ground. No matter how hard he tried to stand, the room continued to vibrate, rattling his brain and forcing him to curl into the dirt. He could barely lift his head to watch.

Lily's body collapsed on the stairs. Where she had once leaned against the wall, she now lay motionless and empty on her side. The whole room began to hum with electricity, and the lightbulbs from the top of the stairs and each of the small rooms flickered wildly. They illuminated and darkened the space like a strobe.

Maren watched in horror from the ground as the shadow man stood tall in the center of the room, unbothered by the overwhelming energy that swam around it. The edges of its blackness rippled like water as its arm lifted toward the ceiling, basking the doll in the flashing, blinding lights.

Adrenaline surged through Maren's body, willing each limb to move before it was too late. Whatever was happening, he knew it would be irreversible. He knew this was his final chance to save his daughter.

His right hand felt around at the wall behind him as he pushed himself up with his left. He could hardly feel the pain of his severed bone where the shadow man had struck him, crunching and shifting beneath the weight of his body. All he cared for was Lily.

His fingers wrapped tightly around something solid, something slightly loose in the wall, and ripped it free. A thick, rotting piece of wood easily separated from the rest of the old beams with one good pull.

The air in the basement swirled around his body as he stood, shaking with fear and resolve. The only thing keeping him standing was Lily and the picture of her that he held in his mind—the picture of his daughter safe, smiling. He *needed* to get her back.

Maren lifted the rotted wood in the air, pulling it back with as much strength as he possessed and stabbing its sharp end through the shadow man's back. It lodged deep into its blackened skin, pouring black, sap-like blood from the gaping hole. He ripped it back out with both hands, letting its energy bleed out. All at once the room stilled. The thick dark storm was no longer swirling and the lights no longer flickered. A heavy darkness settled again in the room, blanketing the shadow where it stood. It stayed eerily still.

Maren jumped forward, tearing the Lily-Doll from its large black hand and gripping it as tightly as he could bear. The pain from his shattered bone was heavy now, traveling through each finger as they curled around the cold porcelain. In his right hand, he grasped the wooden stake, still dripping with the figure's black blood.

The shadow turned, bobbing its broken neck and preparing to pounce from the corner where it stood. Maren shouted, keeping it in place.

"*STOP!* I'LL BREAK IT!" His hand constricted around the doll as he pointed the sharpened end of the wood toward its small, fragile skull. His entire body was drenched with blood and sweat, dragging with each wound, but he stood tall. "If you take one step toward me, I'll *shatter* it."

The shadow waited, unmoving. The silence was thick. His daughter's weak body slowly lifted from the stairs as John's energy returned to it. She sat straight up.

"*You . . .*" John's prickly voice scraped from her dry tongue. Her face was terribly pale, shining in the moonlight that slid through muddied windows. Her black eyes gleamed. "*You have no idea what you're doing,*" he hissed from her lips, mockingly.

"I *know* that you need this doll to take my daughter away." Maren's throat stung with tears. His body threatened to break beneath him, but he pushed forward, ignoring it. "I *know* that she isn't in here yet, or all of this would have been *pointless!*"

He was lying through gritted teeth. He wasn't sure of anything. He had no idea where Lily was or what was happening, but he studied John's reaction, waiting for a tell.

"If I shatter this doll," he continued, "Lily will have nowhere to go. Her body is dying . . . You're *killing* her." His voice cracked, letting the tears escape from his eyes as he spoke. "You will lose."

John rasped weakly through Lily's lips. "*Her name is Alina. She is my—*"

"*HER NAME IS LILY!*" Maren screamed, crying out each word through sobs. He was still holding the wood over the doll, waiting to smash it. His fingers twitched with anticipation.

"Her name is *Lily.* Not Alina," Maren sobbed. "She is *MY DAUGHTER!* She's my little girl and you're *KILLING*

HER!" He slammed the wooden stake against the dirt then returned it quickly to the doll. A warning.

"*My daughter . . . my Alina,*" John pleaded. "*She is here. I know that she's here and I know that you took her. I'm taking her back.*" Each word was a prayer.

Lily's body was growing weaker by the second, and a pool of blood was gathering around her on the stairs.

"*ALINA ISN'T HERE, JOHN!*" Maren wept, collapsing into the dirt. "You're killing my girl! My *only* girl . . ." He could barely keep a hold on the weapon. His shoulders shook.

"*She is already dead,*" John whispered, distorted and slow. His heart felt unbearably heavy, but he chose to ignore it.

John had been searching for Alina for so long. So many hopeless, empty nights of pain and suffering. He had never felt such loneliness as he had within the doll, searching for her spirit, staring at nothing. It wasn't until *she* had found him that the life within him finally sparked again. He had found her, *his daughter.*

She cared for him. She loved him. Her blonde hair and her blue eyes and the warmth of her pale skin, she looked just like *her.* Lily was sweet and adventurous, like Alina was. She was alive and breathing. She was *here.*

Slowly, John convinced himself she had finally come back to him. After all this time, she had found him again. His precious girl. He forced himself to believe it to numb the pain.

But tonight, as he crouched in front of the fireplace remembering Alina's face, he knew it wasn't true. The storm of his realization boomed from his mind, sweeping all over the house and filling each corner with that same returning dread. The *loneliness.*

Alina was dead. Alina had been dead for a long time. But he had already made up his mind.

None of that mattered now. He would not return to the emptiness and the torture of his life, trapped within the house and unable to leave. Now he had *Lily*. He had someone to share his burden with.

Maren could no longer take her away.

"What did you do?" Maren pleaded, coughing up each word. John was silent. "*WHAT DO YOU MEAN, SHE'S ALREADY DEAD?*"

Lily's body rose from the stairs, slowly descending. Her black eyes dug through the air. The shadow man flinched in the corner of Maren's vision, turning its broken neck toward him.

"*I didn't kill my daughter. You did,*" John growled from Lily's lips, reaching the bottom of the staircase. He placed her feet into the dirt. "*We have both already lost. I won't let you take her away again.*"

Maren seethed, contorting his face into a horrible grimace as he lifted the rotting wood into the air, sending it down with all the power of his rage to crush the doll's head.

The shadow launched toward him through the darkness, knocking the sharpened wood from his grasp before it could collide. The weapon clattered into the dirt. Maren's fingers desperately stretched toward the doll, missing it by centimeters as his body crumpled at the impact and landed on the ground.

The Lily-Doll clattered to the dirt at the shadow man's feet. It didn't even look down.

The dark figure moved slowly across the basement floor, closing in on Maren as he forced himself to stand once more. With hot anger pouring through him like fuel, he pounced forward, ignoring the pain in his broken arm and all over his weakened body and toppling the shadow man to the ground.

He knew this would be his last fight.

Thirty-One.

Maren used every ounce of his strength to take down the shadow man. They collided into the dirt, writhing around on the floor of the basement.

The dark figure seemed smaller this time, weaker. Maren could barely get within inches of it before, and now he was able to take it to the ground. John's hold was loosening, he thought. He was getting weak.

Maren scrambled over the figure, trying to get a hold on it before the opportunity slipped through his fingers. His mind raced, searching for a plan.

Just a moment before, the wound that was left by the rotting wood had been enough to stop the figure in its tracks. Now as it was held beneath him, Maren wondered what else he could do to destroy it completely.

The shadow man's neck had already been snapped, with its head hung to the side. He couldn't strangle it, he couldn't smash its skull, and he couldn't rip it apart—not as weak as he was now. Maren scoured over the darkened basement searching for the stake. It was his only hope.

In his desperate search for the weapon, a sudden realization crept over him like a spider. His heart rate quickened.

Lily's body was nowhere to be found. The room was empty with the exception of himself and the shadow underneath him, struggling in the dirt.

"*JOHN!*" Maren called out, shaking his entire body at the power of his scream. "*JOHN! BRING HER BACK!*"

There was no answer, only the sounds of the shadow sliding against the floor of the basement as they fought. Rage crashed through him, fresh and hot. His eyes turned red.

He needed to hurry. He needed to find Lily.

At the edge of his vision, the sharp end of the rotting wood gleamed in the moonlight that pierced through the windows. The thick dark blood of the shadow still soaked it.

Maren rocked to his side, straddling over the dark figure and keeping it in place with his good arm. He reached toward the weapon on the ground with shattered bones, fighting through the pain and the stabbing feeling in his forearm. The shooting agony reached down to each of his fingers as he touched his fingertips to the wood.

He slowly drew the stake into his palm, inching it closer with each pull until his hand was able to wrap fully around it. He grasped it weakly, rocking back on his heels to crouch over the shadow man.

The figure continued to weakly struggle, shifting back and forth beneath him while he transferred the weapon into his right hand. He wrapped his fingers around the makeshift handle as tightly as he could and lifted it high above his head. A scream let loose from his throat, webbing around the room as he buried the sharp end into the thick chest of the shadow.

The darkened figure groaned softly, stilling around the wood that plunged deep inside of its skin. Maren felt the shadow's bones shift and its skin break. Its whole body loosened, softening against the dirt.

A deep sigh drifted from its mouth.

Maren stood slowly, shaking with adrenaline that still coursed through each vein. His mind raced and his lungs contorted. The shadow's life was draining into the basement floor, now covered in its thick red blood. Maren searched each corner of the room for Lily, for John. He needed to find them. There was no telling what John could have done to his defenseless daughter by now.

He hurried toward the stairs when something shifted at the corner of his eyes. It was so dark he could barely see, rolling his gaze over the abandoned room. It landed on something at the edge, something tall. Maren squinted.

Buried deep within the blackness, the shadow man stood motionlessly in the corner, exactly where it had been before it jumped at him to attack. It stared blankly forward like it wasn't really there, like it still waited for John's instructions.

It was dissolving into the air like ashes.

An eerie feeling draped over Maren, rapidly filling the room. His teeth grinded.

Softly, a dull, distorted noise lifted to his ears from behind where he had left the shadow to die. It sounded horribly familiar. Maren turned his stiffened body toward the noise, letting the terrible truth embrace him. It infiltrated his lungs, his stomach, and his heart as the reality around him deepened.

John had tricked him.

"No . . ." Maren breathed, beginning to shake violently. *"No, no, no, no, no . . . NO!"*

He melted to his knees before the *shadow* on the ground as the darkness evaporated from around it, revealing his daughter's bleeding body beneath.

Her black eyes gleamed up at him as did John's weak smile that still painted her lips.

Maren sank defeatedly into the dirt, pressing both palms around the gaping hole in his daughter's chest where the rotting wood still protruded from her.

His emotions were overwhelming, pouring over him like molten lava. His entire body burned and his chest was caving in, rib by rib. He was breaking, falling apart from the inside. His thoughts were *loud. Swarming.*

She's dying.

She's dying.

SHE'S DYING!

"GET OUT OF HER!" Maren shrieked, so hard he felt his throat tear. His sobs echoed through the basement and bounced off each wall. Lily's blood was puddled around her, soaking into her father's clothes and all over his trembling hands, darkening them.

"She was never here," John choked out from Lily's lips while blood rose in her mouth. He gently closed Lily's blackened eyes as his smile faded.

Maren couldn't accept it. His blood rushed like a tidal wave as he scrambled to save her. His daughter's blood streamed between his fingers.

Lily's body was empty. Her mind had been pushed out far before Maren had stabbed her. John couldn't keep her inside any longer, jumbling with his mind. All she had done was distract him and keep him from his goal. She could have stopped it, and he could not let that happen.

She floated now, somewhere deep within the house like John had before he settled within the gray doll. No matter what might happen to her body, her fate had already been set. The plan was almost complete, with one final piece.

John needed Lily's body to die inside of the house. He needed his spirit to be released from within her, to cloud back into the air and sink back into the walls like it had before—in this very basement.

He would fall back into the house, filling each crack, each room, and each hallway with his aura. With the gray doll destroyed, the house was now his home.

This time he wouldn't be alone. This time, he would have Lily. She was waiting for him now. She would fall from the air and into Lily-Doll, and they would be together forever.

Maren had been the biggest key to his plan.

What do I do?

What do I do?

What do I do?

Maren's panicked thoughts formed a shroud over his head. No matter how hard he pressed, the blood continued to pour from Lily like the spout of a fountain. Maren's mind was going numb. He could barely breathe.

I could go upstairs, call 911, his thoughts scrambled. *They can help her; they can save her . . .*

He stared down at his hollow daughter while her body slowly died, and he knew that he couldn't leave. He couldn't call the police, he couldn't find help, he couldn't do anything at all. She would die any second now, and he could only watch.

Maren's sobs erupted from his lungs as he collapsed over her, wrapping his broken body over hers. If he could do one thing for her now, he could be here with her. He could make sure she wouldn't die alone.

"Lily . . . my Lily. *I'm so sorry.*" His cracking words were barely audible through the tears. "I failed you. I failed you over and over and over . . ." He scraped his bloody fingers through his hair, pulling at it until his scalp stung. The pain in his chest was unbearable.

"I love you. I love you, I love you, I love you so much that it *hurts.*" The words crawled from deep within him, swarming out. "I'm so sorry I couldn't be the father you deserved. *I'm so sorry . . .*" He stroked her face while the life drained from her.

"My Lily . . ." Maren could hardly speak. His voice fell weaker with each word. "Out of everything I loved about your mother . . . the best thing she ever gave to me was *you.*"

Lily's small, frail body exhaled, releasing its final breath. Each muscle relaxed against the dust.

Maren's scream ricocheted from his core. His body shook, melting over his daughter where she lay empty on the dirt floor of the basement. He cried so hard his chest heaved, sucking in the thick air of the room that scratched his throat while both of his fists pummeled into the ground. Any life he had left inside of him disintegrated, pouring from his burning eyes, and the pain in his body went unnoticed.

The room felt painfully hollow. Each beat of his heart bounced from the walls and crashed into his ears as her dark blood slowly dried against his skin, branding him while he waited for his daughter to go cold.

It should have been me.

"Li—" Maren sputtered, his voice failing. His reddened hands reached forward to caress her face, soaking her in one final time. Her innocence and beauty were no longer blighted by John's presence. Only his own.

Silence fell around them like a blanket, broken apart by a soft voice.

"Dad?"

It was quiet, sweet like sugar. It wasn't the same horrid, distorted sound that had been tearing from his daughter's lips. It was hers, untainted by John. It was *Lily.*

"Lily? Sweetheart?" Maren rose slightly, hovering over her face and staring intensely down at her closed eyes.

"*Dad . . . I'm so sorry,*" she spoke again. Her eyes were still closed, her mouth unmoving. Maren searched the room desperately for the source of her voice, but it was everywhere. "*I love you too.*"

The ground around him began to shake gently. The dust lifted from each surface and small rocks slid across the ground as it vibrated.

"Lily . . . *wait,*" he begged as her voice went silent inside his mind. His emotions bubbled over while he pleaded for one more moment with her. "*Please,* wait. Lily . . . *LILY!*"

Maren led his eyes around the trembling basement as each light flickered from above. The dust swirled in the shadows, splashing around him where he stood and pushing rapidly toward each corner of the room.

"Lily . . . *please* come back," he choked out past the tears, still searching the room for any sign of her.

On the ground, the small blonde doll still sat in the dirt where he had dropped it. Staring at it with blurry eyes, a thought poured over him, one that he couldn't bear. An impossible choice.

He stood over his daughter's hollow body while the night quaked at his feet. It was an image that would forever be etched in his mind in black ink. His mind raced, pulsing behind his temples like a mallet while tears streamed down his face. He couldn't bring himself to move, speak, or even think.

Before he could consider, he launched for the doll, dropping his knees into the dirt and snatching it quickly from the ground. He held it tightly between his fingers, squeezing bloody fists around its porcelain skull.

He couldn't let this happen. He couldn't sit by and watch his daughter's soul be chained to this house, to this *doll.* What kind of father would he be if he condemned his only daughter to this endless hell?

His fingers curled around the porcelain, feeling it begin to crack.

The dark aura of the house swirled around him. Each light bulb pounded beams of white across the basement over and over, like a spell.

Her body was gone, *dead,* and she had nowhere else to go. Once the doll was destroyed, her soul could escape. She would die.

The thought stabbed at him.

She would die.

He halted, second guessing. How could he be so sure that Lily would be free? What if he destroyed the doll, leaving her stuck inside of the house with John? What if he was only robbing her of a place to go, cursing her to roam the halls at night like a lost ghost?

What if, he thought, she *was* set free, gone forever? What if he truly could never hear her sweet voice in his head again? His thoughts battered him, each one worse than the last. He was too weak.

I can't, he confessed, *surrendering.*

The doll dropped from his grasp, falling softly into his lap. His thoughts swirled as violently as the air within the room, stabbing him the same way the lights stabbed at his eyes each time they flickered.

He knew somewhere deep that destroying this doll would save her. He knew despite his doubts that without the

Lily-Doll, John's plan would not have worked. She would be free.

I can't let her go.

Tears filled his eyes, slipping down his cheeks and soaking into the thick material of the doll's yellow dress.

Suddenly, the basement air stilled over his skin. The dust settled throughout the room, drifting over each surface. The small rocks stopped sliding and the lights stopped flickering. Maren inhaled a shallow breath.

Lily-Doll lay against him in his lap. He could feel her cold, hard porcelain through the thick material of his clothes as it began to warm.

After everything that had happened, he was still a coward.

Thirty-Two.

Maren stared blankly into the fireplace while the chair rocked gently beneath him. The heat of the fire crackled and popped within the cage of red bricks.

The house that encased him was overflowing with emptiness, screaming with silence. Each day now was always the same.

He would wake up, though he never slept. Eat breakfast, though he never ate. He would sit in his favorite chair downstairs and wait until 9:00 a.m. Lily was never one for waking up early.

He would crawl back upstairs, turn down the hallway, and stare into her closed door waiting for her to wake up, though she never did. He would knock on the wood from outside her bedroom, though she never answered.

The house was quiet, as it always was these days. He went through his usual routine.

The leather chair released him, sending him away from the warmth of the fire. Each step up the stairs felt heavy and dull.

His right hand gripped the rail tightly while he trudged to the second floor. His left arm was bandaged to his chest with a makeshift sling, still pounding with pain along with the rest of his battered body. He didn't seem to notice.

Each of his heavy footsteps echoed off the hardwood as he walked down the hall toward his daughter's bedroom. Photos had been taped to the walls, dulling the blinding white of the house.

Everywhere he looked, his daughter's smile penetrated him. Pictures of Lily, Jewel, their once-perfect family, spread out over each surface. He emptied every photo album he could find, ripping photos from boxes, books, and out from storage. Even the frame that had decorated his desk now lay empty.

Each photo was meant to be a motivation, a push to keep going—a reminder that he needed to see this through, though he couldn't seem to bear the weight of it.

It had been days since he last heard Lily's voice. He begged and pleaded to the empty house to bring her back, to fill the void that engulfed him. Each night he only stared at the ceiling awaiting her sweet words to embrace him in his mind, but each night they never came. He had tried everything, to no avail.

Still, he waited.

His hand curled into a fist as he raised it against the wooden door of his daughter's bedroom. He had messily repaired it for her after it cracked against the wall a few nights prior. He knew that his daughter preferred her privacy.

Her voice didn't come to welcome him inside, it never did, but still he waited a moment before pushing the door open with a soft palm. He didn't want to scare her.

Lily-Doll was tucked away inside the bedroom within the comfort of Lily's large bed. He had left her beneath the warm covers, which stretched up to her chin like she preferred. She looked exactly the same as he had left her when he tucked her in the night before. He grimaced.

She had always been a restless sleeper.

"Lily?" Maren's soft tone broke the thick silence of the bedroom. "It's time to get up."

It was perfectly clean. Maren had painstakingly plucked every chip of the smashed dollhouse and each fleck of Mr. Doll's gray porcelain from the carpet.

The bed had been properly made, with folded blankets and tucked sheets. Her colorful clothes had been returned to the closet, and each drawer pushed tightly against the frame of her dresser. It was just how she wanted it.

"Lily?" he asked again, pulling the thick blanket away from the doll's small body. His head was quiet, stilling his thoughts and searching hopelessly for her voice.

Maren reached a delicate hand toward Lily-Doll, lifting her from the bed. Her cold porcelain burned against his palm.

"How did you sleep, Lily-pop?" His quivering finger lifted to her tiny face, stroking her cheek.

He hadn't felt her since *that night.* He hadn't felt her warmth on his skin or her voice in his mind. It was like she had completely disappeared. Maren searched for her every moment of every day.

An overwhelming darkness burned inside of him, scratching at his chest as he stared at the images of his daughter. The pictures from the hallway had found their way inside of her bedroom as well. He hoped to draw her back to the doll with images of her life. He thought that he could remind her of who she was and how much her father truly loved her—even though he had failed to show her.

As he stared at each photo, he realized that every happy memory of Lily was slowly being erased, replaced with a screaming need to hurt a man who was already dead—the man who had taken her from him.

He couldn't stomach the thought of his daughter floating around in this house, chained to the monster who killed her. It made him shudder.

Every image of her beautiful smiling face was gradually sinking away. They slowly morphed into a version of her that now plagued him each time he closed his eyes—ghostly pale skin; deep, blackened eyes; and blood pouring from her chest all over his hands.

He grasped tightly to Lily-Doll, lifting her up to his face. The doll that was supposed to save her.

He hoped and prayed with every ounce of his being that his daughter was still here, somewhere close. Maybe she was hiding deep in the dirt of the basement where he had buried her body, or wandering the shadowed hallways at night searching for him. He wondered if she was angry with him for leaving her alone.

He thought maybe when Lily died she was lost within the house. Maybe if Maren were to join her, he could track her down deep inside. He needed to see her, even if only once.

He pulled Lily-Doll back away from his face, and her empty blue eyes stared up.

Was she looking at him?

He hated himself for what he had done, but clung desperately to the reality that he created. He could have crushed the Lily-Doll. He could have released his daughter's spirit, freeing her from this hell. Instead he held tightly to this fragile toy she was tied to. Or was she? He couldn't even be sure.

Maybe he had imagined her sweet voice inside of his head that night. Maybe he had imagined the warmth of her hard skin. Maybe he was so desperate for her to hear his words that he would rather his daughter's soul be trapped here within the house than have to watch her die before he could tell her that he loved her for the last time.

No matter the reality, he had made an unforgivable choice. Maren always seemed to have to choose between two bad options, rarely knowing what the lesser evil would be. This time the evil was palpable, and he chose it anyway.

He couldn't take the guilt of what he had done, or what he had allowed to happen. John had planned this from the start, and it slipped through Maren's fingers. John tore his perfect daughter away from him, forcing him to dig rotting wood through her flesh. He couldn't scrub the feeling from his hands. Her skin tearing, her blood escaping over his fingers . . . Bile rose in his throat.

He held the small doll in his hands, not caring if it was empty—he only needed a piece of her. He couldn't bear to leave without telling her goodbye.

"I love you, my sweet girl. My Lily." He gently held Lily-Doll to his lips and grazed a soft kiss on the side of her small face. The cold porcelain stung against his skin. "I'm so sorry," he whispered.

A tear rolled down his face, dropping from his chin.

He put the doll back into bed, returning the warm covers over her porcelain flesh and taking one last look at his daughter—her short blonde hair, her bright-blue eyes, her bewitching smile.

Maren turned out of the room as fast as his bruised body could carry him. He needed to move quickly before he had the chance to change his mind. Turning a corner, he released a shaky breath and descended the stairs. He had just one more moment of this life left inside of him.

Arriving at the bottom of the stairs, the mouth of the fireplace welcomed him. Flames reached out toward him like stretching fingers, calling him to it.

Maren steadied himself while his hands continued to tremble. He needed to be strong, for Lily.

The bucket was heavy in his grip as he lugged it around the house with his one good arm. He poured the thick liquid down the stairs first, soaking the basement below before moving up to the second floor.

He tore each photo down from the wall, soaking them with the gasoline that slicked the hardwood. It fizzled into the air, burning his nose and eyes, but he couldn't stop.

Hurriedly, he poured it into the carpet of his bedroom and trailed it all the way down the hall before stopping outside his daughter's empty room. Gasoline dripped from the lip of the bucket and onto his shoes while he pulled himself back from opening the door once more.

Is she in there? he wondered.

There's still time to clean up this mess. I can take it all back.

You can't.

What if she's in there? What if she's waiting for me inside of the doll?

She isn't.

His thoughts argued back and forth as he stood for what felt like ages. His fingers were aching at the weight of the bucket still perched in his hands.

I'm sorry, Lily.

Maren pushed the door open, barreling through the entryway and spilling the gasoline all over her room. He soaked the carpet and drenched the bed and the warm blankets, sending gasoline seeping into Lily-Doll's pretty yellow dress and blonde hair. The horrible scent filled the room.

He ran from the bedroom, silencing his thoughts and continuing on his mission back down the wooden stairs. The liquid from the bucket spilled over them as he descended, pouring down into the living room. He splashed it on the couch, the floor, and his favorite chair, soaking every surface before his thoughts could stop him. The flames of the open fireplace teased the sopping wet house as they popped.

Maren dropped the empty bucket, clattering it against the floor as his sunken eyes landed on something in the corner of his vision—a bright-pink book where it sat on the counter.

It had been ripped up, handfuls of pages torn out. It was the same book that John had used to burn the gray doll's body.

In Waiting.

Maren snatched it from the counter as his chest tightened around his broken heart. He ran a wet finger down the face of the book, coating it in gasoline.

His deep-brown eyes welled as he opened the bright cover of his wife's precious gift, ripping out a handful of pages and tossing the book back to its spot on the counter—the book he would never get to read.

He took the same lighter from the same drawer with the same blue handle as John did. He stared at it with a blank, cold expression, fingering the trigger until a thin flame bloomed at the top. He swallowed hard.

He quickly placed the papers on the floor, soaking the pile into the gasoline that spread over it. The tip of the lighter gleamed orange with the flame as he held it steadily over the papers, threatening to light them.

Maren held his breath, considering. His burning eyes stared deeply into the fire of the lighter, reflecting the bright-orange color.

He saw Lily in his mind, young and careless. He saw Jewel guiding her over the edge of a swimming pool, laughing and kicking her feet. He saw Lily's wide, toothy grin across the table from him while he let her win in a game of checkers. He saw all of the things they had done together, and all of the things they would never get to do. Each piece of her slowly fell from the air, sinking into the wet wood beneath him.

He released his finger, sending the flame back into its case.

"I can't do this," he whispered to the hollowed expanse of the house. "*Not again.*"

The gasoline continued to soak into the papers, wetting them completely into the floor as Maren surrendered. He set the lighter on top of the side table, dropping his head into his hands.

He had been too weak to save his daughter, too weak to admit his fear, and now too weak to let her go. He begged silently for someone to save her, for someone to do for his daughter what he had never been able to do—the *right* thing. The house answered.

The fireplace cracked, shattering the moment. Maren's head rose just in time to see an ember erupt from the fire and throw itself onto the soaked floor, igniting it.

The small ember grew wildly into an enormous flame. It rippled in all directions, following the long trail of dark liquid.

The fire raged around him while each flame licked the walls and infected the entire house—the couch, the doors, the staircase, even the air.

Heat embraced him, engulfing each room and shattering the windows. The fire crawled up the stairs, down the hallway, and ate up each drop of gasoline, growing larger with each gulp. It trampled through the door of Lily's bedroom, swallowing it in flames. Lily-Doll caught fire in her bed, shattering her porcelain.

The basement rolled in heat, soaking into the dirt and down to Lily's hollow corpse. Maren could see the flames crawl up from the basement and burst through the open door from his spot on the floor in the living room. Agonizing cries tore from his throat as his flesh seared from his bones and his clothes melted into his skin.

While the house burned down around him, destroying what was left of his life, he whispered a silent gratitude to the red bricks of the fireplace, to the pop of the flames that saved his daughter when he couldn't.

As he drew his last breath, one final image flashed through his mind.

Lily.

Discussion Questions:

1. In the first line of the book, the author mentions that good parents kill the parts of themselves that don't benefit the child. Which parts of himself did/didn't Maren kill?
2. Maren's nightmares play a big part throughout the book. How do you interpret them? Are they warnings, a peek into John's mind, or something else?
3. What are the key causes of Maren's ultimate unraveling?
4. What is the significance of Jewel's book, In Waiting, to the plot?
5. What does Lily ultimately want and do you think she ever receives it?
6. Do you think Lily's spirit is inside of Lily-Doll at the end of the story? If so, why do you think the doll is still cold and unresponsive to Maren?
7. Why do you think John is not active in the house during the final chapter of the book? What does his silence mean?
8. In the final scene, the fire pops and ignites the gasoline, burning the house down and killing Maren. Do you think this is Lily's doing, John's, or a coincidence? If it is intentional, why?
9. Which aspects of the conclusion shocked you, and which had you predicted? Were there any unanswered questions?
10. What is the significance of the last line of the book?

<u>Author's Answers:</u>

<u>Q1: In the first line of the book, the author mentions that good parents kill the parts of themselves that don't benefit the child. Which parts of himself did/didn't Maren kill?</u>

A: Maren was unable to kill his pride and his ego. He wasn't able to move on from Jewel or kill the part of himself that still needed her to function. When it came down to it, he also wasn't able to do what was right for Lily.

<u>Q2: Maren's nightmares play a big part throughout the book. How do you interpret them? Are they warnings, a peek into John's mind, or something else?</u>

A: The dreams are basically pieces of John's mind and his past that filled the house and filled Maren. John's thoughts infected Maren, manifesting in his dreams and subconscious. John had convinced himself that Maren was the intruder, which is what made Maren act out the scenes of the night Alina died as he was sleepwalking.

<u>Q3: What are the key causes of Maren's ultimate unraveling?</u>

A: The key cause of Maren's ultimate unraveling is his ego, which doesn't let him admit his fear or make necessary decisions based on that fear. He ignored it until it was too late.

Another cause of his unraveling is his pain, which doesn't allow him to move on from Jewel's death or appreciate and love whom he has left. He abandons Lily in his grief and forces her to seek love out wherever she can find it. Also, his guilt makes him turn against himself, which only gives John more influence over him.

Q4: What is the significance of Jewel's book, In Waiting, to the plot?

A: Jewel's book serves as a vessel for Maren's guilt. He is unable to read the book for years after her death, and when he finally does, he poisons it with his own thoughts of Jewel's anger and blame toward him for what is happening. His perspective of Jewel hating what he has become is simply a reflection of what he thinks of himself. Through the story he creates in her book, he foretells his own future of failing Lily, and failing Jewel.

Q5: What does Lily ultimately want and do you think she ever receives it?

A: Lily is desperate for love and belonging. She feels so lonely and invisible, and all she wants is someone to love her and need her the way she feels Mr. Doll does. Even if she ultimately learns the truth—that she isn't his real daughter and is just a replacement—she would still trade that feeling for a sense of belonging. After her death, she realizes it was never real and regrets her decision.

<u>Q6: Do you think Lily's spirit is inside of Lily-Doll at the end of the story? If so, why do you think the doll is still cold and unresponsive to Maren?</u>

A: Lily's spirit does end up inside of Lily-Doll. She warms in Maren's hand to comfort him and say goodbye, then recedes. She realizes she is dead and trapped inside the doll with John, who doesn't truly love or care for her, and finally sees how much her own father loves her. She also knows that if Maren realizes she is inside the doll, he wouldn't have the strength to free her from it, so she stays hidden.

<u>Q7: 1. Why do you think John is not active in the house during the final chapter of the book? What does his silence mean?</u>

A: By the final chapter, John has accomplished his goal. However, after all is said and done, he sees it was all for nothing. He knows that Alina is still dead and that Lily can't replace her. The mind games he played with her no longer work in the face of the truth, and he is alone again with what he's done. Not only is Alina still dead, but now he has destroyed Maren and Lily in the same way the intruder destroyed Alina and himself. He knows it is all over, and he's filled with a sense of emptiness and regret.

<u>Q8: In the final scene, the fire pops and ignites the gasoline, burning the house down and killing Maren. Do you think this is Lily's doing, John's, or a coincidence? If it is intentional, why?</u>

A: This is intentional. The house always responds to John's thoughts when he is emotional, like the door handle that shocked Maren when he is angry. This time, there are two spirits in the house who are struggling to cope with how everything unfolds. They are both filled with regret and want the fire to wash it all away. It is up for interpretation whether the fire popping was a conscious decision from one or both of them, or if the fire simply reacted to their emotions, but ultimately it is what both of them want.

Q9: Which aspects of the conclusion shocked you, and which had you predicted? Were there any unanswered questions?

A: There are a few unanswered questions by the end, like where does Lily go, and when? What happens after the house is burned down? What is inside the book Maren never got to read? These and others were intentionally left unanswered, up for the interpretation of the reader.

Q10: What is the significance of the last line of the book?

A: The last line explains that Lily is Maren's last thought before he dies, which shows the development of his character. Throughout the book, he can't seem to put his daughter above the thoughts and memories of Jewel. He could have been thinking in his last moment that he was ready to see his wife again in death. Instead, he is thinking of his daughter, thanking the house for making the decision that he couldn't, and setting her free—setting them both free. It also serves as a final example of how Maren is a mirror of John, who also spent his last living moment thinking of his daughter during the flashback in chapter twenty-one.

www.ingramcontent.com/pod-product-compliance
Lightning Source LLC
Chambersburg PA
CBHW031335010826
48972CB00012B/349